—◀ THE DARK DANCER ▶—

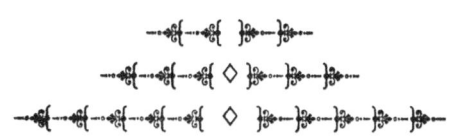

The Dark Dancer

FREDERIC PROKOSCH

FARRAR, STRAUS AND GIROUX

NEW YORK

Copyright © 1964 by Frederic Prokosch
Library of Congress catalog card number 64-11268
First Printing, 1964
Published simultaneously in Canada by
Ambassador Books, Ltd., Toronto
Manufactured in the U.S.A. by H. Wolff, New York
Designed by Adrianne Onderdonk
ISBN 0-374-52658-3

An ominous ambiguity hangs over the historical documents which touch on the reigns of Jahangir and Shahjahan. I have taken advantage of this ambiguity and have adapted certain episodes as well as certain settings to suit my own purposes.

CONTENTS

PART ONE

A Tryst and a Wedding

There had been rain in the afternoon, lightening the burden of the heat. There was a smell of wet grass and a misty sheen hung over the ricefields. Village folk were swarming idly along the puddle-filled road, laughing and chattering at the prospect of the evening festival. The grunting of marsh-frogs rose from the river; a flock of wild ducks went circling over the cattails.

The Princess Arjumand sauntered down the path through a copse of willows. At the bottom of the path lay one of the inlets of the river Jumna, which shone through the boughs, brown and torpid as tea. Now and then a lingering drop would fall from a branch overhead and leave a dark stain on her pale orange shawl. Once a drop fell on her cheek and trickled down like a tear. Her face was tense and expectant: a thin, childlike face with large chestnut eyes and a petulant little mouth.

The path suddenly curved. Three large elephants stood in the shallows. They were being bathed by a quintet of soap-spattered elephant boys. The elephants kept waving their trunks about playfully, spraying the naked brown boys, who squealed with excitement as they brandished their brushes. Overhead some long-haired monkeys were swinging about in a casuarina tree, tossing twigs in the water and cackling insults at the elephants.

The Princess followed the path toward the Emperor's boathouse, which was a scallop-roofed shed with pointed eaves of a carved vermilion. She paused by the veranda. Half-hidden behind a column stood a slender young man, robustly handsome in the Kashmir manner.

"You're late," he whispered, "my darling," and he drew her gently into the shadows.

"I can't help it. The Ranee Mahil insisted on having a little chat with me. They're all gossiping about the Emperor's festival. There will be some Javanese dancers tonight and tomorrow there'll be a Persian magician. And the day after tomorrow the Sultan Shahriyar is staging a play. It was written especially for Shahriyar by a young Chinese poet."

"Do you like all these people? Do you like that preposterous Shahriyar?"

"I neither like him nor dislike him. He amuses me," said the Princess.

"Amuses! I see nothing amusing in a pompous little pederast."

"My dear Sirkandar," said the Princess irritably, "you are not in a position to give me orders. I shall choose my friends as I wish. I am neither a snob nor a puritan. I don't suggest that Shahriyar is a person of profundity, but he's much friendlier than that pudgy Parviz and much nicer than that sinister Khurram."

Sirkandar smiled. "No," he muttered, "you are neither snobbish nor puritanical. After all, you're a noble princess and I'm a common little cavalry officer. Come. Hakim's gone home. It's cooler down in the boathouse."

They walked across the gravel toward the back of the boathouse and stepped through the doorway into the reed-smelling darkness. A painted barge lay floating in the water, a frivolous vessel built by Akbar which had fallen long since into neglect and corruption. The gilded carvings were stained with moss, the silken curtains were tattered, the massive ebony oars lay helterskelter across the deck. The smell of old slime and dead lilies filled the air, tinged with the musk of stale satin and stale amours. Through the arches shone the dazzle of sunlight on the water; they could hear the cries of the elephant boys and the scolding of the monkeys. Sirkandar knelt on the ground by Arjumand and drew her gently to the floor, which was covered with mats and cushions of raffia. They made love in the sultry silence; but there was a listlessness in their lovemaking. It was hurried, preoccupied: there was something they were afraid of.

They lay motionless in the shade, half-concealed in the watery half-light. Arjumand lifted her head a little and peeped out into the sunlight, where the dragonflies were darting over the listless green water. Then she looked at Sirkandar lying silently beside her. After that bodily intimacy he looked strangely remote. His eyes were closed; she studied his flesh with a casual detachment. The throbbing veins in his temples, the tiny nipples and concave belly, the arrow of hair pointing downward toward the dark deflated genitals—there was no mystery in it any more, no secret menace and no immediacy, and she felt aloof and almost indifferent, like an old, old woman.

After a while she said softly:

"My dear old grandfather used to say that women are like water and men like earth, but I think he was mistaken: it's the men who are water and the women the earth."

"Words," said Sirkandar. "Nothing but words. They're all just people, both men and women. They're flesh and blood, they're equally helpless, they're equally baffled by the puzzles of existence."

"You are charming," murmured Arjumand, "when you turn into a philosopher."

"When we're frightened," said Sirkandar, "we clutch at the vapors of philosophy."

He drew his mouth along her arm and then slowly across her shoulders, and then he said: "Words, words! How silly they are! I'm filled with a hidden whirlpool, but what are the words to describe this whirlpool? Is it love? What an empty word! How little it means! How little it tells us!"

There was silence for a while and then Sirkandar said quietly: "Yes. I know. You'll never marry me. There are bigger fish waiting to snap at you."

"I will never marry again," said Arjumand.

"Never?" said Sirkandar. "It's nothing but a word!" He leaned over her in the darkness; his eyes were as dark as the water.

"You are free. Completely free. I'll never deny you your freedom."

"I have never asked for it, have I?"

"Because you were never in doubt of me. And you were never in doubt because you were never really in love with me."

"Now it's you," said Arjumand softly, "who are toying with words."

They rose and strolled back into the sun-sprinkled woods. Sirkandar took her hand and said gravely, "Listen, Arjumand. Let us leave this horrible city. Let's ride into the mountains and forget the rest of the world."

"I should like to," said Arjumand slowly.

"But you can't? You don't dare?"

"My poor darling," said Arjumand, "no woman is in control of her existence. All women are at the mercy of circumstance, or the cruelty of society, or their weakness as women."

"Yes. I see," said Sirkandar quietly.

"Do you? Do you?" said Arjumand.

They stood in the shade for several moments and looked silently at one another. Then they parted without a word and the Princess wandered up the path again.

II

On the banks of the river stood a grove of flowering citron, and beyond lay some irrigated fields of corn and millet. The fields shone a rich vivid green under the clouds, which drew discs of gray shadow over the land as they passed. A young man in a dark-blue tunic was strolling idly through the grove, pausing briefly to look at the women beating their laundry on the shore below. His movements were supple and casual but at the same time tense, catlike. His eyes were black and brooding; his lips were sullen, contemptuous.

A wall covered with ivy rose at the far end of the grove and next to the wall, tucked in the shade, stood an old Hindu temple. The young Sultan (he must have been a Sultan—he wore a sapphire in his turban) crossed the clearing in front of the temple and paused by the doorway. A skeletal man in a drooping loincloth was sweeping out the temple. He paused when he saw the Sultan and did a lopsided salaam.

"You look mournful, Dhritshtra," said the Sultan.

"You are right, Your Highness. I feel mournful."

"Why, Dhritshtra?"

"It's my day of mournfulness, as it happens," said Dhritshtra. "Yesterday was my day of cheerfulness. Tomorrow's my day of composure. And the day after tomorrow, if all goes well, it's irritability. That's the rhythm, Your Highness. It can't be helped. I'm growing old."

He was a frail-looking man with a large, quivering Adam's apple and ears as delicate as a kitten's, dark yet translucent. There was a look in his eyes both capricious and terrified. Whenever the Sultan spoke to him his body started to tremble and an aureole of alertness played over his features.

"Will you do me a favor, Dhritshtra?"

"With enthusiasm, Your Highness!"

"Mutter a charm for me tonight."

"What kind of charm? Erotic? Monetary?"

"Neither. Just a charm. I need luck. I need excitement."

Dhritshtra peered at the Sultan slyly. He seemed to smile inwardly. Then he bowed with an air of obsequious complicity. "Quite, Your Highness. I comprehend." He tucked his broom behind the door, peeped perfunctorily into the temple, and went scuttling into the bushes.

The Sultan stepped gingerly into the half-ruined temple. It was no larger than a gardener's cottage; it stank of antiquity. One wall was elaborately decorated with wormeaten carvings and the opposite wall was covered with a series of crude, faded paintings. The Sultan stared at the carvings with distaste. Yes, he recognized these writhing deities: they were the gods of a contemptible tradition, the sleek, grinning demons of a superstitious populace. There was Vishnu in the shape of a lion striking at a cringing blasphemer; there was a suave and smiling Vishnu squeezing the bowels out of a victim. There was Siva the Unappeasable dancing the many-armed *tandava* and there was Siva the Inexhaustible crawling out of an enormous phallus. But whatever their shapes and attitudes, there was a sameness about them all: they all exuded an air of sensual cruelty and dark disquietude.

The Sultan walked slowly along the wall toward the orchard. He passed the darkening orchard and entered the path that led to the boathouse. The day was growing late; a coppery light played on the Jumna. The dark, squealing link-boys were driving the elephants out of the shallows.

III

A small dark woman in an orange shawl was walking rapidly through the trees. She paused briefly when she saw the Sultan, then lowered her head and kept on walking.

The Sultan paused in the middle of the path. He started to move on, but then thought better of it and nodded his head politely.

"You've lost your way?" he said gently.

"Not in the least," said the Princess airily. "I've been out for a stroll. It's a beautiful park, Your Highness. Especially toward sunset."

"So you know who I am?" said the Sultan.

"I could scarcely fail to, Prince Khurram. I met you at the picnic yesterday, and at the polo the day before."

"Yes, precisely," said the Sultan quickly. "How very stupid of me. Of course." He groped in his mind for an instant. "You are Nawab Aliya Begam."

The Princess smiled. "You are perfectly right. But I have a simpler name. Arjumand."

"Quite," said Khurram, brightening a little. "You were dressed in purple at the picnic."

"Mauve," said the Princess.

"No doubt," said the Sultan. "My eye for colors is not like Shahriyar's."

"So many parties, so many visitors. One could hardly expect you to remember them all!"

Khurram frowned. "I avoid the ballet. I dislike the theatre. And I loathe these picnics."

"I thoroughly agree with you about the picnics. But the dances," said Arjumand, "I rather enjoy." She raised her finger to her chin with an air of appraisal. "Not those men from the mountains, mind you. The Baluchis are too noisy. But the ones from Cambodia. And the ones from Rangoon."

Khurram glanced at the Princess with something like hatred. But then the look suddenly softened, his lips curved into a smile and his face melted into a shy, uneasy kind of sweetness. He said quietly: "How long are you staying?"

"Two more days," said Princess Arjumand.

"And then?"

"I am visiting a cousin down in Khandesh. The Ranee Sita."

"Don't you care for these festivities?"

Arjumand smiled with an inner amusement. "What am I expected to say, Your Highness? Oh, yes, I thoroughly enjoyed them; more than you, I imagine, but I shouldn't care to live in such an atmosphere."

Khurram looked at her thoughtfully. There was something in
Arjumand which both puzzled and irritated him. She looked
prim and reluctant, with those luminous childlike eyes, but at the
same time she carried an air of casual poise, even a glitter of irony.
No, he decided: she wasn't beautiful. Too frail, too wispy to be
beautiful. She looked more like a little boy or even a wood-sprite
than a woman.

"I am sad," he said gravely, "that you disapprove of Agra."

"Disapprove? Not in the least, I assure you," said the Princess cheerfully. "It is merely that I prefer the provinces. I am a
widow. I value my solitude!"

"A pity," said the Sultan rather affectedly.

"Is it really?" said Arjumand, raising her eyebrows.

She fluttered her fingers in a perfunctory gesture of farewell
and went hurrying up the path toward the yellow-roofed guest
house.

The Sultan walked slowly in the direction of the palace. The
sun was just setting and a whiff of coolness passed through the
air. The reeds down by the river were tipped with fire, like burning knives, and as he watched they turned gradually to a thin,
steely blue. He frowned; he cleared his throat. A tiny vein
throbbed in his temple.

He clasped his hands together and unclasped them again. Then
he nodded twice abruptly, as though in reply to some invisible
questioner, and hurried across the garden toward the Tower of
Jasmines.

IV

A swarthy man in an apricot turban sat in the shade of a palm
tree, thoughtfully fanning himself with an ivory-handled fan. He

had an aquiline face with a deep blue scar across the cheek. His brows were thick and ominous; his eyes were an icy gray. This man was Asaf Khan, the richest nobleman in Jahangir's empire. He fixed his gaze on the middle distance, where a path curved toward the guest house. A young woman stepped from the veranda and walked slowly across the lawn. He watched her with a cool and listless solicitude as she approached him. The fan kept swaying rhythmically; he pointed a finger to the leather cushion.

"Here, sit down in the shade, child. You look tired. And a little vexed."

His voice was thin and delicate, like an elderly matron's. It seemed a bit grotesque as it issued from that vulturelike countenance.

"I do feel tired. As well as vexed. I don't like Agra," said Arjumand.

"Nor do I," snapped her father. "Neither the climate nor the inhabitants."

His pale, close-set eyes regarded her with a secret amusement. "Where have you been? Down by the water? Yes, it's cooler down by the water." He raised the handle of his fan and pressed it musingly to his cheek. "You feel vexed, do you say? No wonder. With all this gossip and triviality. My dearest Arjumand, please listen carefully. I have something to say to you. I have just enjoyed a most agreeable chat with a charming member of the Imperial family. Yes, you've guessed it, I can see. I find Prince Khurram extremely personable. A shade aggressive for my tastes, but both vigorous and resourceful. I was rather startled, though not unpleasantly, when he made an earnest proposition to me. He finds you thoroughly sympathetic. There, don't fidget, please, Arjumand. I shall be candid. He suggested, and with an excellent display of reasoning, that I consider the possibility of his marriage to my daughter Arjumand. I tried to look rather aloof as he elaborated on his theme. I didn't wish to convey an awkward impression of enthusiasm. Nor, I may add, did I feel an uncontrollable enthusiasm. He has a naughty reputation. He looks difficult to tame. But I feel that I should mention, in all fairness to your own well-being, that Prince Khurram is by way of being Jahangir's favorite son, and when I contemplate the other three I can't resist the suspicion that Prince Khurram will inherit the throne before long. Yes, I know what you're thinking. His motives are not entirely idyllic. They are not—how shall I put it—wholly free of an element of expediency. But please consider for a moment. I am a weatherbeaten patriarch. Nothing is farther from my mind than the wish to force you against your will. But I have had some opportunities to observe the mysteries of human nature. I've seen love turn into hatred. I've seen passion turn to boredom, and I've seen indifference gradually turn into a deep and lasting affection. I suggest that the Prince may be a stimulating cohabitant, if you'll allow me to say so, as well as a source of prestige. Think of yourself ten years from now, please. Or twenty, if you can manage it. And think of your children. Your earlier marriage was by no means a fortunate one and you have a right to love and happiness. If I were in your own advantageous position, my dear Arjumand, I should consider it a brilliant and audacious challenge!"

v

The musicians were playing under the lantern-decked trees. The Emperor was proud of his taste in music, which he thought of as unusually subtle and daring. He had imported some lutes from Portugal as well as some Siamese zithers, and this curious concoction of instruments, accompanied by some large Tibetan rattles, had been ordered to play a series of fashionable melodies. The effect was uncanny: the sounds went drifting among the shrubbery, twisting and darting and recoiling like some tortured little ghost.

Princess Arjumand watched the Empress walking toward her through the dusk. She was frightened of Nurmahal; she sensed an antagonism in Nurmahal. Or perhaps it wasn't quite antagonism; it might have been a sinuous kind of curiosity, or some probing and even tender sort of feminine cruelty. Whatever it was, she felt curiously uncomfortable in Nurmahal's presence, which suggested the musky nearness of some great silky cat.

The Empress' eyes were tense and alert. "What do you think of this hideous music?"

"It sounds like music out of the jungle. It sounds bloodthirsty," said Arjumand.

"I find it loathsome," declared the Empress. "One of Jahangir's new hobbies. I wish he'd stick to his butterflies, or those pretty Malayan seashells." Her pupils narrowed a little. "May I offer you my felicitations? I've just heard about it from Indira. I am delighted. And so is Jahangir. A niece becoming a daughter-in-law: it sounds cozy as well as useful. I have always approved of binding our families close together, as you know. And now, well, there is a special sort of festiveness about it. I am fond of you, my Arjumand. I wish you every kind of happiness. You're still children, you and Khurram. You are nineteen and he is twenty. Children are impulsive. They must learn caution and discretion as well as patience. Forgive me. I don't wish to sound like a dreary old governess. But a friendly little warning or two might be appropriate. Don't feel frightened, my child. Khurram is like that curious music. A little junglelike and dangerous, but with hidden possibilities."

She took Arjumand's hands in her own and gazed at her with a blank composure; then leaned over and pressed her broad, frozen lips to the Princess' forehead.

VI

It was a thick, sultry evening. The smell of rushes hung in the air. The bats loped over the inlets, chasing moths and mosquitoes. Sirkandar followed the path that led down to the boathouse, pausing now and again to flick an insect from his arm.

Old Hakim, the cross-eyed boatman, was squatting on the edge of the pier, mending the cable of one of the newly painted boats. He squinted gloomily at Sirkandar, and, holding a string between his teeth, he muttered sourly:

"Filthy weather, isn't it? Weather for the rats. That's what I call it."

Sirkandar stood on the pier and looked down at him silently.

"You look sad, my boy," said the boatman.

Sirkandar laughed. "I look sad, do I? Listen to me, Hakim. There's no one in all of Agra as happy as I! Look carefully! Just look again! I'm as happy as a bird in a tree!"

"You're drunk, Sirkandar."

"Drunk, am I? Oh, Hakim, what a clever man you are! Sad and drunk! My lovely Hakim, I'm as sober as a fish in the Jumna!"

"What's been happening, Sirkandar?"

"Happening! Happening! Nothing's been happening! Things go on. Men are men, women are women, beasts are beasts. Nothing changes in men's souls. They grow older, that's all. Love crumbles, that's all. But men are men and beasts are beasts."

"Something's wrong. You're miserable, Sirkandar."

Sirkandar hiccoughed into space. "Look, Hakim. Do I see a star? One single star! Look carefully, Hakim."

"Yes, there's only one star, it's always the first one to come out. It's the Star of the Golden Crocodile and it's always the first one. But wait. Two more minutes and you'll see another one if you're patient."

"Patient, patient—that's what I've never learned to be, my good fellow! Patient! Why? To wait till I'm old? To wait till I shrivel up and die?"

"No," said Hakim, stroking his rope, "merely to wait till the pain blows over. Just to wait two more minutes for a second star to come. Look at me, Sirkandar! I'm a penniless fool and you're beautiful and tall, with your life still before you! There's nothing to be sad about, Sirkandar. Nothing at all, nothing at all. . . ."

He tossed the cable into the boat, tucked his knife under the cable, took the string from his teeth and said softly: "Look, Sirkandar. There's a second star shining. That's the Star of the Yellow Frog. Do you know what it brings? It brings comfort and consolation. Just keep looking at it, my boy, and you'll feel the comfort in your soul. And look! There's a third one! It's the Star of the Insidious Grasshopper. It brings painlessness and indifference in the face of human misery. You can wait for the Star of the Bull and the Star of the Hermit Crab. And after that come the five little Stars of the Forgotten Maidens, which bring piety, tolerance, potency, good manners and the cure for blindness. But the main thing to look for is the Star of the Grasshopper. Just look at it for a while. You'll feel the comfort creep through your veins. . . ."

Hakim rose, rubbed his palm over his pockmarked face, then lumbered up the path until he vanished under the willows.

VII

Sirkandar stood motionless for several minutes, lost in thought, or what seemed like thought. The sickening sultriness was gone and the sky was filled with the light of the stars. He walked slowly across the pier and climbed down into the boat. The boat swayed uneasily; ripples floated across the water and the reflection of the stars turned into a wandering quicksilver.

Sirkandar knelt down and reached under the cable. He took Hakim's fish knife and looked at it carefully. He closed his eyes for a moment. Then he stretched out his arm, held his breath, raised his head and glanced steadily at the Star of the Grasshopper. With a sharp sideward thrust he buried the knife in his belly, sank down in the bottom of the boat and folded his arms across his chest.

He felt no pain—none whatever, merely a queer chilly breathlessness. The boat kept rocking lazily: then it gradually stopped rocking. The lake lay still as glass. Night fell and all was still until the voice of some quarrelsome nightbird shot out of the shrubbery.

VIII

The Princess Arjumand woke at sunrise on the following morning. There was a heaviness in the air, as though the rain were about to fall again. She tiptoed down the steps and crossed the empty courtyard. Then she hurried across the lawn, which was drenched with a heavy dew, and entered the twisting path that led through the willows down to the shore. She had no particular reason for strolling toward the water. She felt restless, that was all; she felt hesitant, preoccupied.

A bearded man in a tattered dhoti was sitting under a tree. He was nibbling cheerfully at a handful of blackberries. "Good morning!" he cried in his thin, bleating voice. "It's early in the day for a fine young lady to walk through the willows!"

The Princess had a nebulous impression of having seen the man before. She paused, pressed her finger to her brow and said: "Who are you?"

"I have no name," said the man sedately. "I'm a *kusilava*, that's all." (A *kusilava* was an itinerant story-teller.) "I've walked all the way from Kandahar telling my stories, and I'll wander on to Orissa, telling more of my stories."

"So many stories," said Arjumand. "How do you remember them all?"

"They're all part of a single story. If you remember the Big Story you also remember the little stories."

"But all those villages! All those cities! How do you remember their different languages?"

"I know thirty-three languages and eighty dialects," said the *kusilava*. "And if I come to a place where I don't happen to know the dialect I just tell them a story anyway, and they all enjoy the weirdness of it, for their dialect transforms a fish into a pitcher, a king into a mouse and a witch into a soup-bone."

Arjumand folded her arms and said quietly: "Won't you tell me a story, please?"

"What kind of story?" said the *kusilava*.

"What kinds can you tell?"

"Three kinds," said the *kusilava*, pursing his lips rather primly. "Stories about the Sufferings of the Unfortunate, about the Tricks of the Ingenious, and about the Triumphs of the Impassioned. Take your choice, my dear lady."

Arjumand reflected a moment and then said somewhat shyly, "Suppose you tell me a tale about the Triumphs of the Impassioned."

"Very well," said the *kusilava,* closing his eyes in concentration. "I'll tell you a story I once heard as a boy in Golkonda. Once upon a time the nymph Urvasi, sitting in a tree and playing her harp, looked down and saw King Pururavas ride by in his glory. She fell in love with his glittering eyes, and he looked into the tree and he fell in love with her supple body. And so the two of them, after a delicate exchange of mutual compliments, agreed to get married and to live in the royal palace. But the nymph set one condition. 'You must never let me see you naked, my darling, for that is the invariable custom among us nymphs. If I ever see you naked I will have to say goodbye to you.' One year passed and although the nymph was already swollen with his child, she had never seen the King in the nude, either in the morning or in the evening. All went smoothly in the palace and the King still loved Urvasi. But the heavenly nymphs in the clouds, the great Gandharvas, were beginning to miss her. 'This Urvasi has been staying among the mortals much too long,' they said to each other. So they thought of a trick. Urvasi had two lambs, one white and one black, which she kept in her bedroom. One night three Gandharvas swooped out of the sky and stole the black lamb, and on the following night the white one was stolen in an identical manner. Urvasi cried to her husband, 'What's wrong, Pururavas? Why do you put up with this? One would think there wasn't a man in the house to protect me!' So the King jumped out of the bed and started to rush after the thieves. But at that moment the sly Gandharvas sent a flash of lightning out of the sky and Urvasi saw her husband's naked body in the doorway. And customs being what they were among the heavenly nymphs, poor Urvasi quietly vanished like a wisp of smoke through the chimney."

"And she never saw him again?"

"That's the end of the story. I presume that she never saw poor Pururavas again."

"I'm afraid," remarked Arjumand, "that you picked the wrong story. This is the story about ingenious tricksters and not triumphant lovers, the way you promised me."

The *kusilava* frowned. "So it is. I quite forgot. But they're all the same in the end, my dear—the tricks, the sufferings, the triumphs. They seem different at the moment but that's only a passing phase. When the story comes to an end the same thing happens to them all."

The Princess slid a sapphire-colored bead into the story-teller's hand. Then she wandered along the path to the edge of the water. The grass licked at her ankles; all was still, nothing stirred.

IX

A sheet of mist hung over the shore, which was cool and deserted. The sun tipped the dew-soaked willows with a rosy sheen. A parrot rose from a bush and flew low overhead, so low that the Princess could almost touch it as it passed her. She stepped on the pier and tossed a pebble into the water. The ripples spread outward, then died in the huddled mist. She was brushed by a wing of memory as she watched the widening ripples: she was a child staring at a puzzle whose answer still eluded her. She almost had it: one more flicker in her brain and she would have it. But the answer rippled away beyond her mind, like the plum-blue water.

She walked out toward the little green boat which was tied to the pier. It was rocking very slightly in the ripples. She could smell the fresh paint in the morning dampness, and then she saw a dark hand clinging motionless to one of the oarlocks.

x

The trees were empty of fruit but a hundred laborers had been set to work, filling the boughs with paper flowers and gilded pineapples and grapes. The footmen were dressed like birds, with great red plumes sprouting from their shoulders, and the waiters were dressed like savages from the hills of the Brahmaputra. The wedding guests strolled by under the brocade umbrellas—provincial lords and maharanees as well as a scattering of Western ambassadors.

"A curious marriage," said an elderly Brahmin to a visiting Siamese philosopher. "Look at their faces. He looks bored. She looks miserable. They're not in love."

"Maybe she's miserable," hinted the philosopher, "precisely because she is in love."

"Possibly," said the Brahmin. He lifted his brows. "But not with him, most regrettably."

"Love is rare," said the philosopher mournfully, "among the powerful and the luxurious."

The Empress Nurmahal sat in the shade beside the lotus-filled pool, chatting with Ranee Mahil, who lived in the outskirts of Gwalior.

"It will be a disaster," murmured Nurmahal. "She is neither beautiful nor witty."

"Certainly not witty," nodded the Ranee. "But I find her quaint, with those long sad eyelashes."

"And as for Khurram," said the Empress acidly, "he is quite incapable of amorous devotion."

The Ranee smiled and lowered her eyes. "He's still young, dear. Give him time."

Up on the terrace Sultan Parviz waddled bashfully up to the bride. He held out a scroll tied with a narrow black ribbon. "I have no gift for you, dear Arjumand, except this poem which I have written for you. It isn't much, I'm afraid. But it comes from the heart. Old Kausiki muttered a charm over it and Krishnadev-araya gave it his blessing, so perhaps it will bring you luck. We all need luck, even the lucky ones!"

The shabby Parviz was followed by the spruce and handsome Shahriyar, whose long azure tunic was sprinkled with silver dragonflies. He held out a casket which he opened with his little finger. A golden duck lay inside it, with eyes of ruby and a beak of topaz. "It's from Shanghai," he whispered, "Hu-Shin-Po brought it along. Stroke its beak on a moonlit night and all your wishes will come true!"

The oldest of the Sultans, the disinherited and half-blind Khusru, emerged from the crowd and groped his way toward the Princess. He had been freed from his imprisonment for a three days' visit to the ceremonies. He looked pale and disheveled; he carried his head thrust forward myopically and his fingers kept fluttering nervously in front of him.

"Forgive me, Arjumand," he murmured. "I have neither gold nor a talent for poetry. All I can give you is this flower which I picked in the woods." He held out a small blue flower which was shaped like a daffodil. It drooped feebly between his fingers, half-wilted already. "It's the Flower of Eloquent Perception. It grows only in hidden crannies. Tuck it carefully in a book, my dear, and one of these days it will start to speak to you. It will tell you those marvelous secrets that even the Vedas don't know about. . . ."

XI

The Emperor climbed wearily down the circular stairway. At the bottom of the tower he stepped out on the balcony. The smell of the oil lamps seeped through the red lacquer screens and the sound of stringed instruments rose from the courtyard, thin and querulous.

From the balcony with its marble balustrade he could see as far as the horizon. Not as far as the shaggy hills that embraced the jungle, but far enough. He could see the clouds of gray dust quivering over the dry, depleted prairie and after the glare of the day the land took on a different sort of vastness, not that earthy and desolate and slightly sinister immensity but a spaciousness of violet and amethyst, half-insubstantial.

He stepped back through the silk-fringed curtains, crossed the terrace and descended the steps. With a look of bored reluctance he wandered slowly across the garden, preceded by four linkboys who carried hanging lanterns. Dusk fell brusquely at this time of year and a deepening gloom followed the Emperor's footsteps. The light of the lanterns grew sharp as the light in the heavens grew dim: it fell on the Emperor's turban, which was woven with diamonds, and on his trousers of white sarsenet embroidered with pearls. It fell across his face, blurred and pendulous and panting, and it shone on the broad virile face of the man beside him, a bearded old Turcoman whose name was Ahmed Khan. They came to a halt in front of the Emperor's aviary, which was a large iron cage elaborately decorated with twirls and curlicues. It stood on the edge of a pool and was filled with a variety of tropical birds which ranged from a Burmese goose to a Javanese cockatoo.

"The pheasant was badly cooked tonight, I thought," said the Emperor petulantly. "There was something wrong with the sauce. Did you notice it, Ahmed?"

"I tasted it too. It seemed sweetish," said Ahmed carefully.

"Do you suppose. . . ." Jahangir's voice trailed off in wistful dejection.

"I shouldn't worry, Your Highness. Probably some new Malayan recipe."

The Emperor peered into the aviary. "What is that bird in the corner, Ahmed? That tufted little gray one? I've never seen it before."

"A kind of duck, I think, Your Majesty. It has just arrived from Sumatra."

The Emperor reached into his tunic, took out a gold-encircled box, took a pill between his fingers and slid it dreamily into his mouth. The dusk swiftly deepened. The birds blinked their eyes as the lamplight flickered uneasily across their feathers. The Burmese goose buried its head under its ample gray wing; the Tibetan hawk opened his beak and closed it again with a baleful expression.

"Those lanterns—they make everything look a little ghostly, don't they, Ahmed? Ghosts, ghosts! We're nothing but ghosts, both we and the birds, aren't we, Ahmed?" He chuckled faintly. "I'm a rather prosaic sort of person, dear Ahmed, but sometimes strange thoughts come popping into my head. Note that down, please, Ahmed. The world is a jungle filled with lanterns and the lanterns shine on a face, or the beak of an angry bird. But only for a moment. Beyond lies the darkness. But is it the darkness which is the reality or is it the lantern? What do you think?"

"Both are real," said Ahmed equivocally, scribbing away in his notebook.

Jahangir turned away. He suddenly hated the birds. He felt nothing at this moment but a moral fatigue that bordered on nausea; he felt that he was being slowly and remorselessly sucked into an invisible quagmire. Thousands of things, thousands of people! Nothing but words and things and people! Not to mention all these birds, all these lanterns and curlicues! Oh, for emptiness, he thought despairingly. Oh, for the peace of a vacuum!

A woman crossed the lawn and paused with a smile beside the Emperor. She wore a gown of rippled silk embroidered with yellow roses and over that a short-sleeved jacket of indigo striped with gold. A triple string of pearls hung around her narrow neck and from her ears dangled a pair of long ruby earrings.

"My Arjumand," said the Emperor, and a glint of pleasure crept into his eyes again. "How very pretty you look out tonight. Are you getting along with Khurram?" He scratched his cheek and regarded her thoughtfully. "You must be patient with Khurram, you know. He's moody. He's difficult. He hasn't Shahriyar's charm or Khusru's high-mindedness. And he hasn't that certain something in poor Parviz, shall we call it poetry? He has always been hostile to me. There is a well of antagonism in him. He feels hostile toward absolutely everything—his father as well as his brothers, the tigers as well as the elephants, and even those poor sacred cows. . . ."

He took Arjumand's arm and led her back toward the terrace. "These sons of mine; tell me, Arjumand, what on earth am I to do with them? I've been unduly severe with poor old Khusru after that idiotic rebellion of his. It was needlessly severe, I suppose, to keep him locked in his bungalow all these years. But Khusru's ideas are egalitarian. Not that the Empire has no use for philanthropy. But Khusru's notions were distinctly fanatical. They would have led to ruin and anarchy. And as for Khurram, he's a bigot. He poses as a Follower of the Prophet but all that he believes in is himself, unfortunately. Isn't it true, my dear Arjumand? He reveres nothing, nothing except power. He is a militant Moslem not out of a spiritual conviction but out of an inner intolerance, a purely personal turbulence. And then Shahriyar! Shahriyar, I regret to say, is a flibbertigibbet. He has no use for anything but chic and elegance. Quite aside from certain less presentable tendencies, mind you. And finally Parviz. God help us, what can we say about poor Parviz? He is floating away into nothingness with all those misty meditations. I love Parviz but I am oppressed by his similarity to myself. I shall never appoint him my successor, that much is certain. And so the whole deplorable matter boils down to that rascal Khurram. . . ."

They stood for a moment on the edge of the terrace. The moon peeped through the clouds. It shone faintly on Arjumand's necklace and on the diamonds of Jahangir's turban.

Jahangir looked at her thoughtfully with the casual tenderness of the old and ailing. She would suffer a little, he reflected; she would certainly suffer, but did it matter particularly? There was a stubborn animal strength in that small, sharp-chinned face; the resilience of a child coupled with the tenacity of an elderly woman. There was strength but also confusion. Her lips began to tremble. What was wrong? What was she afraid of? Was she alarmed at the thought of all that glory which was awaiting her?

"You look distrait," said the Emperor. "Have you been listening, my dear Arjumand?"

Arjumand nodded her head solemnly. "Yes, yes, I've been listening."

"Attentively?" said the Emperor teasingly.

"Oh, yes! Attentively!" said the Princess.

Jahangir looked at her lovingly and took her fingers between his own. "There is a bewilderment in your head. Isn't there, my kitten?" he said slyly.

PART TWO

The First Murder

The men from the pale, eccentric West were beginning to seep into the Empire. Jahangir welcomed them; they amused him. They gave "a spice to the sauce," as he put it. Three-masted vessels came gliding into the listless harbors of India and their passengers went swarming through the drab coastal settlements. The French landed in Chandernagore and in the south at Pondicherry; the Dutch came to Pulicat and Sadras and Nogapatam; the English settled in the new sprawling suburbs of Bengal and the Portuguese in the inlets of Bassein and the isle of Diu.

The fashionable young Rajahs invited the strangers to their palaces. Bungalows and rest houses were built for the visitors from Goa and Surat. Brocaded suites in the summer pavilions were reserved for the guests from London and Coimbra. European manners were *à la mode*. European sauces were stirred in the kitchens. The poems of Ronsard were read in the salons and the paintings of Antwerp were hung in the loggias. Gloves from Paris, furs from Muscovy and lace from Venice appeared in the wardrobes. The Maharajah of Mysore had a musical box from the Lake of Geneva.

The English factors in Surat lived in especial pomp and elegance. In the ships of the East India Company they imported copper and quicksilver, as well as clocks from Buckinghamshire and gentlemen's slippers from Bath. And the ships returned to England laden with printed cotton goods, with sugar and spices, with opium and indigo. Now and again there was trouble. In 1612 a ship called the *Dragon*, which was commanded by a Captain Best, and another ship, the *Osiander,* commanded by a Captain Nathaniel Salmon, met some vessels from Lisbon and fought a brief but bitter battle. In the following year a group of Portuguese seized four of the Mogul ships, slaughtered the deckhands and plundered the cargoes. And quite aside from commercial rivalries there were delicate religious tensions. To the already chaotic conglomeration of Indian deities the pale-faced missionaries now added the Christian God, with his hymnbooks and crucifixes.

In 1615 Sir Thomas Roe was sent to the court of Jahangir as the duly accredited ambassador from the court of King James I. He landed in Surat and traveled by coach to the Emperor's court, which happened to be in Ajmer at that particular moment.

One autumn day Sir Thomas and the Emperor were strolling idly through the park. It was a calm musky evening; bees were flickering among the honeysuckle.

"Tell me, please," said Jahangir amiably, "about this England of yours. I have some difficulty in visualizing it."

"It is greenish," said Sir Thomas. "There are no deserts in England, and very few snows."

"There are fogs, I hear," said the Emperor.

Sir Thomas nodded. "Fogs and drizzles."

"And the animals. You have no elephants?"

"We have foxes, as well as otters."

"Do you eat these foxes and otters?"

"Not as a rule," muttered Sir Thomas. "We eat mutton and fish, and occasionally a slab of beef."

"What has struck me," said Jahangir thoughtfully, "is the English composure. You smile but you never titter. Your faces freeze but you never grow angry. Is it that you feel no powerful emotions? Or do you make a point of concealing them?"

"We try to cultivate," said the ambassador, smirking slightly, "the art of indifference."

"And is it true," said Jahangir, "that the English are allowed only a single wife?"

"It's quite true," said the ambassador with a glassy expression.

"Doesn't it seem," said the Emperor jovially, "a trifle joyless, just between the two of us?"

Sir Thomas looked stern. "I was recently informed," he said coldly, "that last year in the Deccan, on the death of a certain Rajah, sixty of his wives suddenly decided to jump into the flames. It's all a question of what we choose to consider joyless, Your Majesty. Our climate is cool and our passions are subdued, relatively speaking."

Jahangir smiled. *"Autres pays, autres mœurs,"* he said wistfully. "There are times, my dear Sir Thomas, when I wish that our ladies had a foggier temperament!"

11

There were certain things in the Mogul Empire which distinctly shocked Sir Thomas Roe. Certain habits, certain mannerisms, the sacred cows and the ubiquitous nudities, not to mention the popular dances, which he considered deplorable, and the Grand Mogul's architecture, which he thought appalling. He was struck by something vulgar and even ramshackle in the Imperial Palace. The Hall of Audience, with its marble and porphyry, bordered on a puerile ostentation: it was littered with irrelevant objects, cuckoo clocks and velvet umbrellas and scattered bits of embroidery which were covered with dust and bored with mothholes.

And another thing which somewhat troubled him was a conspicuous indifference toward human life. One day he happened to go hunting with the Emperor Jahangir. Jahangir, who had hitherto impressed him as a kindly sort of man, lost his temper when a servant spoiled his shot at a nilgaw: he had him promptly executed on the edge of the woods. And once, during a battle which was staged between two raging elephants, one of the handlers was badly injured; being of no further use, his body was tossed into the Jumna.

Sir Thomas was a tall, tapering man with ruddy hair and oyster-gray eyes set in an oval face which was flushed with blood vessels. Sometimes a flickering of intensity stirred in the pallor of his eyes and the veins in his cheeks darkened to a fine shade of mauve. But aside from such fleeting symptoms he never displayed superfluous opinions and his relations with the Emperor were cordial and correct.

"You have just remarked," he said to Jahangir as they strolled past the flowerbeds, where some Chinese chrysanthemums were beginning to flower, "you have just remarked, if I understood you correctly, that evil is inherent in being an individual, that is to say, in being a separate and unique human being. Let us assume that this is true. But on another point we disagree. I argue that good is also inherent in these separate human beings. A capacity and a yearning for excellence is also inherent in them. You say that only as a firmly governed group are men productive of good, and only a benevolent tyranny can successfully guide them toward achievements. I disagree. Eliminate their separateness and you may eliminate some forms of evil. But you also eliminate the more delicate forms of human nobility. Man's destiny, Your Majesty, does not lie in grandiose cities or glittering armies; it also lies in spiritual insight, in the flash of poetry, in secret joys."

"Perhaps," said Jahangir with a mellow look, "you have misunderstood me a little. I have no wish to eliminate evil. That is impossible, unfortunately, just as it is impossible to eliminate the plague or the cobras. Indeed, I'm not quite sure that we should eliminate the plague and the cobras. Evil is inherent in the scheme of things and to eliminate this weight of evil would be to threaten the world with a dangerous imbalance. No, Sir Thomas, we all do evil, we are fated to do evil. And doing evil brings remorse; it brings pain and expiation. You were shocked the other day—don't deny it, please, Sir Thomas—when I had that stupid Ghopal killed for his inexcusable clumsiness. Very well; it was rather impetuous of me. But Ghopal's life was nearing its end in any case. He had taken to drugs. He beat his wife. He brought no pleasure to anyone. And I suspect that his death brought displeasure only to me, who had a silly nightmare about it, and possibly to you, with your English humanitarianism! Ah, Sir Thomas, if we never did evil we would never suffer remorse, we would never learn to expiate, we would never have nightmares. We'd be shadowless creatures, vapid and contemptible in the eyes of Nature, which are so incomparably wiser and more penetrating than our own!"

Sir Thomas glanced covertly at the Emperor. There was a curious texture to his skin; it had the iridescent and slightly morbid sheen of mole fur or Venetian velvet. It looked deeply unhealthy and faintly inhuman. And his darting black eyes suggested some trapped little beast which was screaming for rescue from that huge, hideous body.

III

Sir Thomas said goodbye to the Emperor, stepped into his coach and started homeward. The road led through the hunting grounds and along the outskirts of the city, where scrawny children with bloated bellies crouched in front of their dirty huts and wilted men with dung in their hair squatted in saintly meditation. Usually Sir Thomas drew the curtains of his coach as he passed this region; the naked squalor and the dismal apathy were distasteful to his nerves. But today, in the evening light that sprayed like gold through the atmosphere, he looked at these suffering people with a deeper attentiveness. Their life seemed so subdued that hardly a ripple passed over it. It was like a long-neglected cistern, filled with twigs and dead leaves, with nothing to hint at what lay buried far below in that murky water. No sign of passion touched their faces. There was only an all-engulfing quietude. Were they unhappy, after all? Or were they merely comatose? Was their suffering merely physical? Did they have their secret joys? But then he grew disgusted with the smugness of such speculations, closed the curtains briskly and rode on toward his villa.

The road went coiling through a shadowy stretch of euphorbias. He caught sight of a temple half-hidden among the boughs. The light of the setting sun fell on the dark writhing statues and for an instant Sir Thomas thought that a group of dancers had gathered in the forest and were performing some secret, orgiastic sort of ritual.

He asked the coachman to halt and strolled toward the temple. An Untouchable covered with sores was pleading for alms beside the entrance and a *saddhu* sat motionless under a nearby tree. Nothing stirred: neither the *saddhu* nor the begging syphilitic, neither the insects in the leaves nor the obscene dancers. As Sir Thomas stepped gingerly past the moss-stained temple, studying cautiously and a little guiltily the arching hierarchy of postures, he grew aware of the nuzzling nearness of something satanic. He was neither shocked nor exactly titillated by these fornicating friezes: hundreds of nude, expressionless lovers in hundreds of lewd fantastic attitudes, porous breasts, rain-streaked buttocks, members green and wispy as asparagus—they had lost all traces of human sensuality, they resembled a great cascade of strange, half-rotten vegetables. These innumerable bulging bodies, spotted by birds and mutilated by the centuries, all these interwoven demons with smiling faces and upturned fingers—what on earth were they trying to say? That evil was good? Was that it? That all was confusion, that love was illusion, that suffering was illusion, that even God was illusion and a pointless proliferation engulfed the world like a nightmare? Was this all? Was this the answer to man's hope and his suffering?

Sir Thomas walked thoughtfully back to his coach and rode over the carpet of dead, crackling leaves.

IV

Prince Khurram was sitting in his bedroom in Agra one day, writing a letter to his wife, who was visiting a cousin in Patna. He was telling her about the battle he had recently won in the Deccan, where he had subjugated the powerful old fortress of Ahmadnagar. "My father," he wrote, "has rewarded me with the title of Shahjahan. Thirty thousand men and twenty thousand horses have been placed under my orders. Are you proud of me, dear Arjumand? The emoluments are vast, the prestige glitters. All seems well. And yet, and yet. . . . When will I have the actual power which my dreams keep dangling in front of me?"

The thin, bleating whine of the muezzin swam through the air. He put down his pen and glanced toward the balcony. It looked like rain: purplish clouds were racing past overhead. The leaves rattled faintly as the wind blew through the branches. Below he heard the creak of an oxcart on its way to the vegetable garden. A flock of sparrows danced over the lawn, which was yellow with dust.

A little red carriage drove rapidly along the driveway, swaying in the random gusts of wind and spreading wings of dust behind it. The door swung open and a woman in an azure veil stepped under the portico. Three minutes later there was a sharp little knock on Khurram's door.

"Come in," he called softly; the curtains parted. It was Nurmahal. She wore a dress of emerald green embroidered with silver lotuses and her sea-blue slippers were sprinkled with silver stars.

Khurram stepped to the window and lowered the blinds, so that the light of the sun dropped golden ladders across the wall. Nurmahal's tall, powerful body was striped like a tiger's. Only her face was lost in shadow, floating in the darkness like a mask.

"Good evening, my dear Khurram."

"My name," said Khurram, "is no longer Khurram."

"And what is it, may I ask?"

"I am Shahjahan, the Lord of the Universe!"

Nurmahal stared at him stonily. "I too have changed my name. I'm no longer merely Nurmahal, the Light of the Palace. I'm the Empress Nurjahan, the Light of the World!" She laughed aridly. "Do I blaze and glitter? Do you want to know the truth, Khurram? Night of the Soul they should have called me. I detest the light; I detest the world!"

"Our titles," said Khurram sententiously, "are meant to hide us, not to expose us."

"No doubt," said Nurmahal, suddenly bored. "You've been writing letters, I see."

"I've been writing to Arjumand."

"Ardently, I hope?"

"Politely," said Khurrah.

"I am pleased to hear that you're polite, at any rate."

"Am I ever impolite, my dear?"

"It was an idiotic marriage."

Khurram flushed. "Do you feel qualified to judge the matter?"

"It was a brutal, calculated business."

"Those words sound rather quaint coming from you, my love."

"No doubt," said Nurmahal. "I am your stepmother, but I am not precisely blinded by maternal solicitude."

She walked across the room and knelt on the cushion beside the window; Khurram stared through the blinds and nervously fondled the golden tassel. The tension between them was the tension of lovers outgrowing their love, a little stale yet still disturbing, a little guilty yet still petulant, a little bored with their lovemaking yet still jealous, suspicious, vulnerable.

"You came in your beautiful new coach, I see," said Khurram.

"It arrived last week from London. It's a gift from Sir Thomas."

"Is it comfortable?" said Khurram absently.

Nurmahal smiled. "It is fiercely uncomfortable. Being from London, it is smart, but I prefer a palanquin or even an elephant. . . . Look, my darling. See what I've brought you." She placed a box on the table and drew out a phial filled with rosewater, and then she unwrapped a large onyx which she held up to the sunlight. It was engraved with a naked Eve offering an apple to a lustful Adam.

"Charming, isn't it? French, I imagine. A bit salacious but not really. There are three things in the world that never lose their purity, no matter what happens: women, water, and gems. You can read it in the *Mahabharata.*"

Khurram glanced at her warily. He caught the musk of patchouli. His very fear and distrust of Nurmahal acted perversely as a kind of stimulant. Even his feeling of guilt produced a certain defiant gusto. It was as though their very resentment kept their lust still alive; the faint wind of cruelty still fanned the dying embers.

They lay on the couch, drugged and listless, dejected, and now the stripes of light on her flesh made her tigerish posture more plausible. She opened her eyes, glanced toward the table and picked up a paper knife. She pointed it to her belly and laughed softly. "What would you do if I really killed myself?"

Khurram stared at her sardonically. "Yes, I know. You are sick of life."

"Not of life, quite," said Nurmahal. "Sick of love. Or what passes for love."

"What is love?" muttered Khurram.

"God only knows," cried the Empress wearily. "All I know is that I've imagined it a million times in my dreams but when I'm awake, I don't know why, it seems like a farce and a filthiness."

"Because," said Khurram, "you feel nothing."

"Not what I should, at least," said Nurmahal.

Khurram said: "You should have been a man."

Nurmahal laughed. "You may be right, my boy."

They lay naked side by side, lost in thought, limp, melancholy. Khurram turned and glanced furtively at Nurmahal's body: flat-breasted, Amazonian and muscular, with nipples small and puckered as raspberries, tufts of fox-colored silk sprouting from her armpits and sexualia, and skin glossy with heat, delicately creased with the gathering years. They lay without speaking in the plum-smelling sultriness and finally she rose and slipped on her garments.

After she had gone, the Sultan put on his robe and stepped out on the balcony.

The little carriage with its two black horses was disappearing in the distance; only the cloud of dust from the hoofs still hung in the windless air. The storm clouds had passed. No rain had fallen after all. Two link-boys were sprinkling the rosebushes with pitchers of water.

V

Two days after Arjumand's return they left for a visit to
Fatehpur-Sikri. They were accompanied by Indira, one of Khurram's earlier wives: a blond-haired beauty from Kandahar, with
the sharp blue eyes of a Kirghiz. Fatehpur-Sikri was a city of artifice, built for glory by the Emperor Akbar and already falling
into dinginess and decay. The pools were dried up, arteries of
ants darkened the flagstones and the grass was seething with
vipers and salamanders. But the whimsical tracery of its turrets
was still visible in the level distances, and the Himalayan vines
were still tended by the gray-haired gardeners.

Arjumand strolled through the grounds toward the summer
pavilion. This was a fanciful wooden structure built on the
side of an octagonal fishpond. The pillars were peeling and the
gilded shingles were crumbling but the delicate silver bells that
hung from the eaves still tinkled faintly. A monkey on a chain
was playing on the lawn in front of the pavilion, teasing a big
green parrot strutting among the flowers.

She stepped into the pavilion. The smell of dankness filled the
place. No one had been here for weeks. Dead hornets littered
the floor. The shutters were closed but beams of light pierced the
slats, cutting viciously across the darkness like white-hot knives.
Some mildewed cushions lay scattered on the floor, a dusty fan
lay on the windowsill.

She started to move through the empty rooms, listening to her
footsteps echoing eerily. In one of the rooms a bowl of roses had
spilled its petals across the tiles. They lay sprinkled like butterfly
wings, bursting crisply under her feet. In another room some chil-

dren's toys lay heaped on a table: tiny coaches and cradles, a lion with sawdust oozing from its belly, and a doll with its arms flung skyward and a hole in its chest. As she peered at the little doll a great red spider popped from the hole and shot across the table and dove into space.

The adjoining room was filled with discarded theatrical costumes. They hung in a row along the wall—Rajput warriors and Tibetan lamas, clad in clouds of yellowed lace and tapering crowns of rusty tinfoil. All were spotted and stained; a stench of vinegar hovered about them. On the opposite wall hung the masks—black-cheeked witches and white-cheeked courtesans, as well as some Persian demons with shaggy manes and fangs like a tiger's.

Arjumand glanced into the mirror which hung by the door. The light was dim in the dusty glass: her face looked like a ghost's. The cracks in the quicksilver drew narrow wrinkles across her cheeks. She wondered: "Was I ever beautiful? Does anyone think that I am beautiful? Oh, how soon will I be shriveled and utterly hideous, like old Kausiki?"

A wave of horror, such as she was experiencing more and more frequently, suddenly engulfed her: outwardly it was a horror of old age, of bodily decay, of an ultimate lovelessness, but its flavor was so permeating that it infected everything around her—the very air stank of cruelty; even the light had a deathly sheen to it.

Something was stirring behind her: a thin pale shape in a long white gown. Some troubled phantom out of the past, some dim denizen of these rotting precincts? She wheeled around: it was only Indira, who had come to look for her.

"What are you doing here?" said Indira. "All alone! You look terrified!"

"No, not terrified," said Arjumand. "Merely sad. With all these phantoms."

"Come. It's late," said Indira. "The guests are waiting in the Room of the Water Lilies."

"Tell me, Indira," cried Arjumand, clasping Indira's hand suddenly, "what do you think? Will he ever love me? Is it possible that he will ever love me?"

"Who?" said Indira, pale and expressionless.

"Who do you think?" said the Princess quietly.

"Oh," said Indira, raising her brows. "I almost thought for a moment—" But then she smiled at Arjumand blandly. "Of course he loves you. In his own strange fashion."

She drew closer to Arjumand, kissed her gently on the ear, then took her by the hand and led her back into the hard, dry sunlight.

VI

"Last night I saw a ghost," muttered the Empress, lifting her head.

"Where did you see it, my dear?" said the Emperor drowsily.

"In the jungle of my dreams!"

"And what was it?" whispered the Emperor.

"It was a woman with the head of a jackal and her breasts all covered with hair. She came up to me," said Nurmahal, "and said, 'Beware, Mihru-n nisa. The snakes are rising from the heat-blistered banks of the Godavari!'"

"And what did she mean, this jackal woman?" said Jahangir, rubbing his eyes.

"Something unpleasant," said the Empress bitterly, "but I can't imagine what. She crept up through the dusk and placed her finger on my throat, and there was something in her eyes which looked vaguely familiar. She whispered, 'The time of the centipedes is coming, Mihru-n nisa!' and then she faded like wood smoke among the branches."

"Odd," said the Emperor. "I've dreamed of elephants but never of jackals."

"It was an omen. But of what? I cannot imagine," said Nurmahal.

She rose and stepped to the window. The far-off plains were shimmering with heat. The slopes in the west were shawled in a grape-colored mist. The mist grew tinted with rose: then with opal and then with gold. For one more moment the waste land still shone with an unreal splendor and then it sank into the sun-baked desolation of the day.

Nurmahal dipped her face in the bowl to freshen her eyes a little. She paused by the mirror and ran a comb through her hair. Then she sank on the cushions beside Jahangir. She glanced down at his face: tiny tears clung to his eyelids, which were swollen and slightly purple under the effect of the drugs. His shaggy chin sagged over his throat; his wrinkled cheeks were peppered with gray. His naked brown body, encased in rose-tinted cushions, looked hideous and diseased, almost deliquescent: purple veins bulged from his belly, large green splotches covered his legs, and his shrunken genitalia were completely hidden by a thick gray moss.

"Tell me," said Nurmahal a little absently: "how do you feel about Khurram?"

"He has just won a beautiful battle at Ahmadnagar," said Jahangir.

"But what are your feelings?"

"Fatherly affection, tinged with alarm," said Jahangir.

"Are you sure of his loyalty?"

"Not in the least," said Jahangir, blinking.

"Do you love him? Do you admire him?"

"I love and admire him," moaned the Emperor, still stupefied by opium, "since I must choose at least one son to love and admire." He smiled wryly at Nurmahal. "Khurram has fire in his soul. He must be a splendid hot-blooded lover. . . ."

Nurmahal's eyes froze slightly. "Please forgive me if I say so, but I've never thought of Khurram as a suitable successor to you."

"Oh! Really?" said the Emperor mockingly. "And whom do you suggest?"

"Khusru is out of the question, naturally. I've thought of Parviz, but poor Parviz! He lies the whole day long in a kind of adipose stupor and it's painful to imagine our dear Parviz on the throne. Khurram has his points, of course, I grant you. But he's treacherous. I don't trust him."

"I always thought you were rather fond of our little Khurram," said the Emperor bleakly.

"I have no feelings toward Khurram, either friendly or hostile. But I have opinions. And my opinion is that he would cut your throat if he could, Jahangir."

The Emperor turned his bleary old eyes toward the window.

"Those are disparaging words," he murmured, with a sad little sigh. "I think of Khurram as a bit of a scoundrel but not precisely as a parricide."

"His ambition," said Nurmahal, "amounts to ferocity."

"Well," said Jahangir, running his tongue over his lips, "that leaves Shahriyar."

The Empress looked remote. "It does indeed. What do you think of him?"

"Shahriyar is a donkey," said Jahangir.

"He is not as silly as he seems," said Nurmahal.

"Let him dabble about with his draperies!"

"Shahriyar has taste," said Nurmahal thoughtfully.

"My dear child," said the Emperor, wincing, "I have no objections to his choice of colors, although chartreuse has never been a favorite hue of mine, and I am perfectly willing to overlook his choice of bed-companions, although that stableboy from Peshawar seems difficult to swallow. But when all is said and done, my mind rebels at the thought of Shahriyar. My real objection to Shahriyar is the following: he's superficial. He's a dilettante."

"I suggest," said Nurmahal thinly, "that you meditate on the matter. I'd rather see a harmless pansy on the throne than a black assassin."

Two Kashmir servants parted the curtains and entered the room. They set the breakfast tray on the ottoman which stood by the bed, filled two goblets with rice wine, two more goblets with the milk of a coconut, and two tapering blue cups with warmish tea from Darjeeling.

The Emperor picked up a goblet. He peered at it glumly and set it down again.

"Masks," he whispered. "Nothing but masks. That's all I see —just a world of masks. Khusru wears a mask, Khurram wears a mask, our beautiful Shahriyar wears a gilded mask. What are they like underneath, will you tell me? When are we really ourselves? Is it at public moments, when we act in accordance with our outer convictions and build up an image of our character for the rest of the world? Or is it in private moments when we sit in the shade of a tamarind, listening to the strumming of a zither or the chattering of the birds? Or is it in moments of passion, when love or hate comes surging over us? Which is it, Mihru-n nisa? When do we shed those horrible masks?"

"At none of those times," answered Nurmahal. "Neither with the crowd nor in solitude. We are ourselves only in the jungle of our dreams, I think, Jahangir, and even in our dreams we still wear masks. Those grinning masks are our true identity."

She drank her glass and crossed the room and stepped out on the shadowed balcony. Now the whole land lay stunned, strangled in the clutch of the Indian sunlight. All that vastness! All those multitudes! Thousands and thousands of nameless villages sprinkled like seeds over the immensity of burning prairie and steaming underbrush. Even the colors were crushed by the sunlight. The grass was grayish, the pond was grayish, even the overhanging sky receded into a dead hollow grayness.

Far off, beyond the trees which fringed the banks of the Jumna, she could see a thin black column wandering westward through the dust.

VII

It was in the year 1616 that the plague struck the Punjab. The pestilence spread slowly through the rest of the Empire, northward as far as the mountain passes and westward to the sands of Baluchistan, and it raged for seventy months before it finally dwindled away. First the rats and the mice were affected. Then it spread to the Untouchables. Then it filtered across the Hindu populace, who perished in droves, and then through the Muslims. Only a few scattered cities like Fatehpur-Sikri escaped. In Allahabad the bells kept tolling the whole night long and in Gwalior pyres were lit to keep the vultures from the heart of the city. In Benares the corpses were dragged to the ghats and hurled to the crocodiles, who refused to devour them, so that the Ganges was choked with flesh. In Ajmer one whole quarter of the city was burned to the ground in the hope of sealing off the contagion. And in Panipat the last survivors went chanting through the gates, leaving the dead and the dying to fester in their blankets.

In the villages the people did not grasp at first what was happening. They saw their families one by one develop strange greenish swellings. Two days later they started to suppurate from deep purple abscesses. They danced a Dance of Death to the sound of the village flute, trying to exorcise the demons with incense and music. The roads were filled with terrified processions fleeing westward, and the sick were left ruthlessly to die in the fields. Whole towns were exterminated. The temples were deserted. Jackals crept through the empty streets, looking for random tidbits. And the pest spread even to the seas, where ships sailed aimlessly on the tepid water, their sails flapping idly and their decks covered with skeletons. In the monasteries the monks wandered about in their saffron robes, murmuring endlessly: "All the Substances of Humanity are Evanescent. True Wisdom comes only with the calm of Self-extinction."

But the curious thing was that with all this prevalence of dying and this fearful ubiquity of every aspect of death, men stopped thinking about death and the meaning of life grew more intense to them. It resembled the stirring of some precious fluid in a delicate phial, shining more and more faintly through the black inhuman wilderness.

VIII

One autumn evening Sultan Khusru was sitting in his small mountain bungalow. The wind whimpered fitfully as it swept through the woods, and through the noise of the wind crept other, more delicate noises: the far-off chattering of angry monkeys, the mournful cry of a lonely hill-bird.

"You must try to comprehend, Your Highness," said the old man softly.

"I do not comprehend," said the Sultan, "nor do I wish to comprehend. The faith of Islam is like a knife, sharp and hard and to me repugnant, but at least it is a religion, clean, plausible, coherent. Christianity I comprehend. Zoroastrianism I comprehend. Even the Gods of the Baluchi tribesmen and the Naga savages I comprehend. But my dear Ani, what are we to think of this shadowy and amorphous religion which swarms through India like a horde of locusts, nibbling away at her blood vessels? No one knows what it really is. I have often asked but no one can tell me. It is like a mist, vague and blurred, slightly malignant, filled with phantoms. It is merely a feeling of dark religiousness and not a true religion. It has a thousand different faces, it is a blending of myths and magic, it is everything and nothing, it's just a feverish conglomeration."

"It hints at everything," said the old man, nodding.

"And tells us nothing," said Prince Khusru.

"It is like a poem. It sings. It lingers."

"A black, nightmarish poem."

Ani Rai reached over the table and picked up his *vina* and sounded a tentative note on it. Then he started to sing in his squeaky old voice:

> *"The wind keeps on blowing.*
> *The clouds from the heart of midnight*
> *Blind the eyes of the little moon-lady.*
> *I listen; I wait. The leaves*
> *Tremble gently on the rhododendrons.*
> *The snake lies coiled on the precipice."*

Khusru stared at the old man, but all he could see in his semi-blindness was a shriveled gray shape with a dark brown face that looked like a crabapple, with the deep clever wrinkles catching the gleam of the candle. He still could see, but only dimly: the colors were ill-defined and watery and the shapes melted together like a herd of cattle in the fog. And with this vagueness of vision reality itself relapsed into vagueness. His memories had grown confused. His thoughts were growing

troubled. Even the people round him seemed to dissolve into ambiguity. And his own face, as though in response to the impre-
cision of the outer world, had taken on a kind of moonlit pallor.
The blinded eyes were set deep under their heavy oily lids and
only the mouth retained its expression, pained and reluctant, uneasily smiling.

For a while they sat in silence. Then Khusru said absently:

"Tell me, Ani, why does power and the lust for power bring
such murderous cruelty? We see the poor and the weak living in
peacefulness and tolerance. But the rich and the powerful seem
to live in perpetual fury."

"There must be powerful ones in the world, just as there are
tigers in the jungle."

"And must we accept this?" said Khusru.

"Just," said Ani, "as we accept all evil things. Even the worst
of us," he added, "carry gold locked up in our hearts, and even
the best of us carry dark little bottles filled with poison."

He struck a note on his *vina* and started to sing again:

> *"The wind keeps on blowing.*
> *Where are you, my love?*
> *The dust swirls over the cactuses*
> *While I lie and weep in the darkness.*
> *Leaves rattle in the deodars*
> *And a bird swoops down from the hills.*
> *The stones dig at my breast*
> *As I lie and sob for you, my love."*

They sat silently and the wind went whistling past the bungalow, and as they gazed through the open doorway they saw a
party of horsemen approaching. Rajput horsemen they seemed
to be, in their flapping robes of indigo: they were riding up the
path, followed by some slaves carrying a palanquin.

The first of the horsemen, a lean dark man with a face like a hyena's, stood in the doorway.

"Yes? What is it?" said Ani Rai.

"We have come for the Sultan," said the soldier hoarsely.

"You have orders?"

"We do," said the soldiers, thrusting a document in front of Ani.

"And where will you take him?" whispered Ani.

"To the Jhelum," said the soldier.

"The Jhelum," said Ani, expressionless.

"It's Asaf Khan," said the soldier uneasily. "It's Asaf Khan who's his new protector, and the orders have come straight from the Emperor. That's what it says in the paper, isn't it? It's Asaf Khan, that's who it is, and we'll be carrying him all the way to the river Jhelum, according to the orders."

Khusru was listening in silence. Ani Rai glanced at the floor. The silhouettes of the horsemen were barely visible under the trees and the curtains of the palanquin fluttered feebly in the darkness.

I X

The flamingos swept down from the Oxus and came to rest on the shores of the island. Their feathers lay scattered in the grass like rosy petals. Prince Khusru sat on the veranda: the shapes of the birds crossing the sky looked like ribbons of fire to his half-blinded eyes. He could see their beautiful wings as they floated gracefully across the sunset, but they vanished from sight as they sank into the reeds one by one.

A boat moved toward the island from the opposite shore. Three men were in the boat but the Sultan could not see their faces.

"There is a boat, isn't there, Azam?"

"There is, Your Highness," said the fat young Muslim.

"Who is in the boat? Can you tell?"

"I see a man with a scar on his cheek."

"It sounds like Asaf Khan."

"That's who it is, Your Highness. Unquestionably."

"And who else?"

"A man with a scimitar."

"A soldier, could it be?"

"It is a soldier, definitely, Your Highness."

"And the third?"

"The third is a boy. He is wearing a cloak with a golden collar."

"Dawar Baksh," said Khusru softly.

"Dawar Baksh," said Azam, nodding.

The boat nuzzled its way through the stiff blue cattails. Dawar Baksh leaped onto the pier and ran up to the veranda while Asaf Khan waited on the pier for the soldier to fasten the cable.

Dawar flung his arms around the Sultan and kissed him on both cheeks.

"Dawar! Dawar!" grunted Khusru. "You're as tall as I! You've turned into a man, my darling."

"Can you see me, father? A little?"

"Yes, I see you," said Khusru.

"I was on my way to Srinagar, but Asaf Khan said I could come if I wanted. So I came. It's only for a moment," said Dawar breathlessly.

"So you came. Yes. Sit down, Dawar." He waved at the fat little Azam. "Bring us a platter of grapes, please, Azam." He looked tenderly toward Dawar Baksh, whose lean young shape he barely discerned in the shade of the veranda. Dawar Baksh was a beautiful boy, rosy-cheeked and slightly effeminate, with long silky lashes shading his huge sea-blue eyes.

"I've never been in Kashmir. Is Kashmir pleasant?" said Dawar judiciously.

"No place in the world is so lovely as the Vale of Kashmir," said Khusru calmly.

"The flowers," suggested Dawar.

"Yes, the flowers," said Khusru sadly.

"And the poplars," said Dawar.

"Yes, the poplars. The azaleas. The roses."

"And the mountains!" said Dawar eagerly.

"Oh, the mountains! Those terrible mountains! Nothing in the world is so grand and ghostly as those mountains."

"Some day," said Dawar timidly, "I'd like to visit the rest of the world." He took his father's hand in his own and leaned forward, staring at Khusru: he saw the vacancy in his eyes and the smooth gray vagueness of his features and only in his mouth a hint of intensity, the uneasily smiling lips.

"What is it like, the rest of the world?"

Khusru's head sank a little. "To the north lie miles of snow. Just range after towering range, blazing with that terrible white snow and shrill with the everlasting tempests. To the east lies the jungle with the Brahmaputra roaring southward. To the south lies the hot blue sea. And to the west lies the desert. That's the world. Jungle and desert, the hot blue sea, and those terrible mountains."

"And still beyond? When you go further?"

"Mystery and evil," said Khusru gently.

"Persia? Arabia?"

"Nothing but mystery. Nothing but evil," murmured Khusru.

Asaf Khan stepped onto the veranda, followed by the soldier with the scimitar, and Dawar Baksh strolled into the house, eager to explore the curtained rooms.

"It is a pleasure, Asaf Khan," said Prince Khusru, rising from his chair. "As well as an honor, I should add. If only I could see you a bit more clearly. Is the look in your eyes a friendly look, or is it irritable, my good Asaf?"

"Oh," said Asaf, "I've long ago given up being irritable, Khusru."

"Have some grapes, please, my dear Asaf."

"They look delicious, my dear Khusru."

"Tell me, Asaf. How are things?"

"Dreadful as usual. Needless to say."

Asaf grinned and spat the grape seeds across the veranda. "Have you ever known things to be other than dreadful in our miserable Empire? Fortunes spent on incompetent officials, extravagant banquets for contemptible foreigners, bad news from Bengal, where there is a famine, bad news from Orissa, where there is a rebellion, and bad news even from the Punjab, where there is a disease among the cattle."

All that Khusru could see was Asaf's turban, bright as a nectarine, and the violent black eyes, which shone like jewels in the foggy half-light.

"It's just as well," said Asaf silkily, "that you're out of it all."

"Just as well, just as well," repeated Khusru, smiling wryly.

"You were never intended for power," said Asaf Khan. "Nor was poor Parviz."

"Is Parviz well?" said Khusru carefully.

"He lies on his couch the whole day long. Sipping sherbets, reading the Persians, listening to the parrots, dreaming dreams."

"And Shahriyar?"

"Precisely as usual. Exquisitely perfumed, implacably cheerful."

"And Khurram?"

"Oh, none of us ever really knows what to make of Khurram. We're all frightened a bit of Khurram. There is something tigerish about our Khurram."

"There are times," said Khusru quietly, "when curious

thoughts creep into my head. That what I see, or almost see, has no existence, no force, no body. That everything we witness and experience is just a charade, an interminable charade. All our beliefs, our traditions, our ceremonies, our laws, our systems—nothing but pantomines! Nothing but dances being danced against an impenetrable darkness. Why are some of us rich and powerful and why are others wretched and untouchable? Is it an accident? Is it caprice? Can you tell me, Asaf Khan?"

"The Brahmins will explain it for you," said Asaf Khan with a certain acidity.

"We're not Brahmins! We are men of reason! I cannot accept it," said Khusru wearily. "I am well out of it, as you say, but I cannot accept it. I cannot accept it."

"Suffering," said Asaf, relenting a little, "will always exist in one form or another."

"Let men suffer from the inevitable things," said Khusru, leaning forward, "if suffer they must. From death, from loneliness, from spiritual turmoil, from unreciprocated love. But not from the things which can be avoided. Not from gratuitous misery. From plague. From hunger. From tyranny or cruelty."

"The dividing line," said Asaf, shrugging, "is exceedingly difficult to draw. You are not alone in desiring a better-nourished and a better-smelling populace, my delightful Khusru."

He peeped slyly at Khusru with his foxy, ironical eyes. He was far beyond feeling either tenderness or admiration for another being, but for an instant a flicker of pity shone in those dark, narrowed pupils as he looked at the misty-eyed, miserable little Sultan.

He rose from his chair, stroked his beard and stared out at the twilit water. "Be careful, Khusru. I have the responsibility of guarding your safety, as the Emperor so tactfully phrases it, but who knows what will happen in this tiger-infested wilderness?"

He stood by the door and called: "Dawar!" Dawar came hurrying across the veranda.

"I've been talking to Azam! What an amusing fellow he is, that Azam!"

"Goodbye, Dawar," said Khusru softly.

"Goodbye, father," said Dawar, blushing.

"Don't go traveling too far, my child."

Dawar laughed. "There's nothing to be afraid of!"

The three visitors walked silently down the path toward the reed-edged water. Over the opposite shore the stars were beginning to shine. Khusru stood and stared into the dusk; he could hear the rustling of the cattails, and then the lapping of the oars and the squeak of the iron oarlocks. But he saw nothing beyond the mottled obscurity that hung on the horizon and after a while he heard nothing but the whine of the mosquitoes.

x

Azam came waddling up to the Sultan and touched him lightly on the elbow.

"Look, Your Highness," he whispered tensely. "Someone else seems to be arriving." He pointed into the gloom behind the little bungalow where the lamplight shone on the thin gray tree-trunks.

Khusru stood beside Azam, staring into the gloom of the woods. He watched closely as the half-naked man slid into the lamplight. He was as dark as a Tamil and wore a frayed yellow loincloth; his face had a pinched, rather jackal-like look to it. He walked up to the veranda and bowed obsequiously in front of Khusru. Then he spoke to Azam in a high, nasal dialect.

"What's he saying, please, Azam?"

"He says that he's come to help you, Your Highness."

"Help?" said Khusru.

"He's got a boat, he says. It's down in the cove, Your Highness."

"And what would I do with a boat, please, Azam?"

"It's from a friend, he says, Your Highness. They're trying to save the Empire from corruption. They're going to put you on the throne, Your Highness."

"It sounds a trifle suspicious, Azam."

Azam rolled his eyes ambiguously. "Who can tell? He's got a boat down in the cove and that's the important thing, Your Highness."

"It sounds curious, a bit," said Khusru.

Azam shrugged his fat shoulders.

The Tamil drew a paper from his loincloth and gave it to Azam, who took it between two fingers, opened it gingerly and passed it to the Sultan.

"Would you read it, please, Azam?"

"It's from Mahabat Khan," said Azam. "The Empire is rotting away and it needs your guidance, says Mahabat Khan."

"It seems implausible," murmured Khusru.

Azam gazed at the floor intently. "It is difficult to be sure about these matters, Your Highness."

Khusru grew thoughtful; he stepped back into the shadow of the veranda. He sat down in a raffia chair and stared vacuously across the river. He could see neither the stars nor the faintly silhouetted horizon but he could see, ever so dimly, the cool round pallor of the moon. Then he groped his way into the bedroom, reached for the cushion at the end of the bed, ripped it open and drew out carefully a chain of yellowish pearls, which he slipped into a narrow pocket under his collar. Then he stepped back on the veranda.

"What does it matter, my dear Azam? Life is brief, life is hazardous, and there's nothing to be gained from mere negation."

"You must trust your own judgment," said Azam, impenetrable.

"Or my intuition, more likely," said the Sultan wryly.

"God protect you," murmured Azam.

"You have noticed nothing, of course," said the Sultan.

"Oh, nothing at all, Your Highness!"

"Goodbye, dear Azam!"

"Goodbye, Dear Highness!"

He patted Azam on the cheek with the tip of his forefinger. Then he started to walk haltingly across the clearing. The naked Tamil took his hand and led him silently through the trees while Azam crouched on the veranda and watched them vanish into the darkness.

X I

They left the boat on the shore and made their way through the muddy underbrush. The Tamil held his hand as they dug their way through the marshes. Soon they reached the dry forest and the earth grew firm and fragrant. A path led through the evergreens and Khusru cautiously followed the Tamil, whose loincloth bobbed in the moonlight like a pale floating bird, the only visible object in that leaf-littered darkness. Now and again the Tamil halted and glanced back at Khusru. He muttered a few words but Khusru shook his head regretfully. The land rose. The trees grew sparser. The light of the moon was unusually brilliant and it almost seemed to Khusru that his aching eyes had learned to see again; the soaring trunks gleamed like marble, the motionless leaves flashed like phosphorus. And as they walked it occurred to Khusru that he had wandered beyond reality and that this moonlit copse was merely a dream or not even a dream, merely a kind of posthumous initiatory ritual;

that he had died at some casual moment which he had already forgotten and that he was wandering through the night toward the Land of the Liberated.

Once he stumbled over a root and fell to the ground. The Tamil rushed up and helped him back to his feet again. A nail of pain shot through his knee cap; he felt the blood beginning to trickle. But after a while the pain dissolved and only a numbness remained—a trancelike severance of sensation that permeated his mind as well as his body. Even the weariness fell away. The night had crystallized into a pattern: black trunks rising at regular intervals, the padding of feet falling into a rhythm, the light of the moon drawing its fingers along the branches and the whine of the mosquitoes weaving its drab, insensate music.

He grew aware of a sudden brightness. He caught the scent of fresh woodsmoke, and under the smoke the rich, crisp smell of roast venison. He saw the shapes of the turbaned men crouching in front of the flames. As Khusru approached the fire the sound of their voices subsided and they turned their heads in the direction of the Tamil. The Tamil crept up to the strangers and muttered something in his rippling dialect: two of the men rose from the ground and walked slowly toward Khusru. Without a word, as though they were performing some regretful little ceremony, they grasped the Sultan by the elbows and bound his wrists with a thick black cord.

XII

The plague had spread eastward. It seeped down through Rajputana and the plains of the Deccan were foul with the stink of the dead. As they rode over the prairies, the curtains of the palanquin were carefully drawn but Khurram on his stallion saw the filth and the desolation. The dead had been dragged from the villages and left to fester along the roadside, the young as well as the old, the men as well as the women. One small village had been exterminated and no one was left to drag out the corpses: they lay scattered among the huts, dark and stiffened in grotesque attitudes, some with their arms still stretched skyward, maybe in terror of the circling vultures. But even the vultures had recoiled from this blue infected flesh and even the maggots had left it to shrivel away in the sunlight. The heat waves went rippling over the dry yellow grass and the shapes of the dead seemed to heave and gesticulate.

They finally reached the hills. The curtains of the palanquin were drawn aside. A delicious fragrance rose from the pines and the flowering rhododendrons. The procession climbed slowly up the thin twisting path, the turbaned guardsmen in front, the cooks and coolies in the rear. A feathery buffoon with an ape on his shoulder kept dancing in front of Arjumand and behind the palanquin crept Lakshmi, her cheetah, on a golden chain. They paused to drink tea and sat by a lake fringed with alders, and dusk had already fallen when they reached the rest house on the edge of the precipice.

Khurram glanced into the mirror as they sat by the glowing brazier: he saw a dark and feverish face shining with sweat in the light of the flamelets, with violent black eyes half-hidden in the shade of their sockets. "God help me," he thought. "Do I really look like this? As ugly and brutal and murderous as this?"

He turned and looked at Arjumand, who was sitting on a velvet cushion. Her eyes were fixed on the brazier; dark red shadows stirred on her forehead. Beyond the screens the sky had deepened into the grape-blue of midnight. Somewhere an animal was wailing. There was a crackling of tiny embers.

"I keep trying to understand you," said Khurram. "But you insist on recoiling from me."

Arjumand frowned and glanced at the ceiling. "I don't recoil. I wait. I wonder."

"There is a puzzle in you," said Khurram. "You're as simple as a child. And as subtle as a cobra."

"Anything but subtle," said Arjumand smiling. "You imagine the subtlety. I'm as plain as a sparrow."

"You live in a secrecy of your own. I keep looking for the key but I cannot find it."

"It is you," said Arjumand quietly, "who live in silence and secrecy."

Khurram laughed. "Here we're sitting in the middle of nowhere, talking of secrecies! As though we had never met before! As though we were strangers meeting in the darkness."

Arjumand looked at him tensely. "Do you really detest me? Have you always detested me?"

Khurram spread out his fingers and watched them gleaming in the heat of the brazier.

"I've never known what I really feel toward you. Or what I hope ever to find in you."

"You despise us all," said Arjumand. "You feel a contempt for everybody."

"Not for you," whispered Khurram.

"For me too, though that is irrelevant. There are more important things in the world, but you feel no love or humility toward any of them."

"Oh," said Khurram, staring into the darkness, "I feel bored, that's all it amounts to. I feel restless and impotent. I keep waiting for things to happen."

"Boredom. Restlessness." She shrugged her shoulders. "It lies deeper than that, my darling. Is it merely ambition? Or is it a more dangerous worm that's nibbling away at you?"

"Such as what, for example?"

"Do I need to be specific?"

"Are you thinking of Khusru?"

"Yes, of Khusru. Among other things."

Khurram stared at the ceiling. "Your respected father," he said quietly, "was much relieved to forward Khusru to my personal supervision. Khusru is a problem. He has always been a problem. What's to be done with the miserable fellow? His father loathes him. His brothers pity him. His wife despises him. The courtiers laugh at him. I don't look forward to having him thrust under my roof in Burhanpur."

Arjumand nodded. "Nothing but secrecies! We're nothing but strangers meeting in the darkness."

Khurram rose and crossed the room and peered out into the night. He felt something between a rush of tenderness and a hot, sourceless bitterness. He caught a scent faintly like clover which hung in the air: the smell of Arjumand. The inexplicable thing, as he had said, was that the more he was with her and the more intimately that he felt her, the more she eluded him; as though her physical nearness merely obscured some deeper identity. A fog hung over the valley, the sweeping distances were lost in mist and only the daggerlike glitter of the cliffs shone under the starlight.

He turned back into the room, sunk on his knees in front of Arjumand and buried his face in the folds of her lap.

XIII

Prince Khusru's prison in Burhanpur, where he arrived in late November, was a low dark annex to the Sultan's stables. At the

end of a winding corridor was a little cell where an oil lamp splut-
tered, sending spirals of smoke toward a hole which punctured
the ceiling. Day and night were the same. Rain and sunlight were
indistinguishable. Only the bed was a royal bed covered with silk-
embroidered cushions and the wine was served in goblets of a fine,
tapering amethyst.

Arjumand was permitted to visit him occasionally and she read
him some verses by Kalidasa and once a week Khurram called on
him and told him the latest news from the court.

The relation between these two brothers was curious. For Parviz
Khurram felt contempt and toward Shahriyar disgust, but for
Khusru he felt a lingering esteem which was tinged with affection. And yet the very esteem contained a dangerous element—
envy—and the very affection was poisoned with a deep-seated
rivalry. As for Khusru, who loved Parviz and was amiably amused
by Shahriyar, Khurram remained to the end an unfathomable
mystery to him, darkly impressive, even formidable, but hopelessly alien.

"Tell me," said Khusru one evening, "who was that queer little
fellow sent by Mahabat Khan?"

"I might as well tell you," said Khurram blandly, "that he had
nothing to do with Mahabat Khan."

"Who sent him, then?"

Khurram smiled. "You have no idea? You never suspected?"

"Was it my father?"

"No, not your father."

"Asaf Khan?"

"Not Asaf Khan."

"Nor you, conceivably?"

"Oh, certainly not me. I was in Bengal at the time. I had nothing to do with it."

"It baffles me," said Khusru uncomfortably.

"It will continue to baffle you," said Khurram.

Khusru had grown intensely thin, in spite of the delicacies

from Khurram's kitchen; his hair had turned white, his face was
pale as a moth. He tried to preserve his body by a set of gymnastics every morning, and he tried to preserve his mind by reciting
aloud long passages of poetry—from the *Ramayana* chiefly, and
occasionally a hymn from the *Rig-Vedas*. All he could see was the
tear-shaped flame of the dangling copper oil lamp and the high-
lights caught in the fluted goblets and the silver cutlery. But his
smell and his hearing had grown abnormally acute: he could
smell the windswept shrubbery sending its fragrance into the corridor and he could hear the termites gnawing at the vault of the
smoke-stained ceiling.

One night he was lying on his bed murmuring some lines from
a hymn to Kali when he heard a knock on the door, which was a
grill of woven metal.

He called: "Is it you, Naranji?" Naranji was the oily-skinned
turnkey.

"No, Your Highness, it's not Naranji," said a thick, stuttering
voice.

"Who is it?"

"It's Raza Bahadur."

Raza was a slave who attended the elephants.

"What do you wish, Raza Bahadur?"

"Open the door, please, Your Highness. I have an order of liberation from Agra, as well as an embroidered robe of honor."

"There is something odd in your voice, I can't help thinking,
Raza."

"It's the truth," growled Raza, "that I'm telling you, Your
Highness."

"Does my brother know of your visit?"

"Prince Khurram is hunting in the mountains."

"Does the Princess know of your visit?"

"Princess Arjumand has accompanied the Sultan."

But Khusru, as the result of his blindness, and also perhaps as the result of his loneliness, could smell into the heart of things, and he smelled the purpose in Raza's mind.

"I don't believe," he said, rising, "that you're bringing an order of liberation, and I doubt whether you are carrying a robe of honor for me, Raza. I see your face only faintly but I see the knife gleaming in your belt. However, let's not quibble. Come in, Raza, and let's talk for a while."

He crossed the cell and opened the latch and Raza Bahadur slid into the cell.

"Yes," thought Khusru, "it's just as I thought. He has come to kill me. I can smell the killer."

"Your Highness, please forgive me," said the slave in a dull, flat voice. He was a magnificent bull-like man, with the bloodshot eyes of an Ethiopian, and he loomed with an incongruous majesty over the pale, shrunken Sultan.

"Yes," said Khusru, "I forgive you, Raza." He lowered his head and sat down on the bed. "There's nothing that either of us can do about it, and we might as well accept it gracefully."

"I have orders," said Raza, stuttering. "They are cruel orders but I am powerless."

"We're both powerless," said Khusru quietly. "All we can do is behave with dignity."

"I feel no hatred, Your Highness," said Raza, shuffling uneasily as he stood by the table.

"I know you don't," said Khusru consolingly. "But what do you feel? Come, tell me, Raza."

"I feel a strangeness," whispered Raza.

"Yes? What else?" said Khusru coaxingly.

"I'm not quite sure," said Raza Bahadur. His torso gleamed in the lamplight. It looked like a great dripping column of polished obsidian. He folded his arms and stared down at the table, where the light shone dimly on an empty wineglass.

How very odd, thought Khusru calmly, that at this last lonely moment the only person I should suddenly love is this ugly brute who has come to murder me. Some wild caprice in the heart of destiny has bound us violently and inextricably together. He is the only, the pure participant in my final, triumphant experience.

"Think, Raza. What do you feel?" There was an urgency in Khusru's voice.

"I feel a sadness," said Raza sullenly. "I feel a loneliness; yes, Your Highness, I feel that we're all alone, just the two of us, and the rest of the world has vanished. I feel—how shall I say it—that you and I have entered a darkness and that we're clinging together and nothing will ever separate us."

Khusru nodded. "So it is," he said and he beckoned to Raza.

Raza sunk to his knees. Tears streamed down his cheeks and he clutched the Sultan by the knees imploringly.

"Forgive me, Your Highness!"

"God bless you," said Khusru.

For a while neither of them spoke. Finally Khusru reached down, drew the knife from Raza's belt and placed it firmly in Raza's hand.

Raza took the knife thoughtfully, rose from the ground and looked at Khusru. He leaned forward and kissed his wrist, wiped the tears from his cheeks and then slowly, with a childlike reverence, buried the knife in Khusru's breast.

PART THREE

The Rebellion

Arjumand stood by the window in the rustling privacy of the harem, peeping out through the lattices into the sun-streaked courtyard. The eunuch Shadi was standing below in the shade of the archway—a lean beautiful man with a face that looked like Siva's, suave and ironical, with a hint of despondency.

The curtains parted and the Empress Nurmahal stepped into the room. "Are you ready? The musicians are waiting in the courtyard."

"Almost ready. I can't decide. Shall I wear this yellow veil or the blue one?"

"Try the blue one, my child." Nurmahal's eyes glittered festively. "It's quite amazing, my dear Arjumand. You have suddenly grown quite beautiful."

"I was never beautiful. I'm too dark and too angular. It's the Rajput blood in me."

"Look at me," said the Empress sullenly. "White as death. It's the Persian blood in me." She walked up to Arjumand and glanced through the lattices. "I envy your darkness and you envy my pallor. I envy your frailty and you envy my strength. There it is. No one is satisfied. We all keep whimpering for something else."

Arjumand looked at her thoughtfully. "For something else? Yes, I suppose so. Tell me, Nurmahal, where you ever really in love with Jahangir?"

Nurmahal's face remained expressionless. "Love is a foggy little word. Of course I was in love with Jahangir. And of course I was never in love with him."

"I am puzzled," said Arjumand, wide-eyed.

"I love Jahangir for the power I have over him. And I also love the power within him, which has gradually become my own. And I love him for his utter and preposterous dependence on me, his childlike frailty with all that power, and even his silliness. Even his pomposity."

The air was listless and the flies were buzzing; the eunuch glanced toward the window instinctively, as though aware that the women behind the lattices were peering down at him.

"Why," said Arjumand, suddenly alert, "have you come to hate Khurram?"

"I don't hate him. I merely deplore him."

"You spread that gossip about Khusru's death."

Nurmahal shot a quick little look at her. "It wasn't I. It was Asaf Khan."

"Was Khurram responsible? Is it true?"

"I have no opinion on the matter," said the Empress. She put her arm on Arjumand's wrist. "You feel uneasy and you'll always feel uneasy. Khurram is a killer by nature; I cannot put it more specifically. Not out of cruelty exactly, though I don't deny there's a cruel streak in him. But just as certain men like Khusru are born to be saints and others, like Shahriyar, are born to be clowns, there are some who are born to be killers, just as the tiger is a killer."

"I cannot live with such a thought," said Arjumand, staring through the lattices.

"You'll get used to it," said Nurmahal. "After all, my dear child, it's not as though he were bathing his hands in blood every morning. It is somewhat subtler, luckily. He's half a dreamer and half a man of action and he finds no resting place between the two. His dreams make him ashamed of his actions and his drive to action makes him bored with his dreams. He seeks grandeur and power in action but his dreams keep whispering of other things. He seeks refuge in the secrecy of dreams but the world outside keeps mocking at his dreams. He seeks splendor like a barbarian. Remember, Arjumand, he descends from Tamerlane."

"He is full of complexities," said the Princess absently.

"Full of demons. Like all of us," said Nurmahal. She leaned closer to Arjumand, took her chin in her fingertips and kissed her on the cheek. "My darling," she murmured, "you don't love him. And you'll never love him. You loved Sirkandar and you're still in love with the beautiful vision of Sirkandar. Don't blush, child. You're trembling! Put on your veil. The guests are arriving."

11

Sultan Parviz lived in a small red bungalow in the middle of the hunting grounds with an elderly servant and no luxury except for his bowl of tropical fish, which stood behind his bed with a copper oil lamp shining down on it. There were fish from Ceylon of a tawny gold, striped like tigers; there were fish from the Persian Gulf, thin and blue like the knives from Ispahan; there were fish from Eritrea with bulging eyes and fins of emerald; there were fish from Cambodia, black and veiled, like flying witches. The violent light slid through the slats in the shutters during the day, but at dusk the pine-spiced breeze flowed in from the forest, and after sleeping most of the day the Sultan stepped on the veranda, where he sat and wrote his verses, mostly in the manner of the fashionable Persians but now and then in the style of the old Chinese poets. Parviz was excessively fat, squat and shapeless and prematurely bald; his whole body exuded an air of lassitude, stagnation. A bowl of wine stood on the table and beside it a casket of opium; the very odor of opium had seeped into the smell of his body. Only his eyes still had a small, quivering gleam of intensity —a flicker of desperation, a glint of self-ridicule.

Sometimes toward dusk he strolled through the park into the adjoining pine woods and spoke to the hermit Krishnadevaraya. This hermit was a man in his nineties, skeletally thin and dark as midnight, with skin that drooped from his bones like thin purple crepe.

The hermit would sit at Parviz' feet and read to him from the *Aranyakas,* the Books of the Forest, and as dusk crept through the trees he would talk to him of the transmigration of the soul, which was called *samsara* and which condemned all men to perpetual flux and disintegration. "Salvation," he murmured, "is only possible by escaping from the life of the senses and seeking deliverance from good and evil, which enslave us equally."

"But how," said Parviz, with his usual irony, "can you equate these two, Krishnadevaraya, when the one brings peace to the mind and the other a state of torment?"

"I disagree," said Krishnadevaraya. "Your remarks are unworthy of your intelligence, Your Highness. The peace of mind that so-called good brings with it is only transitory, it is smug and hypocritical, and in the end does nothing to assuage our anguish. Whereas the torment which you mention, which is the aftereffect of wickedness, can equally well purge the soul by cleansing it of smugness and hypocrisy."

"But," said Parviz, smiling faintly, "if that were true, dear Krishnadevaraya, then we'd all be well advised to abstain from virtuous behavior and indulge as much as possible in all sorts of wickedness!"

"Not in the least," retorted the hermit. "You are distorting the sense of my words. Deliberate, self-conscious wickedness is as absurd as deliberate, self-conscious good. True goodness comes over us quite involuntarily, without our willing or controlling it or even our being aware of it as such, and the same applies to true wickedness—it comes in a hot surge of feeling. But neither the one nor the other brings relief or illumination. The only relief is to be found in abdication, which eventually approaches a state of vegetable indolence."

"Precisely the state," hinted Parviz, "which I seem to be achieving, though not for the reasons you specify."

"Life," said the hermit, "is a perpetual tension. The solitude, the stillness keep eluding us. There is *dharma* and there is *artha:* duty and interest—stability and change. And we keep swinging between two, the frantic desire to experience everything and the equally profound yearning for total peace, renunciation. And both, dear Parviz, blend eventually into the same deplorable compromise, which is a mountainous despair which is gradually shrouding humanity."

"It is always encouraging," said Parviz, "to listen to you talking, Krishnadevaraya."

The old hermit brushed away a gnat which had settled on his nostril. He grinned at Parviz mischievously and scratched at his toenail. The last light flickered in the treetops like a flock of orange butterflies. The smell which drifted from the hermit's hut was like the smell of a cesspool, and the smell of his body was like the stench of a hyena.

Parviz gazed at the hermit with a mingling of amusement and disgust. Oh, yes, there was no question whatever about his wisdom and virtue, but perhaps one might as well talk about the wisdom and virtue of a crocodile. A wisdom and virtue totally inert, totally secretive and unproductive, with no influence whatever on the course of human affairs. Well, then, could he really be considered either wise or virtuous after all, with those scrawny bow-legs and that enormous purple scrotum?

"I went strolling through the village yesterday. An old woman had just died. Her body lay wrapped in a thin gray sack. They were performing the rituals," said Parviz.

"What did she die of?" said the hermit.

"Oh, just poverty," said Parviz airily, and a ripple of misery passed over his features. "Just poverty and neglect, just hunger and rot, just the fate of the multitude."

"You still," said the hermit, "feel uneasy, don't you?"

"I have always felt uneasy."

"Calm yourself," said the hermit gently, tugging daintily the Sultan's sleeve. "In the *Rig-Veda* you can read about it. Men are unequal. It can't be helped. When Purusha, the first of the mortals, was finally sacrificed, the priests or Brahmins rose out of his head, the warriors or Kshatriyas rose from his arms, the merchants or Vaisyas rose from his thighs, and the serfs, the Sudras, sprang from his feet. That's how it was, unfortunate possibly, but the facts are clear in the *Rig-Veda*."

"No doubt," said Parviz, "but between the two of us, do you really believe this deliberate nonsense?"

"I both believe and disbelieve it. It is less painful to accept these things as inevitable."

"I can never accept them," said Parviz viciously, "when I see a woman dying of hunger while the courtiers in Ajmer are nibbling at peacocks stuffed with almond paste."

"You will never," said the hermit sadly, "have the makings of an Emperor." He looked at Parviz rather wistfully with his lemur-like eyes. "Good men like you, my beloved Parviz, are not fit to be kings. Look at your brothers. Khurram is a warrior. Shahriyar is a dandy. Neither of the two has your humanity but either would make a better Emperor."

"I have no wish to be an Emperor," said Parviz. "I am a drug-infected poetaster."

"Your soul," said the hermit, "is that of a deer—a wounded, sad-eyed deer."

"And my body," said the Prince with venom, "is that of a bloated old sea-beast."

"We all," sighed the hermit, "rot away."

"But some more swiftly than the rest," said Parviz.

III

The path to Parviz' bungalow led past a stream which encircled the hunting grounds. Arjumand paused by the orchard, which was humming with bees, and she picked a flowering twig from a sweet-smelling plum tree. Then she wandered up to the bungalow and knocked on the door.

"Come in, please!" called Parviz, and she stepped into the half-lit bedchamber. All she could see was the flickering goldfish darting about beneath the oil lamp; but then her eyes grew used to the gloom and she looked at Parviz, who lay in his dressing gown, his face damp with sweat, his eyes blurred with opium.

"Today is your birthday. I have brought you a present," said Arjumand gently.

"Nothing costly, I hope," said Parviz.

"Not especially," said Arjumand. She took an object from her shawl and set it on the bed table: a tiny Siva carved of obsidian, with his six black arms gracefully extended.

"Would Khurram approve of this?" said Parviz.

"Probably not," said Arjumand, smiling. "Even I don't quite approve of it. I bring it as an ornament, and not as an idol."

"What is the news?"

"No news," said Arjumand. "Since Khusru's death there have been no visitors, except for Nurmahal of course and a group of huntsmen from Golkonda."

"And how is Khurram?"

"Restless. Uneasy. There is something weighing on his mind. He is brooding about some project. Don't ask me what. I cannot imagine."

"I am older than Khurram," said Parviz plaintively, "and considerably wiser in my own queer way. But I'm weak. I'm sickeningly weak. I brood all day. But not about projects. Not about doing things or achieving things, merely about eluding things, avoiding things." He rested his elbow on the wine-stained pillow and stared intently at Arjumand. "Do you know what I dreamed last night?"

"What did you dream?"

"That Khurram will kill me."

"Nonsense," said Arjumand, pressing her hands together. "You mustn't give way to these morbid fantasies."

"It was only a dream," said Parviz casually. He suddenly burst into laughter. His pudgy torso rippled in waves of uncontrollable merriment. Then he pulled himself together abruptly, sat up in the bed and looked at Arjumand. "I shall hardly notice the difference, my dear. I shall float away like a wisp of smoke."

A powerful wave of tenderness suddenly swept over the Princess. What she felt for this wreck of a creature was more than solicitude, it was almost love. That moral collapse, that sickening obesity, those oozing cheeks and piglike eyes: could it be that under it all there was a secret triumph, even a hint of magnificence?

"You live in a perpetual state of worry, that's your trouble," said Arjumand impatiently. "You are frightened of life and frightened of yourself. And you mask this fear with invented fears."

"No doubt," said Parviz. "But that's a little true of us all, isn't it, Arjumand? It's true of Khurram, now that I think of it. Khurram invents his enemies to disguise his Enemy." His voice grew softer and his self-despising little pig eyes grew meditative. "I visited the hermit the other day. He had some pearls of wisdom to impart, as usual. There's no such thing as safety or real serenity, said the dear old fraud. We want safety in our lives as well as in our hearts, but there's always death which destroys our lives and the loss of love which destroys our hearts. And the more we devise new means of safety, the more unsafe we become in spirit. And we're better off if we never even look for safety."

"And look for indifference, I suppose?"

"Phrase it as you wish," said Parviz dreamily.

"A woman," said Arjumand, looking intently at the goldfish, "is not afraid of life as a man is, or even afraid of death as a man is. She is not afraid of her own death or even her lover's death. She is only afraid of the death of her lover's love."

Parviz peered at her with a glint of sarcasm. "That feminine vanity. That female possessiveness."

"Phrase it as you wish," said Arjumand gently. She leaned down and kissed him on the forehead.

She paused by the orchard again on her way back to the palace. Dusk was floating through the trees like woodsmoke and the scent of the blossoms was tinged with twilight. And as she stood there, she noticed a shape which had halted behind her among the alders: an elderly one-eyed slave with a wispy beard whose name was Hemu. She turned around and beckoned to Hemu, who came sidling up to her sheepishly.

"Have you been following me, Hemu?"

"Oh, Your Highness, I wouldn't dream of it!"

"You're stuttering, Hemu. You've been following me."

"Oh, Your Highness, what a cruel suspicion!"

For a moment she stood in silence, staring with rage at the cringing Hemu, whose hairy arms dangled limply on each side like an orangutan's.

"Well," said Arjumand, "you can tell whoever sent you, and I can easily imagine who sent you, that I called on the Sultan Parviz and had a highly refreshing conversation, and I brought him a little present, since it happened to be his birthaday."

And she turned and walked slowly past the dusk-shadowed orchard.

IV

There were moments when Khurram felt an inner disquietude that bordered on frenzy. He would rise in the middle of the night and pace across the bedroom, fling open the blinds and stare out into the emptiness. The plain spread below him. The dome of the mosque rose in the distance. Beyond the mosque shone the blaze of the time-destroying stars. The world looked so vast, so chaotic and unfathomable, how could a single small man ever hope to penetrate its meaning? How could a single miserable creature hope to bring order into all that chaos? Indeed, it seemed that even the hope of penetrating the meaning and of ordering the chaos was itself a symptom of man's helplessness, his pathos, his defeat. And yet, with the feverish intensity of his needling little brain, Khurram knew that whatever happened, whoever loved him, or whoever betrayed him, he would never cease trying to conquer that helplessness. He stared across the plain, trying to detect the hidden animals—the jackals, perhaps, or the night-roving pariah dogs. And after a while he crawled into bed again and laid his head on the pillow and Arjumand could hear him panting in the darkness as he lay there.

"Are you awake?"

"Yes, I'm awake."

"What are your thoughts?"

"God knows," said Khurram. "They aren't thoughts, they're too black for thoughts, they're just bitterness and disgust."

"Yes," she murmured. "You are bearing the burdens of your imaginary empire in your brain."

"The real empire is decaying. The Emperor is decaying. Islam is decaying."

"Why do you despise your father, Khurram?"

"I've told you already. He is sick and senile, his mind is corrupt, the court is corrupt, Nurmahal is tightening her grip on everything and all of Agra is vile with degeneracy."

"Is that all?"

"Not quite all."

"Yes? What else?"

"He's my father." He turned his face slowly toward Arjumand; his eyes shone in the darkness. "Oh yes, you think it shocking that I should hate my own father, but there it is. I can't help it. I've always hated him. I'll always hate him."

"Be careful, Khurram."

"Don't ask me to be careful. I've discussed it thoroughly with the Rajahs of the Deccan. It's all been planned. It will happen. Nothing will prevent it from happening."

And two months later, according to the plan, the Sultan's rebellion got under way. Thirty of the noblemen at Jahangir's court joined forces with Prince Khurram. The Emperor himself was in Lahore, sick with a lingering attack of dysentery, and Nurmahal was with him and the palace in Agra was half-deserted. The Emperor's horsemen were hurriedly gathered from the hills beyond Agra and at Balochpur, just south of Delhi, a battle was finally fought. The Princess Arjumand went riding with the army in an iron-plated howdah. The lances flew; the Chinese cannons rolled into action. The swivel guns were mounted on the camels and the rockets came pouring from the hillocks, bursting like geysers of fire on the heavily armored Imperial elephants. But when dusk fell on the battlefield it was obvious that the rebels had been defeated. As the Princess rode through the woods with the scattered remnants of the defeated army a young Rajput rode up to her and whispered breathlessly:

"He's been captured, Your Highness! I saw it happen with my own eyes. He was crossing the river and three men rode out of the thicket. They drove him into the quicksands and flung a rope round him. Then they led him back to the camp of Rajah Salim . . ."

Arjumand turned to Ahmed Khan, who was riding beside her, and said: "Is it true, Ahmed?"

"It may be true," said Ahmed discreetly. "But I know the Rajah. I know his opinions. And I know Khurram. I shouldn't worry about it. Khurram is a cat, a great black cat that will always land on those clever little feet of his!"

v

The morning rain was beginning to fall, rapping gently on the blood-red canvas. The first light of dawn was creeping westward from Bengal and the dew was beginning to shine on the hides of the dozing elephants. Behind the trees rose the amber-striped tent of Rajah Salim; the horses were stirring uneasily in the shadows.

Khurram glanced at the guardsman who was squatting on the trunk to keep watch over him: a Mongol-like man with protruding teeth and a slate-blue beard.

"And what was it like in Darjeeling?" he muttered.

"Dull," said the guard. "Like all those places. Nothing to do the whole day long. Just squabbling and dicing and dirty jokes, and the women all stinking of rancid goat cheese."

"And the mountains?" said Khurram.

"Yes, the mountains, of course," said the guard. "You get used after a while to those big white mountains. They stop looking so big, they look quite commonplace and ordinary. They look like a row of wise old women with long white hair streaming over their shoulders. Each of the peaks has a special face; sometimes it smiles, sometimes it scowls, but who cares whether a shriveled hag happens to smile at you or scowl at you?"

"True, true," murmured Khurram.

The guard yawned thoughtfully. He lowered his head and closed his eyes.

In a corner of the tent lay a woodman's axe which was used for the tentpoles. Khurram crawled across the ground and squatted in the darkness beside the axe, turning the blade with his elbows and grasping it firmly between his knees and softly grinding the rope that bound his wrist across the edge. Finally he unwound the severed rope and picked up the axe. He sprang forward and lifted the axe and brought it crashing on the guard's skull, which cracked with a low, brittle sound like a breaking coconut. For an instant the Prince stood there, watching the blood spurt over the ground and the brains ooze slowly over the dead man's shoulders. Then he slipped through the door of the tent, glanced quickly about and entered the forest.

The sun was beginning to rise when he reached the edge of the forest. The plain of Balochpur spread featurelessly below him, tufted and tawny, like the hide of a camel. The river moved slowly past the flat grassy banks—so slowly that it scarcely seemed to be moving at all. Khurram slid off his tunic, sprinkled his body with dust, tossed his bracelets into the underbrush and started cautiously down the hill.

At the bottom of the hill the empty prairie spread eastward. Drops of dew still clung to the grasses, which were as tall as bamboos, so tall that his head just barely rose above them. The stalks clanked like knives as he elbowed his way through them; sharp as knives they were, too, and after a while he was spangled with blood. His whole torso was crisscrossed with tiny lines which burned like wasp stings. The sun rose higher and now the heat of the day crept over the plain, the insects started to buzz and the crows swooped overhead. Khurram glanced toward the woods and saw four horsemen galloping toward him. He ducked swiftly and started to creep through the grass on all fours, very slowly and fastidiously, so that the stirring in the grass was hardly perceptible. After a while he stopped moving and sat quietly in the gold-striped shadows, waiting for the peasants in the distance to pass him by on their way to the fields. He felt as though he were hiding in some primitive world, invisible to other men, frequented only by the ants and the grasshoppers. All around him there was nothing but tapering stalks of tawny grass, which began to look as tall and imperturbable as treetrunks. There was a ceaseless vibration of innumerable wings, some of them so small that they were hardly visible, and the buzzing of their wings blended into the clicking of the grasshoppers, so that the secret world of the grasses was filled with a multitudinous orchestra, now shrill, now subdued, playing its own exotic music.

The heat grew suddenly intense. The peasants had disappeared and he was about to move on again when he saw a shape rise up in front of him. His sense of proportion had been disordered by the eerie world of the grasses and for a moment the serpent looked as large as a dragon. But then he realized that it was only a snake, one of a million other snakes, no larger than the others and no more venomous than the others. He stared at the cobra without moving and the cobra stared back at him. Its eyes were as bright and hard as rubies. He knelt motionless in the dust. The cobra swayed gently, flicking its tongue with curiosity, trying to appraise the man's intentions. Then it thrust its head forward, uncoiled its body with a slow, wild elegance, moved casually past Khurram and disappeared in the rustling grasses.

VI

"But we all," said the Emperor plaintively, "have our private intuitions. You accuse me of being eclectic. Very well, I am eclectic. I've listened to the Buddhists and the Brahmins, the Zoroastrian sages and heretical Sufis. I've listened to the Christians and Confucians. I've listened to men who pray to the crocodiles. But somehow I still feel that I'm entitled to my own intuitions."

"Intuitions," sighed Father Joannes. "It's a vaporous word, Your Majesty. We must try to formulate our beliefs, however brusquely and arbitrarily. It's not enough for a lonely man to confront Eternity with his intuitions."

Jahangir frowned a little. Then he tapped the priest on the shoulder. "I believe you are trying to trap me. I refuse to be trapped, Father Joannes! I shall flit from faith to faith like a butterfly. I shall believe in the spur of the moment. I refuse to betray my intuitions."

They were sitting in the marble gallery which overlooked the blue-tiled fountain. The evening light played in the spray, turning the drops into opals. It crawled up the columns, turning the marble to a fleshy pink. Along the walls of the gallery hung Jahangir's collection of paintings—some scrolls from Peking and some beautiful Arabian miniatures, as well as works which his ambassadors had brought him from Europe: portraits of the Pope and the King of Spain and the Duke of Savoy, portraits of Saint Anthony and John the Baptist and Bernardino of Siena. In the center hung a painting of "The Adoration of the Magi," recently brought back from Lisbon by Ruy Lourenço da Tavora.

"Listen," said the Emperor, stroking the parrot perched on his shoulder: "I am not a Muslim at heart. I cannot believe in Muhammed's grandeur. Nor am I a Christian, needless to say. I cannot accept these tales of a Resurrection. I do not follow the Zoroastrian rites and I wouldn't dream of adopting the Hindu practices. I think of the usual hodgepodge of Hinduism as a wicked and disreputable religion. There's no reconciling the Muslim and the Hindu. The Buddhist, yes, but never the Hindu. The Hindu thinks that everything dissolves and is annihilated in the terror of things. He believes only in vastness, in multiplicity and mystery. The Muslim believes in order and self-discipline and exactitude."

"And you yourself?" said Father Joannes.

"I flutter merrily between them all. Taking my choice, sipping the honey," said Jahangir, chuckling.

"Do you believe in a God?" said the Jesuit, who was a mouse-like man with beady eyes.

"Ah, yes, my dear, I believe in a God, but a God whom I prefer not to visualize as a God, a God so elusive that His features remain invisible, a Power moving through the bushes, hovering in the sunlight, shining in the water. Look," said the Emperor, pointing to the fountain, "don't you see Him out in the sunlight? Dancing ecstatically, making fun of us, tantalizing us, perpetually eluding us?"

"Your religion," said the Jesuit, "is a wayward deism of your own invention, Your Majesty."

"Is it?" said Jahangir, peering into space. "Very well. Then so it is."

A look of sadness crept over his face. Jahangir's health was in decline. He had grown grotesquely fat and his skin had turned a strange dead color. He sat in a heavily cushioned chair in a dirty velvet jacket with a sweat-stained fez on his head, too lazy or indifferent to indulge in elegance. His ears were pink and hairy and his face was like a baby's, with tiny pale eyes of an almost idiotic innocence.

In his growing detestation of power, in his growing languor and cynicism, in his gathering pain and despair it seemed to him that everything was turning into its opposite. Lust had turned into satiety and power into impotence, protectiveness into panic, curiosity into indifference, and the fabric of daily life was merely material for caprice. All that he really still enjoyed was watching the sunlight on the fountain, the butterflies darting in the acacias, the elephants gamboling in the pool. Everything tinged with order and reason had begun to bore him. Everything tinctured with humanity was beginning to disgust him.

Father Joannes rose to go. "And what is the news," he said, "of the rebellion?"

The Emperor yawned and drew his palm over his swollen gray cheeks. "Oh," he said, "you can tell the Viceroy that everything has been successfully settled. Khurram escaped, the clever devil; he has fled to Bengal, but he is already beginning to make the appropriate overtures. It will all end peacefully, I assure you. I love my Khurram. I forgive him. You know," he whispered, leaning forward with a confidential air, "with all his virtues I found Khusru a terrible prig. And with all his wicked rebelliousness I find Khurram close to my heart."

"And so," said the Jesuit, "you forgive Prince Khurram what you never forgave Prince Khusru?"

"Exactly," said Jahangir, lifting his finger. "There may be subtler motives involved, but call it my Tartar whimsicality. I love a fine black-hearted rascal!"

VII

Prince Parviz crossed the withered lawn. The leaves hung dead from their stems. The grass, what little there was left of it, had turned an ugly ochreous color. Two little boys crouched over the rosebushes, plucking the rose-lice from the stalks. An old Untouchable was squatting in the shade, combing the long-haired Persian kittens.

Parviz walked up the steps and crossed the long marble gallery, where the freshly sprinkled curtains created an air of fragrant coolness. He strolled up to Jahangir, bowed slightly and kissed his forefinger.

"Shocking, isn't it?" he murmured casually.

"But scarcely surprising," said the Emperor. He peered dyspeptically at Parviz. "You're looking shabby, my dear Parviz. There's a soup stain on your sleeve. And is it conceivable that you need a shave?"

Parviz blushed imperceptibly. "You are right, I am afraid. I'm growing careless."

"Is it the poetry?" said the Emperor mockingly.

"It must be the poetry," said Parviz, smiling.

"I have never properly appreciated literature, much to my sorrow," said Jahangir. "My forte is the visual arts. My eye is keener than my intelligence. Far be it from me, however, to condemn your dedication to verses. There is nothing wicked about verses. Provided that they don't interfere with our hygiene. Listen to me, Parviz. I have a rather serious suggestion to make to you."

Parviz folded his pudgy arms and glanced mildly at his father.

"Now that my Khurram has misbehaved so appallingly," said

Jahangir, "I am driven to make a choice. It lies between you and Shahriyar."

"You know my weaknesses," said Parviz calmly. "I am not suited for Imperial power."

"No one is suited for power," said the Emperor. "Was I suited for power? Is anyone suited by nature for the evil tensions of real power?"

"Akbar was suited for power, I think."

"Only briefly," said the Emperor thoughtfully.

"And Khurram is suited for power, I imagine."

"He desires the power but he hasn't experienced it yet. He does not know the implications, the strains, the unease, the disillusionments. Unquestionably Khurram is suited by temperament for the exercise of power," said the Emperor petulantly, "but the time has come in our history when the grandeur of the Moguls needs no longer to be extended but must be mellowed and modulated. It must be chastened. It must be purified."

"Purity. Chastity," said Parviz. His moonlike face took on a demure expression. "These are words I hardly expected to hear in such a context, father."

"I do use them," said Jahangir, pouting. "I do use them and I insist on using them. They are not only relevant, they are crucial. Purity is not a matter of personal habits, as you yourself are in a position to confirm, my good son; it is a matter of freshness of spirit. Of simple moral honesty. The most outrageous debauché may have a purity of heart immeasurably greater than that of a monk or a grovelling *saddhu*. I see the dirt under your fingernails, but you have purity in your heart, and that is why I am choosing you in preference to that lilylike Shahriyar, who bathes twice a day and sprinkles his members with rosewater."

"I will never be Emperor," said Parviz quietly.

"Why do you say that?" said Jahangir, blinking.

"Because it's true. Don't ask me the reasons. There may be fifty different reasons. But this I'm sure of, whatever may happen, and curious things are likely to happen, my destiny has decided for once and for all that I shall never be Emperor. Oh yes," said Parviz, and a touch of passion crept into his high sexless voice, "I've often thought of what I would do if I were to be the Emperor! I'd give utter and immediate freedom to the slaves and Untouchables, I'd bring sweetness into the lives of the wretched ones, I'd give almonds to the hungry and wine to the thirsty, I'd hang silks in the village huts, I'd spread unguents on the arms of the lepers, I'd destroy the roots of all power and dry up the sources of tyranny; I'd crumble the Empire into a million pieces and let each man find his own salvation!"

He paused and blushed, panting with the effort, and lowered his eyes to the ground.

Jahangir gazed at him wistfully. "I feel saddened, Parviz. I feel melancholy. Partly because I know how impossible of fulfillment our loveliest dreams always are—oh, I know you were speaking with irony, you were merely reproaching me with highflown phrases, but I know how an exquisite ideal grows gradually poisoned by the touch of power. And I'm also sad because I see how false our feelings are to our sense of values. It is you I should have loved above my other sons, Parviz. You're the only one whose soul stirs a birdlike fluttering in my sick old spirit. And yet, why is it I cannot love you, I cannot respond to you, I cannot feel close to you? You're perfectly right, my dear boy, it was only a whim that made me call you to the palace. It will never happen. You will never be Emperor. God bless you, child. Go back to your poems."

VIII

The road to Bengal ran through dusty prairies, withered jungles and dried river beds; it went winding through disconsolate villages and rotting brown fields. The Prince and the Princess were making the voyage in a double palanquin, borne by eight Rajput bearers who wore poppy-red turbans. A column of slaves carried the rugs and the jugs and the sweetmeats. It had ceased being a flight, it had turned into a leisurely excursion, but the heat of the sun was turning the earth to a fine gray powder and the naked black slaves were veiled in clouds of fiery dust.

Arjumand peeped through the curtains. The land was veiled and unreal-looking. The distant hills looked strangely filmy, like threatening clouds on the horizon. Only the sun up in the sky looked absolutely real and alive. What was it, this ball of radiance blazing down at the world? Was it merely a hole in that huge blue canopy? Or was it a concrete object, an enormous bowl of burning metal? Or was it more of an intangible intensity, a kind of conglomeration of red-hot vapors? Or was it stranger than any of these things, an unimaginable, impenetrable mystery? Merely a symbol of some fierce and devastating outer Power?

They rode on. The road rose, threading its way among some hillocks. Three men on gray mules came riding through the dust. They wore voluminous felt hats and black hose and black doublets and their faces were streaked with a dusty sweat.

One of the men rode up to the palanquin and peered politely through the curtain.

"I was told who you were, Your Excellency. Forgive my manners. I am Mr. Kimberly."

"Indeed," said Khurram, rather tartly. "And where do you come from, may I ask?"

"I come from London," said Kimberly festively. "But I wasn't born in London, mind you. I was born in Yorkshire, actually."

"How very fascinating," said Khurram. "Come, let's sit under the trees and chat for a while."

The procession drew up under the shade and the boys brought bowls of coconut juice. Silk cushions were placed in a semicircle under the tamarisks.

"We're on our way to Surat," said the Englishman. "We've made arrangements in Bengal. Purely financial," he added hurriedly. "We wouldn't dream of dabbling in politics."

"Very thoughtful of you," said Khurram.

"We are purchasing silks," said Kimberly brightly. "And we are selling clocks and toys as well as some Scottish cutlery. It seems incongruous," he hinted facetiously, "to dispose of clocks in this timeless country, and toys as well, when I think of it, in this land where the elephant is the norm!"

"You have an agreeable way of phrasing things, I see, Mr. Kimberly."

"Thank you, Your Excellency. Manners in Britain have been steadily improving."

Khurram glanced at Mr. Kimberly. He had thick reddish hair, a round, good-natured face, shaggy wrists and thick calves and a deep, powerful voice. Khurram caught a faint eel-like odor emanating from the body of Mr. Kimberly: was it possible that the English did not bathe very frequently? But there was an indomitable cheerfulness about this queer Mr. Kimberly. Khurram glanced at him and smiled. He was beginning to like Mr. Kimberly.

"You are a Christian, I presume?" he said, fondling his bracelet lazily.

"Well, yes, in a general sort of way," said Mr. Kimberly nervously. "I personally feel no inordinate fanaticism about religion, as it happens."

"I see. Do tell me about London. Is London a beautiful city?"

"It has excellent bridges and magnificent towers," said Mr. Kimberly proudly. "Built in the substantial modern manner. We are making considerable progress in such matters. Culturally too, I might add. In music we're catching up with the Italians. And our new young poets are highly sophisticated."

"Who are your poets?"

"Ah," said Kimberly, "this is a subject close to my heart. I used to dabble in iambics myself when I was a youngster. We have Ben Jonson, who turns out comedies as shapely as any in France, and we have Beaumont and Fletcher, not to mention Marston and Middleton. There was a fellow named Shakespeare, but his works are a bit *passé*. We think him a trifle ostentatious and inflated."

"Would I like London?" said Khurram wistfully.

"You would indeed," said Mr. Kimberly. "You'd find the weather somewhat chilling, but I much prefer it to this conflagration. You'd cut a very fashionable figure in London society, Your Excellency!"

The travelers parted and the Prince and Princess rode on into the hills. The heat had grown less; there was a freshening breeze from the east. They reclined in the great palanquin side by side and gazed at the landscape. Tufts of laurel grew in the nooks and once they heard the sound of a waterfall.

IX

Arjumand was holding a small ripe orange in the palms of her hands. She raised it to her nostrils, sniffing the brisk acid fragrance. She glanced slyly at Khurram. "Tell me," she murmured, "about Nurmahal."

Khurram looked a little startled. "What made you suddenly think of Nurmahal?"

"I felt you thinking about her, possibly."

"I never," said Khurram, "think of Nurmahal."

"But you used to? Long ago?"

"Nurmahal," said Khurram, "is a sinister character."

"But you loved her once? You really loved her?"

Khurram blushed; his jaw twitched. "I was impressed by her. And I was always afraid of her. I was under her spell like a frightened rabbit."

"You don't look," remarked Arjumand, "like a frightened rabbit precisely."

"There's a sickness festering in Nurmahal. It fills her soul with a greed for power. An unquenchable gnawing lust. She's turned Jahangir into a mushroom."

"But why?" said Arjumand. "What does she want?"

"Who knows?" said Khurram. "Vengeance, possibly."

They rode on; the sun sank; fireflies sparkled among the bushes.

The Princess peered at the motionless Prince. A coppery glow outlined his profile, which was slightly oily with the long day's voyaging: the fine thin nose, slightly hooked, with its conspicuous nostrils; the heavy brows and enormous lashes; the girlish lips, both prim and sensual; the tremulous chin, both aggressive and vulnerable. His eyes in repose looked mild and poetic, a little mournful. What to make of such a face, with all those curious contradictions? When she looked at it she hardly knew what she really felt toward it—a flicker of alarm, a twinge of pity, a hint of boredom, a reluctant tenderness.

"And now," said Khurram in a languid voice, "suppose you tell me about Sirkandar."

Arjumand's face remained expressionless. "What made you suddenly think of Sirkandar?"

"Oh," said Khurram, "something in the atmosphere. I don't know quite what to call it."

"Yes," said Arjumand in a low, cool voice. "It is perfectly true. I loved Sirkandar."

"You loved him bodily?" said Khurram softly.

"Yes," said the Princess. "I loved him bodily."

They rode on through the dusk. They reached the top of the hill and below them, in the blue slumbering distance, lay the Bay of Bengal.

x

She woke up in the morning to the smell of the pines. She flung her night robe around her and peeped through the door of the tent. There had been a rainfall before dawn and the drops were shining on the pine needles. Quails were bobbing about clumsily in the deep foam of grass and the sunlight on the clouds was fine and piercing, like the sound of a flute. She watched a scarlet butterfly circling around a clump of honeysuckle and suddenly she was struck with the bizarre and gratuitous beauty of natural objects—the flowers and insects, the exultant clouds, the glittering vastness below them. Was there any particular reason why these things had been made beautiful? Was there a reason for that golden dust on the wings of the butterfly? Or was it purely a human illusion that these things looked beautiful? Was all this beauty merely imaginary, a man-made caprice? But no, she thought, even to a tiger another tiger must seem beautiful, and even for the tiger the butterfly must have a certain beauty, and even to the jackals and vipers there must be an exhilaration in the light of the morning and the freshness of things blossoming and the smell of the mountain pines. They too were capable of happiness, though they might not think of it as happiness, and surely they were capable of sadness too, though they might not know that it was sadness.

And then she wondered, as she turned around and saw the long light-sprinkled bay: What did she believe? Did she believe in anything? What was her faith? Did she have a faith? Was there nothing she was sure of? Was there nothing she was deeply convinced of? Was she incapable of real conviction, of a firm coherent attitude? She vaguely sensed that behind these multudinous movements of nature a single force lay secretly lurking: the flying birds had something in common with her, even the pines had something in comon with her, and every creature living had something or other in common with her. She too was participating in some process that was transpiring in a nameless secrecy, else why did she feel these quick, scattered pangs of illumination which carried with them the ring of truth, the unmistakable heartbeat which echoed from the core of things? But to identify it, to name and formulate it, was hopelessly beyond her. She felt with half of her mind that she was commonplace and colorless, without traits, without opinions, with nothing vivid or distinct in her character. And yet with the other half of her mind she knew that there was an oddity about her, a uniqueness in her soul, a terrifying strangeness in her destiny. And there were times, as she looked into the distances beyond the great prairies, when she sensed that something sinister was waiting beyond the horizon; that all her diversions, her moments of gaiety, were merely islands of refuge, just foam-splashed little islands in a black and murderous sea.

As she glanced at the sleeping Khurram, his face half-buried in the pillow, with the light through the pines stirring faintly on his cheeks, something suddenly rose up in her, it clutched at her throat and took her breath away, and though her fear was as powerful as ever, something new entered her feelings, a spearing shock of recognition, almost sickening in its sudden sweetness.

Khurram opened his eyes. His long black lashes looked damp and heavy. He smiled a drowsy smile; it was hardly a smile, it was merely an awakening. Then he raised himself on his elbow and looked at her wickedly. His naked body still had the musky aura of sleep clinging to it. "Come," he whispered. "Lie down, Arjumand. Lie down, my darling. Let me look at you."

And suddenly the fear came over her again. "Yes," she said, half-faint with panic.

PART FOUR

The Second Murder

Along the shore of the promontory an artificial jungle had been created. Fruits of glass tinkled in the boughs, waxen orchids hung from the trellises. In the arbor where old Draupadi was serving the sherbets, a tame lion from Ethiopia was lolling among the flowers. A swarm of yellow butterflies dangled from black silken threads, shimmering idly in the breeze like flakes of brocade.

"Artifice," purred the Sultan, with a silver hummingbird poised on his wrist. "That's where we seek our consolation. And that's the only place where we'll find it." He looked at the bird which fluttered its wings when he tugged at a golden cord: "The natural bird lives and dies; it rots away and is eaten by worms, but the fraudulent bird is immortal—it will give pleasure throughout eternity!"

He lay on a couch by the water's edge. Velvet rugs lay spread on the grass and in the bushes a boy was singing to a three-stringed zither. Dusk was falling; the lanterns were lit one by one under the willows. The rosy light fell on Shahriyar's face, which was slightly oily with the sheen of unguents. He was darker and suppler and more athletic than his brothers; there was a Siamese look about him, with his sloping eyes and thick, high cheekbones. His expression was cool and impersonal; his gestures were casual and languid. His voice was caressing and musical, tinged with an affectation of melancholy.

"Sit down, Rambha," he said wearily, motioning to the woman who was approaching, a slender girl with hair dyed scarlet and arms aglitter with bracelets. "Let us talk about love. What are your thoughts on love, my Rambha?"

"I have no opinions," said Rambha in her low, grating voice.

"Only experiences. And not enough even of these, I'm afraid. Love! Dear boy, we develop our philosophy of love only when we've stopped experiencing Love!"

Two young men were lolling on the rugs at the feet of the Prince Shahriyar: Sambhuji the singer and Eden the dancer.

"Tell me, Sambhuji," said the Sultan, "do you believe what Rambha is saying?"

"Rambha has had fifteen lovers. Whether they were enough I can only speculate!"

"She says no," said Shahriyar dreamily. "What went wrong with them, do you imagine?"

"She attracts the wrong lovers, presumably," said Eden, waving his fan.

"Or is attracted," said Sambhuji, leering slightly, "to the wrong ones."

"Or has tastes incapable of fulfillment, very possibly," put in Rambha, settling herself into a cushion on the edge of the flowerbed.

Eden was a beautiful Kashmiri, tall and lean, with foxlike eyes. He was naked except for a Paisley-patterned cloth around his hips. Sambhuji was bald and barrel-chested; he came from Madura and was dark as a Negro. Rambha was an actress who habitually performed the role of Kali the goddess. She had emerald-green eyes and an air of dry, depleted bitterness.

"There is nothing," said Rambha, "so unrewarding as this chatter about love. Theories about art are very well, or theories about sicknesses or God or government. But love is like water. It trickles through our fingers when we try to snatch at it."

"And yet," said Eden, "we keep chattering about it. We keep snatching at it and theorizing about it. It's the one thing about which there is never a final, clear-cut certainty."

"It keeps changing like water," said Sambhuji. "All love is a fluidity, I have discovered."

"Ah, there you are," said Shahriyar gaily, "stating a principle!

When there are no principles! Love keeps changing incessantly but it still can be lasting while perpetually changing!"

"You are an idealist," said Rambha bleakly.

"Not in the least," said Prince Shahriyar. "I am merely stating that everything is possible in the kingdom of love. There are infinite varieties and infinite variations and whatever we say, the opposite is also true."

"You've been listening," said Eden darkly, "to that bore Krishnadevaraya."

"Yes, I've listened to him," said Shahriyar, laughing, "but his opinions on love are academic, I fear. I don't think poor old Krishnadevaraya speaks from a wealth of amorous experiences."

"And yet," said Sambhuji, rolling his eyes, "the curious thing is that those very people who have never enjoyed much love in their lives are full of wisdom and intensity about it, while those who've had their fill have neither the wisdom nor the intensity."

"In which category do you belong, my exquisite Sambhuji?" said Shahriyar teasingly.

"Into the first," said Sambhuji sadly. "I am wise and intense. And no one loves me."

A bell was ringing. There was the clash of copper cymbals among the trees.

"Hush," said Shahriyar. "They're nearly ready. Go, tell Draupadi to bring us the joss sticks."

The theater had been constructed on a circular raft which floated below them. A platform of wood stood under a high silken awning and the lamps hung from stakes which surrounded the stage. The actors and dancers were being rowed to the stage, their bracelets and crowns shimmering faintly as they crossed the water. Under the trees sat the guests with their slaves standing behind them, and with the horses and elephants forming a wall still beyond.

The propitiatory words were uttered. The wings of the stage hummed with prayers as the make-up woman ground her powders and the costume mistress hung the wigs. The actors stepped out of the boat. There was the sound of a Chinese flute. All grew still; the curtains rustled; a drumbeat sounded; the play began.

11

Shahriyar's theater had four sets of curtains, as was customary: black for tragedy, red for violence, white for love and yellow for laughter. Tonight they were using the yellow ones. The play dealt with Siva and his seduction of a milkmaid. He appeared as a peacock in a mass of feathers, then in furs as a lion, then in veils as a butterfly, and finally in scales as a fish. It was in his role as a fish that he succeeded in ravishing the milkmaid. The style of the dialogue was tedious in its subtlety and cloying in its pseudo-elegance, but a ripple of humor ran through the performance of the naughty Siva.

After the play was over there was a picnic beside the shore. Crimson cloths were spread on the grass; incense was burned to banish the gnats. Boys in apple-green fezzes served the chickens in aspic and a eunuch in a gilded headdress poured out the rice wine. The Empress rose from her cushions when the music had died away and strolled slowly toward Shahriyar, who was squatting among his cronies.

"I found the play a bit obscure. I wasn't sure quite what to make of it."

"It was symbolical, of course," said Shahriyar, grinning playfully at the Empress.

"All these feathers and scales: do they have a hidden meaning?"

"Certainly," said Shahriyar, looking wise. "People fall into three categories—the earthy, the airy and the watery. We long for feathers or furs or fins."

"Very improper, I can't help thinking," said the Empress crisply.

"But full of poetry, full of suggestiveness," said Shahriyar, tittering.

The Empress looked sternly at Shahriyar. "They tell me that your life is very dissolute."

Shahriyar blushed slightly. "It's even worse than the gossip, I assure you!"

"Do you *try* to be wicked?" said the Empress.

Shahriyar laughed. "What is wickedness? We all have wickedness in us; it's merely a question of what we do about it. Some of us pretend that it isn't there, others struggle to overcome it, others let it fester quietly, others draw it into the open. I prefer to conquer my vices by acting them out. And thus I grow virtuous. Or so I like to imagine."

"Is it your opinion," said Nurmahal coldly, "that we become the opposite of what we do? It sounds a bit far-fetched, my dear Shahriyar, to say the least."

"All things eventually turn into their opposite, that's what the hermit told me yesterday. The gods have two faces. The secret of life is its ambiguity."

"Nonsense," said Nurmahal impatiently. "You're still obsessed with your childlike cleverness. There are those like you who love mystery and those like me who hate mystery."

"The Philistines," said Shahriyar, "and the poets, I suppose."

"The sensible ones and the fools," said Nurmahal.

The water lay smooth as a mirror. The evening mist was beginning to rise. The theater was empty but the hanging lamps still shone through the mist. The servants were strolling about, swinging their bowls of glowing sandalwood, and the smell of the misty marshes seeped through the smell of the incense. The older ladies gathered their shawls and started back toward the palanquins; some of the guests gathered in a group to watch the Nepalese dancers. Several drunken young men sauntered furtively into the bushes. Rambha and Eden and Sambhuji went strolling to the edge of the pier.

"Listen, Shahriyar," said the Empress brusquely. "You must pull yourself together. I've always had a tender spot in my heart for your beautiful naughty face. But we're growing older, all of us. You can't keep on with this cheap frivolity. You've been neglecting your wife atrociously. It's not surprising. She's far from beautiful. It was strictly a marriage of diplomacy, to put it indulgently. But after all, she's my daughter, Shahriyar. I feel involved in the matter. Oh, don't misunderstand me, please. I feel no moral qualms, quite the contrary. I've always been a shade outré myself, as you probably realize. But I must tell you something serious. Khusru is dead. Parviz is in a stupor. That leaves Khurram and you. Khurram is momentarily out of favor, as might be expected, but I know Jahangir's inner feelings about him. I refuse to allow Khurram to wheedle his way into the succession again. And that leaves you, my little dolphin. You may laugh at me if you choose, but I shall insist on your behaving with a certain dignity. We can't have the entire countryside gossiping and giggling about their future Emperor."

"You are most considerate, dear Nurmahal," said Shahriyar after a moment. "I know your feelings. I know your motives. And I thoroughly sympathize with them. I even applaud them. But do you want to know the truth? I despise the rest of my family. Khusru was nothing but a dried-up bore and Parviz is a bloated nonentity and that strange fellow Khurram is a vicious little bully. My father lies befuddled with opium. You are running the Empire for him. Is this grandeur? Is this majesty? Thank you kindly. I prefer my freedom."

Nurmahal looked at him frozenly. "There is such a thing as duty. Not to mention patriotism."

"Duty. Patriotism," said Shahriyar. "Order. Justice. Law. Government. You can take the whole lot of them and toss them into the Jumna. They're nothing but phantoms."

"And what," said Nurmahal, "do you think is real?"

"Freedom. Joy. The creation of beauty."

Nurmahal waved her forefinger and laughed contemptuously. "Creation! As though you were capable of it! And beauty! Just a horde of ephebes! At the bottom of it all there's nothing but laziness and promiscuity."

"Yes, I know," said Shahriyar calmly. "Khurram used to call me a sensualist. But my senses, I can assure you, are governed by a fastidious set of values. Khurram's senses are as wild as an animal's. It is he who is the depraved one."

Nurmahal looked at him inquisitively. "Do you know what I think?" she said. "I really think that you're a perfectly decent and humdrum and sensible person at the bottom of it, and these mincing affectations are just a form of rebelliousness."

"Yes? Rebelliousness against what, may I ask?" said Shahriyar, simpering.

"Against loneliness. Against stupidity. Against the crudity of life," said Nurmahal.

Shahriyar smiled. "You are putting it quaintly, but perhaps you are not inaccurate. And if I ever become Emperor I shall do away with all that ugliness. I shall redecorate that atrocious palace. I'll replace the velvet with *crêpe de Chine*. What India needs isn't more power. It needs delicacy and grace. It needs peace and happiness."

The Empress gazed at him despairingly. "Yes. No doubt," she said quietly. She drew her shawl over her shoulders and wandered silently across the lawn.

III

The Deccan is a land of steamy jungles and suffocating marshes, scorching plains, stinking villages and rocky ravines. Nothing in the Deccan seems gentle. Nothing is humanized or mellowed. But those little stray nooks where there is coolness seem all the more pleasant, and such a place was the house in Burhanpur where Prince Khurram was living in exile.

But the heat of midsummer even here grew intolerable. The stones on the terrace were so hot that it was impossible to walk there and the snakes crawled out of the jungle and took refuge in the cellar.

So Arjumand and Khurram decided to ride into the hills, where a sprawling summer bungalow stood in the middle of a forest, with a crescent-shaped porch all covered with convolvulus. A guest house stood in the shade of a deodar not far away and beyond, on the edge of a cliff, stood the huts for the servants.

It was dusk when they arrived. The horses' hoofs sank into the pine needles and the dew on the pines shone bright in the lamplight. The cook had arrived before them; a smell of curry seeped through the air and the Princess flung her arms around her daughter and laughed with pleasure. They ran upstairs and washed their bodies in little tubs of pine-spiced water, and then they put on their shawls, Arjumand a purple and Jahanara a pink one, and they stepped onto the porch where the lamps had been lit. A net was hung from the roof of the porch to keep off the insects, but their buzzing and whining filled the darkness outside.

After dinner Ali the groom sang a song about the Emperor Tamerlane, and Katyayani the nurse played a game of buttons with Aurengzeb; but then the owls started to hoot and the children were sent to bed and the groom picked up his lute and walked off into the darkness.

"It's so quiet here," said Arjumand. "It's so still I can hear you breathing!"

"It's so still that I can hear dew fall from the pines," said Khurram.

"It's so still I can hear what you're thinking," said Arjumand.

"What am I thinking?" said Khurram.

"You're thinking of Agra," said the Princess.

Khurram scowled. "I feel restless, rotting away in the middle of nowhere."

Arjumand looked at him slyly. She picked up her wine glass and said softly: "My darling Khurram, couldn't we try and forget about Agra! Couldn't we forget about all that splendor and all that horrible intricacy? Couldn't we pack up our bags and go sailing to Arabia?"

Khurram laughed. "There's nothing but desert and murder in Arabia."

"Shall we go to Persia, perhaps?"

"The Persians are filthy profligates."

"Or China, then?" whispered Arjumand.

"Good God! China!" The Prince looked shocked. "In China you'll find nothing but fat yellow infidels!"

Arjumand sighed and placed her forefinger on Khurram's sleeve. "Do you know what I think, my darling? I think that I'd rather die while my eyes are bright than just gradually wither and feel my heart start withering too!"

Khurram knelt down beside her. He ran his hand under her shawl and gently loosened the folds of her dress. Then he took her breasts in his hands and kissed them both, first one and then the other. The peach-colored light fell on Arjumand's flesh and her face grew suddenly strange; it looked like the face of another woman.

"Isn't it odd?" he said quietly. "One day you're as meek as a little caterpillar. The next you're as secret as a snail. And the next you're as darting as a swallow!"

"And you," said Arjumand, tugging at his earlobe, "are as surly as a hornet in the morning, and as nervous as a cat in the middle of the day, and as sad as a marmoset in the evening!"

They lay down on the couch and when their lovemaking was over she crouched over Khurram and drew her thumb across his eyebrows. Then she leaned down and kissed him lightly on the tip of his nose. "The flame is almost dead. I can hardly see you," she whispered.

"I'm ugly," growled Khurram. "It's just as well that you cannot see me."

Arjumand said: "What is it, darling? What is it you're so bitter about?"

"I'm not bitter," said Khurram stubbornly.

"You're alarmed, then," said Arjumand.

"By unknown things," said the naked Sultan, turning his face toward the darkness.

Arjumand nodded. "The unknown! Oh, the terrible wild unknown! Yes, darling, we're all frightened of that snake-faced unknown. . . ."

The flame jumped and twisted. Then it sputtered and died. The breeze rustled gently in the dew-drenched branches. Through the net on the veranda she could see the silhouette of Abdul the cook prowling softly among the trees, gathering kindling for the morning fire.

IV

On the following morning Prince Khurram was awakened by the sound of the ravens. They were squawking below his window on their way to their morning drink. Then the smaller birds woke up and started to twitter in the trees and when he glanced through the window he saw the dewdrops sparkling on the pine needles.

He mounted his stallion Iqbal and rode into the woods. The pines grew so thick that the morning sun was nearly invisible and the smell of the night was still floating among the trunks. He passed the pot-bellied cook who was limping along with a basket of mushrooms.

"Good morning, Abdul!"

"Good morning, Your Highness!"

"Have you seen any strangers?"

"None, Your Highness!"

Khurram rode on. He still couldn't shake off his feeling of uneasiness. The blood-red berries among the ivy had an evil look about them, and the voice of an invisible bird said: "Beware, Sir, beware!" He paused by a stream and the shapes of the fish looked like daggers. A growing tension, a sourceless excitement was beginning to grip him. And the tension was accentuated by his memory of Arjumand's serenity, which seemed a reproach to his own growing restlessness. Everything around him was a challenge to him. Everything called to be subdued. He couldn't bear to feel that something was eluding his power to subdue it. And the very awareness of this impotence and his sense of guilt about this impotence made the restlessness all the more feverish and all the more fanatical. His fingers twitched with impatience; his palms were damp with suspense.

He rode on. Braids of moss hung from the thick gray branches. There were pools of blackish water in the hollows between the trees. Suddenly he noticed a hunchbacked shadow groping its way through the treetrunks. It was Dilras the herb-woman. Everyone knew the Untouchable Dilras, with her face like a frog and her long skinny arms, which looked like the dead, black roots of a palm tree.

"Good morning, Dilras!" called the Sultan.

"Good morning, Your Highness!" cackled the herb-woman.

"Any strangers about?"

"None that I've noticed!" cried Dilras.

Her voice was a sharp little squeal like a whippet's and her breasts hung leathery and hollow and purselike. She had long ago abandoned all pretense of being a woman and her eyes had a cool, bulging glaze like a trout's.

Khurram slowed his horse and paused beside Dilras. He looked at her tensely. "Dilras," he said, "I have something to ask you."

"Yes?" squealed Dilras, fluttering her fingers. "Something about jealousy, I suppose?"

The Sultan shook his head slowly.

"Something about impotence?"

"No," said the Sultan.

"Sickness, then," snapped Dilras impatiently. "I'm tired of sicknesses. Nothing but sicknesses!"

"No," said the Sultan. "It's about my family. Have you any opinions about my family?"

Dilras' eyes rolled in their sockets. "Family squabbles. I'm sick of squabbles!"

"Think hard, Dilras! Look at your leaves!"

Dilras returned the Sultan's gaze. And for a moment there was a strangeness, a kind of flickering between them, like the electrical contact between two lovers. It was as though they had known each other long ago, in an earlier incarnation, with some dark and half-forgotten intensity of feeling. Her mouth shook a little, as though with some painful recollection. Then she squatted in front of the horse and picked up a handful of leaves. She looked at one leaf after another, dampish leaves of the early autumn; she scrupulously studied their veins and discarded them listlessly one by one. Finally she found a yellowish leaf which interested her more than the others. She ran her finger around the edge, licked it with her tongue and lifted it to her nostrils.

Then she quietly raised her huge, baleful eyes toward the Sultan's. A stillness came over her. Her eyes grew veiled; her voice softened. It was almost as though a kind of iridescence were rippling over her body. Her cheeks turned purple and a pale greenish light shone on her hair.

"Very well," she muttered bitterly. "If you insist. I don't care. I'm old, I'm half-dead, what do I care what you do to each other? Killing and killing and still more killing! When will you stop? Not till the mountains swallow you! It's no use asking me questions! Do what you must, but please stop troubling me!"

"Do what, Dilras?" whispered the Sultan.

"You know what!" squealed the woman.

"Tell me, Dilras," coaxed the Sultan.

"Murderer! Murderer!" shrieked the woman. "Kill him if you must! Go on! Poison him! Blood of your blood, flesh of your flesh, and there's nothing bad he's ever done to you! Go on! I won't stop you! It's in the leaves! It's a part of destiny!"

She trembled violently as the evil vision gradually faded and fell away from her. She got up from the ground and placed her hand on the horse's head. Suddenly she seemed to have forgotten all she had seen and all she had said. She leered at Khurram obsequiously. "There's a rainfall coming, Your Highness!"

Khurram reached under his sleeve and drew off a silver bracelet and tossed it through the air in the direction of the herb-woman. Then he flicked at the reins and started back through the forest.

When he arrived at the cottage an oval table had been set under an evergreen. A huge bowl of asters was standing on the middle of the table. The servants were carrying the dishes and cutlery out of the kitchen and Abdul was beating some eggs by an open fire.

Aurengzeb ran up to his father and threw his arms around his waist. "Look!" he cried. "See what I found!" He opened his little hand and there on his palm lay a yellow turtle no bigger than a gold piece.

v

The Sultan Shahriyar and his friends were returning from a holiday near Peshawar. They had left the hills behind them and were crossing the sands which sloped toward the Indus. The day had been hot; the twigs drooped from the saplings. A sprinkle of rain had dotted the dusty gray leaves. Now and again a breeze came up and everything started to tremble—the stiffening thistles and dangling boughs, the manes of the mules, the fringes of the palanquins. The path went twisting among some rocks and then gradually descended. Here and there a black nanny-goat stood on a cliff and looked at them curiously. The land took on a stealthy, conspiratorial expression, as though it were quietly watching and waiting.

The sun grew rosy and bloated when they reached the brink of a hill. Below them lay the Indus, a scalloped pink in the evening light. The path dipped into a ravine and then curved toward the shore, where some scraggly old willows broke the dismal monotony. They climbed down cautiously, two palanquins in which lay Rumbha and Shahriyar, followed by Sambhuji the singer and Eden the dancer on muleback. In front rode the Sultan's bodyguard, an Ethiopian whose name was Bojo, and behind plodded the slaves carrying the tents and provisions. Now and again a cloud of dust shot up when a mule lost his foothold. A stone went tumbling; a bearer cursed. Bojo turned and cried: "Careful, now!" They crossed the pebbles of a dried-up estuary and finally reached the banks of the river. On the opposite shore a wisp of smoke was rising from the hut of the ferryman.

They pitched camp on the grassy banks. It was too late to call to the ferryman. Sambhuji built a fire while the slaves set up the tents and Bojo led the mules down to the water to drink. A strange aroma was in the air: an acidulous smell, vaguely reptilian, as though some drowsy crocodile might be reclining in a nearby inlet. Copper ewers were brought to the tents and the marshy water was sprinkled with lotus oil so the travelers could wash the sweat and dust from their itching bodies. The stars were already shining when they gathered around the fire. Cushions were scattered across the rugs; the roasted pheasants lay sizzling.

"If only," said Rambha soulfully, "we could always live like this! In the bosom of nature!"

"With nothing," said Eden, "to worry us. No plagues, no enemies, no gossip."

"Nonsense," said Sambhuji. "I used to live like this when I was a boy in Madura. There were plenty of plagues and plenty of enemies, though rather different from the ones in Agra."

"There is always something or other to scare us," said Shahriyar, fondling his Adam's apple.

"Growing old," said Rambha dully.

"Loneliness," said Eden, gazing at the river.

"Losing one's lovers," hinted Rambha.

"Or losing one's freedom," said Sambhuji.

The Sultan shrugged his shoulders. "There's something worse. Do you know what it is? Self-disgust. Loneliness and age are nothing to the terrors of self-damnation." He looked desolately at Sambhuji. "Listen," he said. "Do you know what I think? We're just nothings, we're nobodies, and we try to hide from our nothingness in an endless series of copulations. But instead of discovering an identity in all these quaint little orgasms, we merely plunge still deeper into a faceless and soulless nothingness."

"Why do we say of such gloomy things?" said Eden gaily, lifting the wine jug.

"You're perfectly right. We're frightened of ghosts, that's all," said Sambhuji, rising from his cushion. He tossed some twigs into the flames and picked up his lute and started to sing into the huge blue silence of Rajputana.

VI

The sun was just rising when the ferryman stepped on the shore. The tents had been rolled and the travelers were waiting. Only a scattering of ashes and some balls of mule dung marked the camp site. The mules were driven to the ferry; the palanquins were set on deck. The waters of the Indus lay blurred as agate in the morning mist. The boat started to move and soon they were in the middle of the river and the film-covered banks looked strangely distant, like desert islands. The boat shook uneasily in the slow-shifting currents. When they approached the southern shore the river mists had already vanished and the long bleak horizon lay brown and scaly, like a sleeping sea-beast.

The ferryman fastened the cables. The mules were guided

ashore. Shahriyar held out his arm and dropped some coins in the ferryman's hand.

"Be careful, Your Highness. It's an ugly country," grunted the pot-bellied ferryman, who was a Rajput with eyes like an elephant's, sly and jovial and mischievous.

"Yes, it's desolate," agreed the Sultan.

"And dangerous too," growled the ferryman.

"Snakes?" said Shahriyar.

"Yes. Cobras," said the boatman darkly.

They mounted their mules and palanquins and started off into the jungle, which was a tangle of thorny underbrush with a narrow path cut through it. The heat grew intense. Not a breeze stirred the stillness. They came to a grove which surrounded a clearing and in the middle of the clearing crouched a village. One by one the thirsty mules were led up to the slime-green trough. There was something strange about the village. The women and childen hid in their huts; the men peered furtively from behind the treetrunks. Even the cow looked apprehensive, blinking her big sacred eyes.

They rode on. Soon after noon they came to a deserted old rest house which nestled in the shade of a banyan tree. Cobwebs trailed from the rafters and there was a smell of deterioration, of festering wood and fat white termites. Sambhuji lit some incense which he placed in a basin while the servants scurried about, sweeping the floor and laying the rugs. Soon the place seemed almost habitable. A platter of dates was set on the table and only a lingering effluence of something foul hung in the air.

Eden crawled into the thicket and gathered some scarlet blossoms which he laid in a circle around the center of the table. A bowl of curry was brought from the kitchen and the yellow wine was poured into the cups, but a curious depression hung over the company.

"What's wrong?" said Rambha finally. "You all looked terrified. Is this rest house haunted?"

"Something nasty," said Sambhuji, "must have happened here. There's a smell of wickedness."

They placed the cushions across the rugs and lay down for their noonday nap. The flies were buzzing; a monkey scolded. The mules stirred sullenly under the banyan tree. Suddenly Bojo flung open the door and cried in a panic: "Bandits, Your Highness!"

They hardly had time to rub their eyes. Two powerful arms took hold of Bojo and three sweat-spattered cutthroats strode noisily into the room. One wore a mask over his face; he was dressed more gaudily than the others, with a bottle-blue turban and a studded belt and a golden necklace. He flung his arms about exuberantly, shrieking orders in a high-pitched voice while his two shaggy colleagues stripped the jewels from the voyagers.

"You're very lucky, my fine friends," he cried in his shrill birdlike voice. "We could easily enough kill you. But we're not murderers. We're men with a mission. We rob the tyrannical and the debauched. We take their money and give it to the unlucky ones." He took the wine jug from the table and swallowed the wine that was left in it and stalked triumphantly through the door, followed by his ill-smelling accomplices, who were carrying the tinkling jewelry wrapped in a gold-embroidered sari.

The voyagers sat in silence, gazing dejectedly into the wilderness.

"Just as I thought," said Sambhuji finally. "It's a dangerous place. I smelled it in the woodwork."

VII

The Ranee's palace near Gwalior was a turreted, rambling structure set in the middle of a moss-bearded park. The gardens had gone to seed. The weeds were waist-high. The pool was choked with lilypads and the house itself was beginning to crumble, with lizards racing along the corridors and the pantries full of cockroaches. The Ranee was so old that people no longer bothered to visit her, not even her humble relations who lived in Allahabad. She had once been a beauty and a brilliant figure in society but things had gone wrong, the scholarly Rajah had died of cholera and the money had dwindled away and her friends had deserted her. And now she was old, so old that she looked like a phantom, a small blue-haired specter with eyes like a vulture's.

It was here that Prince Parviz stayed for a week on his way to the Deccan. He arrived late one evening after a hot day's journey and the Ranee brought him a sherbet as he rested in his bedchamber.

"Do you think it's wise to travel in this terrible heat?" said the Ranee gently.

"I was sick of Agra. I needed a change. I was feeling miserable," said Parviz.

"My dear Parviz," murmured his aunt, "you have always been given to melancholy. It isn't Agra or Delhi or Ajmer, it's something deep in your blood. I've often wondered about it lately, I have so little else to think about. Why don't you stay for a month or two and try to lift your spirits a little? You're much too fat, that is certain. And your face has a greenish tinge. I don't think you should go to the Deccan in this boiling heat, my dear child."

"Khurram is expecting me," said Parviz. "They're staying in the hills. It will be cool there."

The old Ranee looked at him thoughtfully. "I never cared," she said, "for the Deccan."

"Nor have I. Still, it's a change. I need, how shall I put it, a self-renewal!"

The Ranee stared through the window. "And I've never cared for Khurram. I don't know why."

"Nor have I," said Parviz guiltily. "But it's time I made friends with him."

"Of all the cities," said the Rance, "I like Burhanpur the least. I dislike Patna with its *nouveaux riches,* I loathe Benares with those filthy ghats, and I feel sickened by Fatehpur-Sikri with its faded vulgarity. But Burhanpur is easily the worst. Burhanpur is distinctly sinister."

"I have never seen it," said Parviz.

"It has nothing to offer you," said the Ranee.

Ranee Mahil was one of those ancient indomitable women whose air of ferocity is in proportion to the tenderness in their hearts. She loved Parviz. She saw through that wretched decaying exterior, and she detected the pain and the poetry that lay strangled in all that fat. And her way of showing her love was by scowling at him and growling at him, by rapping his knuckles and perpetually contradicting him.

Parviz got up and waddled slowly through the bleak, disheveled garden. A horde of cats lived in the stables, which were otherwise deserted. A blind old woman was weaving a carpet in the shade of an arbor and beside her sat a boy nibbling at a dish of *hors d'œuvres.* Parviz walked down the drive toward the gardener's cottage. The shed was filled with old flowerpots stacked in rows and veiled with spiderwebs. Iron tools covered with dust lay scattered about in the darkness. The place had the air of some medieval torture-chamber, with its rust-reddened trowels and clotted black shears.

Parviz stepped out into the flat white sunlight again. The shrubs were frozen like corals in the glasslike translucence. Suddenly a battalion of insects started to chirp in the grasses: it was like the screaming of a far-off army of savages.

More and more Parviz had come to feel that he was living in a nightmare. Opium had twisted his senses. Self-disgust had distorted his thoughts. His inertia had gradually turned into a mania, an obsession. Every movement was becoming an intolerable effort to him. Even to raise a glass to his lips brought a fatigue that left him panting. Stepping from one room to another was like digging his way through a quagmire. It was in a last panicky effort to shake off this lethargy that he had embarked on his half-hearted journey to Burhanpur.

He wandered slowly back toward the Ranee's house and entered the drawing room. She greeted him with a cup of palm wine and motioned him brusquely toward the divan.

"You look sleepy," she said. "As usual. But wait a moment. I'll read you some poetry." She reached toward a shelf and drew out a book. She leafed idly through the pages, peeping furtively at Parviz, and finally raised her middle finger and read in a sepulchral tone:

> *"The Daughter of Heaven is rising before us.*
> *O maiden glittering in golden robes,*
> *O empress of all that we have on earth,*
> *O lovely sunrise, shine on us all!*
>
> *"In the sweep of the skies she glows like fire.*
> *The goddess is dropping her robe of darkness*
> *And rouses the world from sleep as she rides*
> *In her burning chariot, the stallions flashing. . . ."*

Parviz looked up with a smile when the Ranee had finished the poem.

"Yes, I know it," he said. "I heard it sung as a child."

"It's a hymn to the lovely Ushas, the goddess of dawn," said the Ranee.

"Yes," said Parviz. "I need to be awakened! I need to ride in a flaming chariot!"

The Ranee closed the book and stared fiercely into the garden, where the roses hung parched in the white, hollow sunlight.

VIII

Nine days later Prince Parviz arrived in the city of Burhanpur and was carried in a litter up to the bungalow in the hills. He was given the little guest house under the deodar and here he spent his mornings, writing in his diary and reading the *Vedas*.

Sometimes he stepped out of doors and went strolling among the pines, but every step was a disagreeable effort to him nowadays. What was more, there was something about nature which disconcerted Parviz: he hated the insects, he distrusted the birds, he feared the reptiles, he was bored by the plants, and the heat of the sun gave him violent headaches. The only things that he liked were the clouds, and after he had put down his pen he'd sit by the window without moving, staring at those ghosts which prowled through the heavens.

There were clouds which were white and bulbous, like great marble domes. There were clouds that moved in unison, like a flock of woolly sheep. There were clouds that hung like ribbons over the pink horizon and there were clouds of a threatening mauve which licked at the sky like a monstrous tongue. But the clouds he liked best were the clouds of no particular character, tufts of cloud that were constantly changing as they moved across the sky, turning from ducks to salamanders, or from porpoises to camels. These clouds seemed to symbolize the transmigration of spirits and he used to wonder what shape he would assume when he finally crumbled. A squirrel perhaps, or a butterfly. Not an elephant, certainly. Possibly a cheetah.

His brother Khurram knocked on the door and stepped discreetly into the room.

"You've been writing?" he said.

"Oh, just scribbling," said Parviz.

Khurram smiled. "Poems, by chance?"

"I've given up poetry," said Parviz glumly. "I've been writing down my thoughts—random, ineffectual thoughts. Most of the time I just sit by the window and look at the clouds."

"The clouds?" said Khurram suspiciously.

"You'd be startled," said Parviz, smiling, "what things one can learn just by looking at clouds. One can see how deceptive are the temporary appearances of things, and how a snake can turn into a rabbit, or a fox into a hen. From watching the clouds I've learned that one must always try to reserve one's judgment. What seems dangerous or grotesque may grow gentle and beautiful a moment later."

"You suggest," said Khurram quizzically, "that nothing remains the same for long, and that nothing as a result contains any intrinsic characteristics? My dear Parviz, I disagree. Isn't the cobra essentially wicked? Isn't the cow essentially kind? Aren't tigers essentially splendid and rats innately contemptible? Aren't the vultures all hideous and the peacocks all beautiful? My clever Parviz, if we started to abandon these human notions of good and bad, God knows where we'd all end up. Everything would turn into everything else and you wouldn't know the difference between a pea and a sapphire. And aren't you denying that nature also has her preferences, her own morals and her own aesthetics? Didn't nature decide to make the hyenas ugly, in view of their detestable habits? And didn't nature give to the tiger his magnificent eyes, in view of his power?"

Parviz sighed and ran his fingers along the edge of the windowsill. "Human fancies! Human illusions! That's all they are, my good Khurram. In the eyes of eternity the little rat is just as splendid as the tiger, and the toad will take his place beside the beautiful long-necked swan!"

I X

After dining among the pines with Khurram and Arjumand, Sultan Parviz strolled back to his guest house under the deodar. The stars were uncannily brilliant; the air was tart with resin. A nightbird was trilling away in the darkness.

He sat down by the window and looked out at the clouds. They were rimmed with silver threads, the vivid clouds of an autumn night. "No," he thought. "I must give up all this poeticizing, this sentimentality. Nothing is beautiful or ugly. Nothing is exquisite or disgusting."

The thought brought him comfort; a wistful smile shone on his lips. And at the same time a large, dirty tear rolled down his cheek.

At that moment, without warning, he felt a jab of pain so violent that his body seemed to crack like a bowl of glass under a hammer. For several minutes he sat motionless, unable to scream. He kept gasping like an asthmatic; his eyes bulged like an idiot's. Someone was walking along the path toward the servant's quarters. He tried to cry: "Abdul!" But there was only a frantic gurgle. He clutched at the sill, then slumped sideways and crashed to the floor.

The pain was so horrible that it ceased being pain, just as cold in its extremity ceases to be cold and turns into numbness. It was a needle which rose into the air with his body pinned on top of it, stiff and faceless as a dried-up insect's. Then it turned into a great white arch which rose over him, spreading outward until he seemed to lie trapped in a giant igloo. And then it turned into a sea, in which his body was an island, just a rocky black island with the waves pouring over it.

From where he lay he saw a long narrow cloud floating in the darkness, stirring faintly among the stars like a kerchief waving goodbye. He snatched desperately at a final thought, like a drowning man snatching for air. "No, the clouds teach one nothing, they mean nothing at all. Only the stars can teach us any-thing. Only the stars never change. . . ."

He heard footsteps in the darkness, but soon they died away again. The smell of the convolvulus came drifting through the window. He rolled over and tried to crawl across the floor on all fours, but then suddenly, as though propelled by some invisible force, he shot forward uncannily, uttered a strangulated cackle, then lay face down on the floor, arms flung sideward, and ceased stirring.

PART FIVE

The Third Murder

The old Emperor felt unwell. It was partly his liver, which was growing weary, and partly his kidneys, which had grown rebellious, but more than anything it was his spirit: a sickening sense of things rotting, a desperate longing for freshness and novelty.

The Imperial summerhouse overlooked the shores of the Jhelum and a canopied houseboat was anchored off the banks. The foothills of Kashmir rose gently in the distance and beyond rose those stupefying phantoms, the Himalayas. Sometimes he'd sit alone in the houseboat with an old Armenian named Papasian, who amused him with his spicy anecdotes about the wickedness of the western cities—the vaulted brothels of Cairo, or the labyrinthine baths of Istanbul.

Papasian was very rich. He had a superb collection of jewels—not only emeralds and rubies and sapphires, but innumerable oddities that he had bought on his voyages. He had a large yellow agate engraved with Leda and the Swan and a moonstone engraved with Minerva and her owl. He had a sardonyx engraved with Isis; he had bought it in Venice. He had an egg-shaped carnelian engraved with the head of Queen Elizabeth. He also possessed some Chinese jades carved into an elaborate pornography and at night he'd sit with Jahangir under the lamps of the houseboat, listening to the sad Kashmiri music and the lapping of the Jhelum. They would fondle the naughty jades and talk of their own long-vanished love affairs.

"Our jewels," said Papasian, "stay hard and shiny. But our loves grow wrinkled."

"True," said the Emperor. "One should learn to conquer these human infatuations."

"Flesh rots, the phallus sags, but the glow of a sapphire lasts forever."

"True, true," moaned the miserable Jahangir. "I wish my body would turn into a sapphire!"

The light of the lanterns lay splintered among the ripples and the smell of the water lilies mixed with the stench of garbage floating from Srinagar. The tiny Papasian, with white hairs sprouting out of his ears, resembled a marmoset, while the swollen old Emperor looked like some sad, wrinkled walrus.

"Look at my sons," whimpered Jahangir. "From whose loins did they spring? Who was responsible for their existence? To whom do they owe their illustrious titles? One after the other they've disappointed me. Khusru rebelled. That I forgave, but not his priggish holier-than-thou attitudes. Parviz drank and took opium. That I forgave but not his horrible laziness. Shahriyar is a bugger. That I forgive but not those simpering, mincing parasites. Khurram rebelled. That I forgive. But I still feel worried about Khurram."

"One should never," murmured Papasian, "expect gratitude from our miserable offspring."

"Not gratitude maybe," said Jahangir. "But at least half-decent manners."

Jahangir's other companion was a dark young fellow named Don Pedro, who had been sent by the King of Spain as a secretary to the Spanish ambassador. The Emperor had taken a liking to him and invited him to Kashmir. He and Jahangir would go roving through the meadows together, picking flowers and catching butterflies, which were the Emperor's special hobby. He and Pedro would stroll through the valley and make lists of all the flowers and sometimes they'd sit in the grass and draw sketches of the magnificent *palas* blossoms. Once in a field of wild flowers he grew so intoxicated with their brilliance that he ordered his soldiers to pick them and tuck them into their turbans.

He cried with pleasure as they rode before him like a column of flower-gods.

He paused with Pedro on the edge of a waterfall and watched the spray grow bright as a rainbow.

"We try to achieve things in this world," said Jahangir, "but what is lovelier than a waterfall? We build palaces and sepulchres but they're filled with the stink of mortals. I'm sick of the stench of mortality! I long to be buried beside a waterfall!"

"Oh, the zest is still in you! You are still alive!" said Pedro merrily.

The Emperor wrinkled his nose. "I haven't made the best of things, dear Pedro."

"In what respect?" said Pedro delicately.

"I was gentle and forgiving," said Jahangir, "at the wrong times. I was cruel and intemperate at the wrong times. I kept wavering indecisively between forgiveness and cruelty."

Pedro looked at him uncomprehendingly, as the beautiful young look at the wretched old. His huge Castilian eyes were both compassionate and utterly ruthless. "We all," he said consolingly, "have memories that worry us a little."

"But you're young, my boy!" wailed the Emperor. "You're still young and still desirable. Women will look at your body and wish to cover it with kisses. But who will look at my bloated carcass and wish to cover it with kisses?" His voice grew softer. "And there's another thing. What God did I believe in? Never Allah. Never Christ. Never a Hindu or a Zoroastrian God or some sleek, grinning Chinese God. I shall pay the penalty. No God will comfort me when I lie down to die. No God will take me in his arms when the death rattle begins!"

II

The old Emperor and his Empress left Srinagar in the middle of October and started across the hills on their way to Lahore. At the foot of the hills there was a village called Chingiz Hatli. Here the travelers came to a halt and pitched camp for the night.

Several times during the night Jahangir had uncomfortable visions. Once an avalanche swept down from the mountains and buried the valley in debris, and once a huge swarm of cobras rose up from the marshes. When morning came he was red with fever. Sweat poured from his belly. He called for a physician, who applied some leeches and rubbed his chest with pickled dandelions.

Toward sunset he suddenly realized that he was about to die. He called the Empress to his bedside and spoke to her softly. He could scarcely see her; great fireballs kept floating in front of his eyes. But he caught the smell of patchouli and knew it was Nurmahal.

He rolled over, touched her elbow and groaned softly: "What do you think, my dear?"

"Be calm, Jahangir. You have nothing to worry about," said Nurmahal quietly.

"And what," he pleaded, "will happen to me afterward? When I'm finally alone?"

"You will always be Jahangir. You will always be an Emperor."

"There are so many things," said Jahangir hoarsely, "so many things that one never knows. So many things that one's never sure about. So many things one should have done differently. I've never learned how to be calm. I've never learned how to be alone."

"It is strange," observed Nurmahal, "that a Mogul Emperor should be scared of the darkness."

"It's even stranger that a Mogul Emperor should be sick with guilt," said Jahangir. He clutched at Nurmahal's hand and muttered hoarsely, "Tell me, Mihru-n nisa. Are there things that you've kept from me? Little mysteries? Little secrets?"

"No," said Nurmahal slowly. "Nothing of consequence. Nothing worth mentioning."

"You've really loved me?"

The Empress nodded.

"And you still love me?"

"Yes," said Nurmahal.

She leaned over him silently. A spasm of terror passed through him. He no longer recognized her face: it was the face of an utter stranger. The terror he felt was no longer the terror of dying, it was a fear even more appalling—that he was being nursed into Eternity by this woman who had always baffled him and whose eerie strength had always terrified him. In the half-light her face turned into the face of the Goddess Kali. Her teeth shone like fangs, the motionless eyes shone like a cobra's.

He rolled back on the couch and buried his face in his arms. Great sobs shook his body. "God forgive me," he whispered.

III

Nurmahal turned and walked slowly toward the door of the tent. Over an ebony table hung a large Peking mirror, with gilded cranes on each side grasping fish in their beaks. She glanced instinctively into the mirror. Her own face was in shadow but she could see Jahangir lying on the bed directly behind her. Something strange was happening to the Emperor. He had rolled on his back. His hands fluttered queerly and pinkish bubbles shone on his lips.

And her own face grew likewise transfigured as she stared at it. Wrinkles crept over her cheeks and her jaw started to tremble. What she saw was not the face of a great Mogul Empress but something cringing and hairy, like an animal being whipped.

She walked out into the night and made her way through the poplars, which rose rigid as sentinels against the distant Himalayas. They looked so clear and so proud and erect in their vigilance, it almost seemed that they had won a victory over that icy immensity. She walked on. She caught the smell of the flowering rhododendron. The leaves of the shrubs cast blue shadows across the ground. And as her eyes grew used to the darkness the mountains grew brilliant; they started to blaze with a supernatural splendor. They were ablaze not with fire but with the opposite of fire, not with the mercy of destruction but the mercilessness of eternal sameness. The air was so clear that she could see the highest peaks—she could see the tusks of blue ice and the diamond glitter of the snowfields. She had never in her life seen anything so beautiful as those seething summits, which looked as though the silence of infinitude had finally materialized.

The Empress Nurmahal was an evil woman, if an insatiable lust for power can be equated with evil. But she was also extremely intelligent and quite aware of the evil in her. And not only was she evil as well as intelligent, she also possessed that deeper grace which gives to evil its tragic intensity. She had poetry deep within her; she was capable of a surging sweetness. As she looked at the mountains, so cold and incalculable in their majesty, the thought of death lost its terror and melted into a far-off mineral harmony.

When she stepped into the tent again she was assailed by a nauseating odor. The Emperor lay on his back. His mouth was wide open. His eyes stared at the ceiling with a look of glassy incredulity. A trail of bloody slime ran down his chin and over the coverlet.

She stood by the bed for several minutes and stared at the corpse. Then she walked to the door and called softly: "Azam! Azam!"

IV

One evening Arjumand was sitting on the veranda with her son, the blue-eyed Aurengzeb. They were drinking wine by the shade of an oil lamp and around the lamp the moths were fluttering, some of them tiny as gnats, others quick and black and furry, and some of them almost as big as fig-leaves, the tremendous honey-winged Atlas moths.

The boy was playing with a crystal elephant with golden tusks and eyes of emerald. He lifted it to his nose and sniffed at it inquisitively.

"Who gave you that elephant, my dear?" said the Princess.

"My uncle gave it to me," said the youngster.

"Your Uncle Parviz?"

"No. Not he."

"Your Uncle Shahriyar?"

"Not he either."

"Well, it couldn't have been your uncle Khusru. Who was it? Tell me, Aurengzeb."

"Oh, some uncle up in heaven," said the boy with solemnity. "Grandfather laid it on my pillow once and said that it came from an uncle in heaven."

"Your grandfather said that, did he?"

"Yes," said Aurengzeb, lowering his eyelashes.

"I wonder what he meant," said his mother, looking at the elephant suspiciously.

Aurengzeb was her favorite child. He was a clever little boy, deeply concentrated in whatever caught his fancy at the moment, and given like his father to fits of vengefulness and depression. He had a scrawny little body which made his mother think of a grasshopper.

The boy looked up at the sky and suddenly he said: "Tell me, Mother. What are those things up in the sky? Are they candles burning? Are they heavenly oil lamps?"

"Ah," said Arjumand, "I wish I knew, dear. They are things that we don't know about."

"Are they alive?"

"I doubt it rather."

"Are they dangerous?"

"No," said Arjumand.

"Couldn't we train one of the falcons to fly up and catch one for me?"

"They are bigger than they look, dear. They are bigger even than elephants."

Aurengzeb wrinkled his nose, trying to visualize a blazing elephant. Then he said: "When are we going back to Agra, Mother?"

"Who knows?" replied Arjumand. "Maybe soon. And maybe never."

She got up and crossed the lawn. Toads were hopping among the clover. Sometimes at moments like this she felt like leaping into the air, like bursting into a dance of brainless joy and sourceless gratitude. There was no reason for these moments. They simply came and went away again. But while they lasted she rolled them about on her senses caressingly, like a cordial on her tongue, reluctant to swallow them.

Behind the garden rose a copse, and a path led through the copse to the edge of the pond. Here the reeds grew in a tangle from the thick reddish clay; fronds of small, spicy jasmine drooped over the flowering lotus. She sat down on a rustic bench built of bamboo and pine logs and stared across the pond, watching the fish snap at the water spiders.

A little boat passed in front of her. In it sat a man and a woman. The oars were trailing idly and the movement of the boat was imperceptible. The strangers sat motionless: suddenly the woman spread her arms and the man leaned forward and pressed his head to the woman's breast. And so they remained, without stirring, and the boat moved slowly past and finally disappeared in the leafy darkness.

Arjumand's heart grew suddenly tight. Her hands gripped the bench. She was reminded of another lake, of another boat and another lover, only the other lake was encircled by willows instead of pines and the lover was dressed in snowy white instead of yellow.

She got up and walked thoughtfully back to the garden. As she opened the gate she saw a silhouette in the shrubbery: a black little man in a dirty dhoti, with a stick in his hands to beat off the snakes.

"What are you doing there, Vasanta?"

"Just waiting, Your Highness!"

"Waiting for whom?"

"Oh, just waiting. For nobody special," said the gardener uneasily.

She walked through the garden and stepped back onto the veranda. Aurengzeb had gone to bed. The flame was guttering in the oil lamp. She grew aware of a cold, needling pain behind her eyeballs, and the leaping in her blood had turned into a dull, slate-gray weariness.

v

On the following morning a messenger from Asaf Khan arrived in Junnar. He had been twenty-two days on his way from the Punjab. He knelt on the veranda in front of Khurram, pink with dust and fatigue, and announced in flutelike tones that the Emperor Jahangir had died.

"How did he die?"

"His stomach, Your Highness. An overindulgence in venison."

"Where did he die?"

"In Chingiz Hatli. In his tent by the woods."

"And who was with him?"

"The Empress, Your Highness. And the Court physician, whose name is Azam."

"And what is Asaf Khan's opinion?"

"That you should come immediately to Agra. Time is short, says Asaf Khan. He suggests that you leave tomorrow morning."

After the messenger had gone Khurram looked thoughtfully at Arjumand.

"What do you think?"

"I should think," said Arjumand, glancing listlessly across the garden, "that my father is probably aware of what he is doing."

The Prince sat silently for a while. He peered furtively at Arjumand. There were moments, such as this one, when he felt a strange indecision, a peculiar weakening of his character, as though it had been mysteriously diluted. He felt an effluence from Arjumand's character penetrating his own and subtly pervading it; not with tenderness but in some covert kind of retaliation. And her own habitual character seemed to suffer from a similar infection, growing crafty and apprenhensive, saying little, subtly eluding him.

He rose and crossed the lawn and entered the path into the woods. The way led through a tunnel-like thicket and then rose and circled the hill. In a dent in the hillside, where a brook ran through the boulders, there was a vine-covered hut tucked among some euphorbia trees. The Prince strode up to the hut and knocked briskly on the door.

He called: "Dataji! Are you there?"

For several minutes there was no answer. Then an old man crept out of the darkness, rubbing his eyes and leaning on a crutch. One half of his face was hideously distorted by wartlike growths; the other had an expression of almost saintly serenity. He scratched his belly, spat on the grass and crouched on a rock beside Khurram.

"Well?" he said rather sourly.

"A messenger from Kashmir arrived this morning, Dataji. My father is dead. Asaf Khan suggests that I leave for Agra immediately."

Dataji shrugged his shoulder and looked across the valley. "Yes," he said. "I was aware that His Majesty had floated away into Infinitude."

Khurram paused for a moment, waiting for Dataji to continue. But Dataji said nothing. He waved at a mosquito and closed his eyes.

"What is your opinion, Dataji?"

"I am concentrating, please, Your Highness."

"There are a few small things that worry me."

"I have no doubt of it, Your Highness."

Dataji knelt on the ground and scooped together a heap of pebbles. Then he ran a withered forefinger slowly over the pebbles. The pebbles fell apart, of their own volition it almost seemed, and made a zigzag pattern in the lemon-hued dust.

"What do they say?" said the Prince, leaning over intently.

Dataji belched faintly and picked up a pebble. "Nothing unusual," he said casually. "Nothing bizarre, as far as I see."

Khurram's eyes grew dark with impatience. "Be specific, please, Dataji."

"Well," said the mystic, "there are certain people who feel resentful toward you, Your Highness."

"Who, Dataji?"

"I think you know."

"The Empress, for instance?" said Khurram carefully.

Dataji didn't answer. He picked up several pebbles and rolled them about in his palm, letting the dust seep through his fingers. And as he crouched there like a monkey, picking absently at his nose, Khurram was filled with a sudden uncontrollable disgust. It was as though Dataji, in order to achieve a purity of insight, had gone to beastlike lengths to achieve impurity of body.

The Sultan looked away, folded his arms and waited silently.

He could hear the gurgling of the brook as it darted across the rocks and the hissing and crackling of a nearby waterfall. The sound of the water was like the sound of tiny voices, mischievous goblinlike voices, secret voices of warning. A parrot shot through the air, catching the sunlight on its wings, and from the dry autumnal valley rose the sound of the cicadas.

Finally Dataji turned his head and grinned connivingly at Khurram. "You have a delicate, subtle soul, Your Highness," he said fawningly. "Yes, a sensitive and reluctant, almost mimosalike soul. But you mustn't let this delicacy interfere with your duty."

"What is my duty, Dataji?"

The mystic looked evasive. "When I look into your soul, Your Highness, I see splendid and mighty things, I see grandiose and golden possibilities waiting for you. But," he added in a softer tone, "you are too deep. Too dark. Too brooding. Cast your eye on the outer world. Be hard. Be cold. Be crystalline." Then he whispered in a voice that was nearly inaudible: "The Empress is determined to put your brother Shahriyar on the throne. Asaf

Khan has taken measures but these measures are insufficient. There is no alternative, Your Highness. You must eliminate the Sultan Shahriyar."

The faintly diabolical look on Dataji's face vanished immediately. A look of almost seraphic blissfulness entered his eyes. He wiped a tear from his cheek, cocked his little finger daintily, and murmured: "It's been extraordinarily lovely weather, hasn't it, Your Highness?"

Khurram frowned; he lowered his head. He stared tensely into the grass. Then he reached into his tunic and took out a gold piece, dropped it silently in the dust and started back through the jungle.

VI

Prince Shahriyar was sitting on the steps of his summer pavilion on the Jumna. His pet monkey, whose name was Rabindranath, was playing with a ball of pink wool, which he was studiously unwinding and wrapping gracefully around his shoulders. There was something about his gestures which was reminiscent of Shahriyar's. Shahriyar was beautiful and the monkey was ugly, but the look in their eyes was the same: both frivolous and grave, with an inky awareness of their singularity.

Through the sun-spotted trees a tall dark figure was approaching the pavilion.

"You look sad, Shahriyar," said the Empress, sitting down beside the Prince.

"I am always sad," said the Prince abstractly. "Feeling sad is a protective attitude. If one's happy there's bound to be a let-down. If one's sad there are pleasant surprises."

The Empress Nurmahal leaned forward and rested her elbow on her knee. Her hair had begun to gray and her skin was growing leathery but she still was extremely handsome, though no longer quite in the style of a woman. She looked more and more like a man, with her jutting chin and piercing gaze. Her whole body conveyed a feeling of latent, high-strung power. There was something faintly snakelike in the movements of her neck.

"Well," she said, "what have you decided?"

"Nothing at all," said Shahriyar indifferently.

"You've had plenty of time to reflect on the alternatives," said the Empress, somewhat crossly. "If you don't succeed, your brother will. And if he does, well, I shouldn't be startled if. . . ."

"Yes," said Shahriyar. "I have pondered thoroughly on the various possibilities. Do you know what I'd like to do? Simply abandon the whole absurdity, shave my head, dress like a monk and sail off to Ceylon."

"It would be a pity," said the Empress acidly, "to shave that lovely hair of yours."

"Oh," said Shahriyar, "that's the least of my worries. I'd wear a wig when I arrived in Kandy!" His face grew wrinkled with annoyance suddenly; he seemed almost on the brink of tears. "Oh, God, why is it," he bleated miserably, "that I can never be left alone? Why do I have all these enemies? Why does your brother hate me so?"

"Asaf Khan was always a puritan."

"It isn't merely that he's a puritan."

"And he disapproved of Jahangir, naturally."

"And maybe he hates you too, dear Nurmahal."

"He does, he always did and he always will," said the Empress savagely. "Asaf Khan is obsessed with envy and it was a thorn in his side to see his sister becoming more powerful in the Empire than he was. But we'll forget about Asaf Khan and his horrid bigotry and envy. I'm stronger than Asaf at the moment. But the moment is brief. We must take advantage of it."

The smell of eucalyptus leaves drifted through the aisles of steel-gray treetrunks. And as they sat there, the Prince and the Empress, something of her vigor seeped through the atmosphere and seemed to impregnate the languid Prince Shahriyar. He smiled. His eyes glistened. There was a touch of gaiety in his voice.

"It is strange," he said, "how I feel toward you. I'm a shocking bad son-in-law, but the fact is that it's you and not your wearisome daughter that I should have married."

"It was impossible, alas," purred Nurmahal.

"I've always loved you," said Shahriyar plaintively. "Oh, not in the usual way, of course, I feel incapable of lust for a woman, but there are deeper and subtler emotions, there are more powerful ways of loving, and the fact is that as I sit here and listen to your voice, dear Nurmahal, I feel a strength and a strange security. I cannot explain it. But there it is."

"And so it will continue, I hope," said Nurmahal. She rose and stood in front of him.

He reached out and took her hand and pressed it gently to his cheek. "May I say something?" he whispered. "I shall die very soon. You'll say that I'm being theatrical but I don't feel in the least theatrical. I shall die, not from sickness or violence but from a terrible ennui. People will explain it in other words, they'll see a variety of reasons for this death of mine, but whatever it may look like and whatever may happen, the reason will be that I longed to die. Does it sound ridiculous to you?"

Nurmahal looked at him tenderly and stroked his hair, which was black and shiny. Finally she said, "Isn't it strange? We used to chatter about our voyages. We used to talk about going to Istanbul and Lisbon and even London. Perhaps we should both pack our bags and sail from Goa."

"Perhaps we should," said Shahriyar listlessly. "But it's too late. Too late for both of us."

VII

One evening, just a week after the Empress' visit, Prince Shahriyar was sitting by the fishpool behind his pavilion. The evening light hung on the water, gilding the ripples above the goldfish, so that the fish looked like reflections of the minnow-shaped ripples. A smell of curry seeped from the kitchen where the Negro Bojo was cooking dinner. The sound of a sauce being whipped crept out through the window. The crickets started to chirp. Twilight came; the pool darkened. Shahriyar was lost in thought. He scarcely noticed the two dark figures who were wandering through the trees in the distance: an old woman with a vegetable basket and a slender boy who was carrying a fishnet. But then he happened to notice his mare, who was grazing under the trees. She pawed restlessly at the ground with her ears turned back alertly.

"Is there anything wrong, Fatima?"

The mare glanced nervously at the Sultan.

"Don't worry, there's nothing wrong!"

But the mare kept flicking her tail uneasily.

Shahriyar leaned back and closed his eyes. The feeling of peace was so pervasive, even the grass smelled of seclusion and even the pool had a scent of permanence. A voice called softly across the dusk: "Your Excellency! Please! Your Excellency!"

Shahriyar turned his head. A barefoot boy was crossing the lawn. He tossed his fishnet into the grass and smiled shyly at the Sultan.

"I beg your forgiveness, Your Noble Excellency!"

"Who are you?" said the Sultan.

"I am Lakshmana," said the boy. "I rove through the forest telling tales."

Shahriyar looked at him curiously. He was a good-looking boy with a smooth golden body and a silky shadow on his upper lip.

"What kind of tales?"

"Tales about witches," said Lakshmana breezily, "and about the terrible devils who creep through the jungle. My father died three months ago. He was the story-teller Amaru. Now I wander alone in the villages, telling the tales my father taught me."

"And what is that net you were carrying?"

"It's to catch the fish in the streams. The villagers give me my bread but when I'm hungry I catch a fish. I cook him over a fire with a sprig of mint and a leaf of rosemary."

"Come. Sit down in the grass, Lakshmana. Tell me a story," said the Prince.

"Very well," said the boy with dignity. He knelt carefully in the grass, folded his arms ceremoniously and started to tell a story.

"A learned Brahmin named Bhasa lost his way in the jungle. As he struggled through the thicket he suddenly fell into a pit. He caught hold of the creepers on the edge of the pit and there he hung like a fruit. And as he hung there he caught sight of a monster below him opening his jaws, and glancing up he saw two mice, a black and a white, gnawing at the creepers. And as if this weren't enough to frighten the wits out of poor old Bhasa, there was a commotion in the trees and an enormous elephant came rushing toward him. This elephant had six heads and twelve legs and a trunk like a crocodile. Well, as it happened, a swarm of bees had stored their honey in a nearby tree, and the honey started to drip onto the Brahmin's hands and he licked at it greedily. . . ."

The boy paused thoughtfully and looked at the Sultan.

"Yes? And then?" said Shahriyar.

"That's all," said the story-boy.

"He just hung there?" said Shahriyar.

"And he's still hanging there," said the boy.

"Explain, please," said Shahriyar.

"Well," said Lakshmana with a knowing leer, "the jungle represents the tangle of Existence. The hanging creepers are Life and the lurking monster is Death. The twelve-legged elephants represent a year and the two little mice are Night and Day."

"And the honey?" said Shahriyar, leaning inquisitively toward the boy.

"Ah, the honey," said Lakshmana. "The honey is our joy in being alive. We ignore the mice and the elephant. We even ignore the waiting monster. We just sip at the honey and forget all the rest of it."

"Do you think that the Brahmin was wise to keep sipping at the honey? Or should he have made an effort to escape from the pit?"

"There was no point in it, Your Excellency. There was that elephant looming above him and there was that monster squatting below him. Bhasa showed wisdom in licking at the honey while there still was time to enjoy it!"

"True," said Shahriyar, smiling thoughtfully. "But I can't help wondering, somehow. . . ."

The boy reached over and fondled the bracelet on the Sultan's arm.

"Very beautiful," he purred, "Your Excellency."

Shahriyar peered at him mockingly. "You'd like to have it, I suppose?"

"Goodness, no," said Lakshmana hurriedly. "What would I do with such a bracelet?"

"You could give up telling tales and embark on a more suitable vocation!"

Bojo stepped from the kitchen with a large bowl of soup,

which he set on a low black table in front of Shahriyar. He glanced at Lakshmana suspiciously and then inquiringly at the Prince.

"Bring another bowl," said Shahriyar, nodding casually toward Lakshmana.

So Bojo brought a second bowl and set it in front of the boy. And after that he brought a duckling, beautifully cooked with grapes from Gwalior, and he brought up the wine, which he poured into the goblets.

Darkness fell. Shahriyar kept listening to the legends which Lakshmana told him and after a while an insidious drowsiness crept over him.

VIII

In the middle of the night Shahriyar woke from his dreams and stared into the night. It was unusually dark: no moon was out, no stars were shining. He felt a drumming in his temples and a curious throbbing behind his eyeballs.

"I drank too much," he thought torpidly. "Very foolish. It doesn't agree with me. . . ."

He reached out his arm, wanting to touch Lakshmana's body. But Lakshmana wasn't there. He reached out further: the bed was empty.

"The naughty rascal," he thought. "I should have known. The little thief."

He fondled his forearm instinctively, expecting to find the bracelet gone. But the bracelet was still there, cool and smooth, with its row of rubies.

And so Shahriyar fell asleep again, and was lost in a series of dreams: about mice with three heads, about a boy with a head like a toad's, about honey which turned into fire and about ivy which turned into vipers.

The following morning Bojo stepped into the bedroom to wake up Shahriyar.

"Wake up, Your Highness! The sun is out! It's a beautiful day and the birds are chirping!"

Shahriyar opened his eyes. "Nonsense, Bojo. It's still midnight."

The Negro drew aside the curtains. "Look, Your Highness. It's as bright as a gold piece."

Shahriyar touched his eyelids lightly: there was a strange, frightening numbness. For a moment he lay still, trying to grasp what had happened. He felt the warmth of the morning sun. He heard the chattering of the sparrows. Then he said softly, "God help me, Bojo. I'm blind! I'm blind! I've been punished for my wickedness!"

I X

After his blindness Prince Shahriyar refused to receive his former friends. His only companion was the faithful Bojo, who brought him his meals four times a day, and led him by the elbow across the lawn and told him the gossip.

Sometimes the whole, unassuagable terror of blindness swept over Shahriyar: this impenetrable darkness was far deeper than merely darkness. It was a negation of everything visible, it was an extinction of light and color, it was the annihilation of all that he loved, the casual grace of human beauty, the subtle expression in a pair of eyes, the sly gymnastics of the monkey Rabin-

dranath, the graceful writhings of the mist over the river Jumna.
Tears rolled down his cheeks when he thought of all that he
had lost, of all that he had carelessly neglected and had failed to
appreciate in its pristine dazzle. He lay in his bed or sat on the
veranda, listening to the myriad small noises—the barking of a
dog or the buzzing of a hornet, Bojo's footsteps, the rustling
foliage; and gradually these sounds took on a new kind of richness and intricacy: they absorbed some of the glitter and preci-
sion of things visible. He sniffed greedily at the air: he caught
fragrances never suspected—the sap in a tree, the scent of a
squirrel, the full moon rising over the deer park—and the variety of visible things was replaced by another kind of variety.
He reached out his hand to touch the monkey's fur or Bojo's
cheek, the rough surface of the veranda floor or the velvety red
of a petal: and he could detect not only the texture but even
the color of things. He could tell by touching his fur the passing moods of Rabindranath, he could tell by touching a flower
whether it would rain or be clear again. And oddly enough,
after the first appalling misery of his blindness certain small compensations crept back into his life, and as these compensations
accumulated Shahriyar found to his amazement a new and unsuspected joy in being alive.

A month went by. He heard stories about Prince Khurram's
arrival from the Deccan, and Nurmahal's quarrel with Asaf
Khan, and the hurried enthronement of Dawar Baksh, the son of
Khusru. But he felt a total indifference toward these squabbles
and intrigues. He was enjoying his isolation, he was almost reconciled to his blindness, and Rabindranath and Bojo were sufficient
in his life.

Once Bojo said softly: "I've finally learned the truth, Your
Highness. It was His Excellency Asaf Khan who sent that horrible
boy to you."

But Shahriyar answered: "Let us forget it, Bojo. Life is too
short to be sullied with resentment."

And he added: "Whatever has happened, it is all my fault, Bojo. They called me Na-Shudani. They were perfectly right. Good-for-Nothing. If I had handled matters more sensibly then all this dreadfulness wouldn't have happened. There's only one thing to do now. To try to be happy with what is left to us."

Bojo sat close beside him and stroked his forehead tenderly. "You have succeeded, Beloved Highness. You've found your joy in the middle of darkness."

Dusk fell; he couldn't perceive it but he smelled it in the air; he could hear it in the stillness, he could even feel it in the touch of the cushions.

"Tell me a story, please, Bojo. Tell me about my ancestor, the glorious Genghis."

So Bojo told him about Genghis Khan, who had died, by a strange coincidence, exactly four hundred years before this very day that they were sitting on the veranda.

"He was descended," said Bojo, "from the maiden Alan-goa, who had been ravished nine months previously by a moonbeam one night. And when he died, twenty horses, the best in the Empire, were buried along with him, as well as forty beautiful maidens, chosen from all over Turkestan. He lived in the saddle and slept in a tent and he drank fermented mare's milk and his habits were those of a simple tribesman. But when he died all the pearls of the kingdom were buried with him and there were loud lamentations all the way from Bangkok to Trebizond."

"When I die," said Shahriyar gravely, "I want no pearls or lamentations. I merely want you to hold my head in your lap when I die, Bojo."

"It will be so," said Bojo solemnly.

"And I'll die peacefully," said Shahriyar, smiling.

x

"Listen," said Shahriyar. "Do I hear something?"

"It's the wind in the boughs," said Bojo.

"Listen again. Down by the marshes!"

"It's only the bullfrogs," said Bojo quietly.

But then Bojo noticed the flickering of torches among the leaves, and he saw a group of horsemen dressed in red riding through the bushes.

"Do I hear some horsemen coming through the trees?" said Shahriyar.

"Four Bengalis, I think, Your Highness."

"Where are they going, do you imagine?"

"They are coming to visit us," said Bojo.

The horsemen sprang from their saddles and strode silently up to the veranda. One of the four carried a torch. The other three carried swords. Without a word one of the three walked up to the blind Shahriyar and swung his great sword in a swift, sickling motion. The wide-eyed Bojo sat stunned and motionless as Shahriyar's head rolled to the ground. And the last that he saw was the second horseman looming over him silently and raising his sword with both hands over his head. His lips twitched queerly and bubbles of sweat shone on his forehead; the light flashed on the sword and that was the last Bojo knew.

XI

The following day, soon after dawn, a woman named Radha was squatting by the river. She was scrubbing at her laundry and watching the soapsuds floating in the current. A curious thing caught her eye. Two dark objects came floating by, and only when she looked more carefully did it suddenly occur to her what they were: two headless men floating past in the misty Jumna and vanishing behind the willows where the river curved eastward.

"Strange things," muttered Radha. "Terrible things. There's no explaining them."

She whispered a little prayer and then leaned over and went on with her laundry.

PART SIX

The Throne

I

And thus it finally came about that Prince Khurram became the Emperor. This was in 1627, when he was thirty-six years old. From now on he was known to the world as Shahjahan, the Lord of the Universe, and the Empress was called Mumtaz Mahal, the Ornament of the Palace.

What had happened was the following. After the death of Jahangir, and in anticipation of a struggle for the succession, the perspicacious Asaf Khan made a journey to Agra. There he met the son of Khusru, who had died five years earlier. This boy was Dawar Baksh, and his nickname was Baluki. He was a good-looking youth, fair and gray-eyed like his father but quick and vivacious, and not an ascetic like his father. Dawar Baksh was hurriedly installed in the palace in Agra and accorded the title of Emperor *pro tempore.*

"Your uncle Khurram is very ill," Asaf Khan told the boy. "He's on his way from the Deccan but it's most unlikely that he'll finish the journey."

Two days later Asaf Khan mournfully announced to Dawar Baksh: "I have pitiful news, my child. Your uncle Khurram has died on the journey. The funeral cortège is moving toward Agra, where he will be buried with all due elegance."

Two days subsequent to this announcement Asaf Khan told Dawar Baksh: "Come, child. The cortège is approaching. We'll ride through the gates and meet it in the outskirts."

Khurram and his cavalcade, which included a leopard as well as elephants and camels, came to a halt in the meadows which bordered the Jumna. The nobles gathered solemnly around the brocade-covered bier. Lamps were lit, the drumbeats sounded, and Dawar Baksh approached the coffin. Asaf Khan with a thoughtful air drew aside the brocade coverlet and Prince Khurram stepped out of the coffin, clad in a bright imperial armor. He raised his arms dramatically, kissed his nephew on both cheeks, and was accompanied into Agra by a long procession of dignitaries, who cautiously murmured to each other en route to the citadel: "Well, it isn't quite the arrangement we had visualized, to be quite frank about it, but maybe it's better to be ruled by a villain than a harebrained stripling."

And so with all the appropriate fanfare Khurram was acclaimed Emperor in Agra, and not long after he received the formal proclamation in Lahore. And in the spring of the following year the coronation was duly celebrated and Khurram took his seat on the gold-embroidered throne.

On the evening before the coronation Asaf Khan told Dawar Baksh: "Unfortunate news, my dear Baluki. Your uncle is a very stubborn man. He has decided to spare your life, an unusual concession on his part, but he strongly recommends that you leave immediately for Persia. In view of the alternatives I think you should follow his advice. Life in Ispahan may well be more congenial than you imagine it. . . ."

And that same night, accompanied by two slaves, the bewildered Dawar rode forth in the starlight on his journey westward toward the river Indus.

11

Lamps were hung from the marble balustrades; garlands were woven of bronze-dipped roses. Arabian rugs were spread in the garden and a red marquee was set up by the pool.

"All this," said Nurmahal acidly, turning to a Ranee from

Ahmadabad, "just to celebrate a succession of brutal murders and fratricides."

Pear-shaped Cantonese goblets shone on the tables under the palms. The Burmese butlers appeared, carrying a row of illuminated trays. Roasted lyrebirds and peacocks with their feathers spread in a fan were followed by ewers of rice and jereboams of wine, and the sweets had been molded into elaborate sculptures—a mosque of marzipan, a tower of dates, and a barge of coconuts floating in honey.

There was a clashing of cymbals. A column of silver-haired slaves led the beasts into a small wooden amphitheatre which faced the audience. A Bengal tiger was made to leap through a series of burning hoops and two elephants danced to some whining Kashmir melodies. Three large cages were carried into the ring and their doors were flung open: a flock of phosphorescent pigeons went flying over the tables. And then some tumblers and magicians marched forth into the ring, tossing swords into the air and twining cobras around their necks. Finally the dancers appeared, their naked bodies painted gold: the men writhed and twisted in imitation of the amorous Siva and the women swayed gracefully in imitation of Kali.

On the opposite shore of the river a horde of onlookers had gathered—peasants and villagers, three old *saddhus* and a scattering of scrawny beggars. Farther off, under a willow tree, huddled a group of sad-eyed lepers. Some fireworks were lit. The lepers' faces shone momentarily and their eyes wandered skyward as they watched the spray of the rockets.

"Krishna, come to us, come to us," chanted a group of little girls.

"Power and glory and perpetual potency," chanted the weather-beaten hags.

"Siva, have pity!" someone squealed, and the village poet sang: "The sun will shine, almonds will blossom, the three-trunked elephant will roar with laughter. . . ."

The heat grew strangely oppressive. The dancers dripped with sweat and the marzipan mosque had dissolved into a shapeless lump. Even the animals were ill at ease. One of the tigers started to bellow. There was a sharp flash of lightning, followed by a cannonade of thunder. The trees rattled, the marquee shook and the lanterns quivered on the balustrade.

And then abruptly the rain came pouring. The gilded dancers were streaked with rivulets and the pigeons went fluttering toward the nearby roofs. The butlers hastily gathered the wine jugs and the birds-of-paradise, whose feathers drooped dismally under the downpour.

The guests gathered their silks and brocades under their arms and went scuttling toward the loggia, whimpering delicately as they ran.

III

"And now," said Khurram, "you will sit on the throne. You will smile and be peaceful."

"It's rather odd," remarked Arjumand, "but I don't feel very peaceful."

"There'll be nothing to be afraid of as long as you live," said the Emperor.

"You really think so?" said the Empress. "I wish I could agree with you, my darling."

The storm had passed and they were sitting alone in the turquoise bedchamber. Far off there was a rumble of vanishing thunder but in the gardens there was only a thin, stealthy drip-drip from the leaves.

Finally Khurram fell asleep and Arjumand tiptoed to the

balcony. It was a relief to feel the cool unburdened freshness of the night. She stood motionless, watching the last of the clouds drift away and the stars grow brilliant over the prairies. A faint miasmic smell rose from the banks of the Jumna. A dark figure, some drunken Rajah perhaps, went lurching across the lawn. Down by the pool lay the discarded loincloths of two link-boys taking a dip. And as she stood there a lingering feeling of unease and apprehension gradually deepened into disgust, and then abruptly into terror.

She crept along the balcony toward the window of the adjoining chamber. "Indira," she called softly. "Are you still awake, Indira?"

Indira, in a white silk night robe, stepped softly toward the window.

"Is there anything wrong, dear?"

"I'm frightened, Indira!"

"Of what?"

"Look! Down by the river. . . ."

"I see nothing," said Indira gently.

"That thing with two heads. . . ."

"I see nothing at all," said Indira.

Arjumand frowned, then nodded wearily. "Yes, you're right. It's nothing at all."

"Just a shadow," said Indira.

"Yes, yes. Just a shadow."

Indira reached through the window and took Arjumand's hand. They stood without speaking, staring listlessly into the darkness.

IV

A bell started to tinkle the moment sunlight touched the roof of the tower. The curtain was drawn aside and an elderly eunuch, Tardi, drew his soft gray palm over the Emperor's forehead.

That was the beginning of Khurram's day. He stepped from his bed and turned toward Mecca, said his prayers and recited a few pious lines from the Koran. Then he crossed the great bed-chamber and stepped into his bath. After the bath the eunuch massaged his body with perfumed ointments. Then he reddened the Emperor's lips with a cherry-colored dye, plucked the hairs from his nostrils and wrapped a kimono around his body.

At a quarter to seven the Emperor appeared at the central window, which looked directly over the banks of the river Jumna. Here a crowd had assembled with a variety of petitions and these were brought to the Emperor on a large green platter. After a cup of dark tea he crossed the garden to watch a ram-fight or even an elephant-fight, a sport which especially delighted the young Emperor.

At a quarter to eight he and his suite retired to the pavilion which was generally referred to as the Diwan-i-am. He entered the hall at the rear and sat on a cushion in the marble alcove; behind him stood the various courtiers and officers of state. All of these men stood quite motionless, hands crossed solemnly and eyes cast floorward, while some Ethiopian slaves waved feathery fans overhead.

In the courtyard outside, which was covered with gold-fringed canopies, stood the lesser officials, some Rajput soldiers and the Imperial Guardsmen.

The *durbar* began. First the paymaster approached the alcove, carrying pleas for promotion from various officers in the Imperial Army. The officers themselves were then presented to the Grand Mogul and received a robe of honor as well as a horse and some weapons.

Then the Emperor received reports from the provincial governors as well as certain officials, such as the Minister of the Treasure Room and the Superintendent of the Pantries. Then the *sadr* presented a list of grants for struggling scholars and penniless poets. And finally the officers of the Imperial stables marched past the door, parading the newly acquired horses.

The Keeper of Scents would go mincing discreetly through the hall, swinging his brazier to banish the smell of sweating bodies and dirty feet; and the Imperial Astrologer would crouch gloomily beside the Emperor, muttering warnings of treason or hinting at possible misdemeanors.

When all this was over Shahjahan retired to the hall of private audience, called the Diwan-i-khas, which was decorated with ancient tapestries. From half past nine till half past eleven he sat with his personal amanuensis, dictating letters, looking at jewels and discussing plans with his Persian architects. Then, accompanied by the Grand Vizier, he strolled on toward the Royal Tower, where he greeted the nobles personally and paused to gossip about more intimate matters. At noon he retired to the harem, where he said his prayers, enjoyed his luncheon, and took his midday siesta, gently fanned by his favorite eunuch.

This was the only time of the day when the Empress herself had an official duty: she sat in an antechamber of the harem, surrounded by a group of twittering secretaries, and listened to the female petitions which dealt with widows, orphans and adulteries.

After his nap the Emperor usually went riding in the park. Sometimes there was an archery contest or a brisk game of polo, and occasionally there was a fencing bout or a bit of hawking or deer hunting. The deer were caught by means of nets which were cleverly draped on the horns of the tame deer, thus entangling the wild ones who inquisitively approached them.

At half past six some candles were lit in the Diwan-i-khas, and the visiting Rajahs gathered to listen to the Royal Musicians. They sipped wine from fluted goblets and plucked nuts out of a bowl and occasionally one of the pets, a monkey or a cheetah, was allowed in the room.

At half past eight the Grand Mogul retired to his harem again, where he listened to some songs sung by the women, alone or in unison. At ten he went to bed, listening to Indira telling a tale or Arjumand reading from a history of foreign kings or a book of travel.

And thus the day came to an end and Arjumand would enter her world of dreams, which was filled with strange visions of lurking beasts and prowling phantoms. Sometimes the beasts had hairy faces which were faintly familiar; sometimes a phantom muttered some words which she vaguely remembered having heard before. But nothing was ever quite certain in these queer little nightmares. Sometimes she found herself standing on the edge of a snake-filled chasm, sometimes she wandered alone through a burning desert. But always on the horizon lurked these half-familiar shadows muttering words from a hidden past or peering at her with their grief-filled faces.

She woke up at dawn to the tinkling of Tardi's bell, and while Khurram said his prayers she stepped out on the balcony. Way in the distance on a meadow a lonely Muslim was laying his prayer mat; he took off his shoes and bowed toward Mecca, just like Khurram. And overhead some jackass birds came wheeling on their way from the Ganges. Their wings caught the glow of sunrise, so that they seemed to be on fire.

v

And in the meanwhile young Dawar rode westward toward Persia. He crossed the Indus: the land grew savage as he approached the towering cliffs of Kirthar.

The two servants who rode with him were called Mahmoud and Hamadullah. Mahmoud was a wolf-faced fellow with a shaggy brown body. He carried a sword in his belt and rode ahead, looking for mischief. Hamadullah was lithe and slender, with eyes like a gazelle's. He rode behind with the water jugs dangling from his saddle.

They passed rocky gorges where the heat foamed like a geyser. They crossed featureless prairies where nothing lived but millions of locusts. Now and then they passed a village squatting dismally among the cactus or maybe a skeletal old shepherd with his matted sheep. There was anger in the atmosphere. The shepherds glared at them sullenly; even the locusts kept screaming with a shrill ceaseless petulance.

On they rode. They passed a nunnery perched on top of a precipice, and further on a Zoroastrian tower surrounded by century-old skeletons.

"What are those skeletons?" said Dawar.

"Oh, just holy men," said Mahmoud casually. "They come crawling up to the tower when they feel the end is coming."

"Yes? And then?" said Dawar uncomfortably.

"They just wait," explained Mahmoud. "They just sit by the tower and wait. After a while the vultures come and it's all over for the holy men, and that's the end of it except for the wisdom, which enters the bowels of the vultures and is scattered like seeds over the suffering face of Hindustan!"

They crossed a plain where the earth had crumbled to a fine blue powder. Clouds of dust steamed all around them, coating the horses and the red-eyed horsemen. Everything grew blurred with dust. Hamadullah kept coughing and Mahmoud wore a thick gray mask of sweaty dust. Even the sun looked blurred and hazy, veiled in its awful immensity.

They crossed a jagged mountain pass. The land grew wild, almost lunatic. Rocks lay cast about at random, as though hurled by a hysterical giant. Far ahead a range of cliffs looked as though they were bleeding in the jellied brilliance.

"Is that Persia?" said Dawar hoarsely.

"That is nowhere," answered Mahmoud. "Neither Persia nor India nor Baluchistan. The Land of Nothingness, that's what it is."

Dawar felt that he had entered a realm where suffering and death meant nothing at all. Whatever he did, wherever he went, whatever he felt: it meant nothing. Everything shriveled into sameness in the fierce yellow light.

"Are you tired?" said Hamadullah.

"Just a bit, maybe," said Dawar.

"What's it like in Ispahan, I wonder."

"Yes, I wonder," said Dawar.

Once they met an old pilgrim who was tottering toward Arabia.

"Just be patient," he croaked feebly: "there's peace and honey at the end of the journey!"

And once they saw an old sorceress squatting in the shade of a grotto.

She shook her fist viciously: "Thieves! Depraved ones! Buggers! Infidels!"

They slept on the sand. The following morning they came to an oasis. Their lips were cracked, their eyes were burning; they gulped frantically at the muddy water. Some men in felt coats were drinking tea from a copper ewer and a woman in scarlet trousers was passing a plate of dried apricots.

One of the men looked at them contemptuously. "You're from the east, from Rajputana. I can see it in your skin. Soft and oily with copulation!"

And another man growled at them: "He's right! I've been in Talamba! The men are women and the women are sheep and even the sheep are whores in Talamba!"

VI

They rode on in the afternoon and entered the desert of Baluchistan. The dusty grayness lay behind them. They breathed the clean bright air of the sands. At sunset they came to a village which lay tucked between the hills. Two old patriarchs were playing dice and smoking nargilehs in the shade of a palm and all round them they could smell the musk of the camels. This was the land of the Afridi shepherds and the barrel-chested tribesmen—powerful men with blue-black ringlets whose capes kept billowing in the desert winds. Some gourds of goat's milk were served to the guests, dervish fashion, and then they rested in the dung-scented gloom of the tents.

That night they sat around the campfire, listening to the monotonous gossip of the desert. Wine was brought and still more wine, wine from the vineyards by the Gulf, which tasted of the dank moldy goatskins in which it was carried. Old Mahmoud sang some lecherous Rajput songs for the tribesmen and Hamadullah got up and did a dance which he had learned in Peshawar. The tribesmen stroked their beards and tittered drunkenly as they watched, and Dawar said:

"Tell me, please. What is it like down at Ispahan?"

One of the tribesmen, a black-toothed warrior, leaned close to Dawar and grunted playfully: "There's everything you want! Roses for breakfast and pearls for lunch and for dinner it's nightingales dipped in honey!"

"I don't believe you," said Dawar, wide-eyed.

"Oh, you're right not to believe me! D'you know the truth? Listen, my boy. It's all just lies you've been hearing about Ispahan. Those fancy palaces, those dainty fountains—they're just lies, like everything else. D'you know the truth? Ispahan's a city just like the rest of them, foul and disgusting. The men piss and the women menstruate, just like here in the desert, only the filth lies rotting in the streets and the rooms are swarming with bedbugs."

"I'm sorry to hear it," said Dawar sadly.

"Listen, my lad," said the drunken tribesman, whose body exuded a stink like a ram's, "you might just as well abandon these fancy notions about Persia. Persia, Persia! What's so fine about Persia? It's full of idiots, like everywhere else. People pretend that it's elegant, with all that poetry and those tinkling fountains, but the fact is you've got to be a Sultan to enjoy the poetry and the fountains while the rest live like pigs, black with fleas, nuzzling at garbage!"

"How about Shiraz?" said Dawar dejectedly.

"I've never set foot there," said the tribesman. "But I bet it's like the rest of them. Just a lot of cheating and fornicating."

"And Kermanshah?"

"Oh, Kermanshah! Just forget about Kermanshah. That's way past Rhagae and Ecbatan—it's almost as far as Smyrna. You can travel for fifty days and you'll never get to Kermanshah. And even if you did, well, I warn you: piss and shit, just like those other places."

One by one they fell asleep, the drunken tribesmen as well as the travelers, and Dawar curled up in a corner of the tent. He could hear the sound of the camels' feet pawing at the sand. He lifted a flap in the tent and stared out into the moonlight. Some Baluchis were rolling their sacks down the path to load the camels and others were dragging their water bags up from the well. It was only midnight, but they were planning to start by the light of the moon, so that the worst of the trip would be over before the day came roaring down at them.

He thought vaguely of Agra, but Agra seemed infinitely remote now. He thought of his few bright days as Emperor, the ringing of bells and the glitter of scimitars, but the vision of himself as Emperor had never been quite real to him. He thought uneasily of his uncle Khurram, who rather frightened him with his snakelike eyes, but it never occurred to him to be angry or indignant with his uncle Khurram. Things were what they were, things happened as they were destined to happen, and now that he was wandering on to Persia a pleasurable excitement filled his senses.

Someone crouched over Dawar: he caught the stench of the gap-toothed tribesman, who fondled Dawar's cheeks and then leaned over and kissed him drunkenly.

"No, no," whispered Dawar.

"You're as soft as a dove!" cooed the tribesman.

Dawar bit his lip with disgust as the enormous drunkard made love to him.

"No," he pleaded. "No, no, please!"

"You're as sweet as a pumpkin," slobbered the tribesman.

But then quite suddenly, in the middle of his ecstasy, he rolled over and started to snore. There he lay on his back, arms flung wide and beard aquiver.

Poor Dawar was half-asleep, nursing his pain and humiliation, when Hamadullah lifted the edge of the tent and whispered in his ear: "Quick! Get up! We'll have to be going!"

"Why? What's wrong?" said Dawar drowsily.

"Someone's told them!" said Hamadullah. "They've seen your jewel-bag! They're planning to rob us!"

"How do you know? You're sure?" said Dawar.

"We heard them muttering! We saw their knives!"

"Where is Mahmoud?" said Dawar.

"He's down by the trees, saddling the horses."

Dawar turned over cautiously, cast an eye over the assembled sleepers, and then wriggled his way under the flap of the woolen tent.

Mahmoud was leading the horses along the wall which surrounded the palm grove.

"Hurry!" he whispered. "It's nearly dawn! We'll follow the caravan as far as Phra and then we'll take the little side road that leads toward Carmana. . . ."

The stars were growing pale; dew shone on the palm leaves. Soon they were out in the yellow wastes again and the memory of the oasis was like a mirage.

"You saw their knives?" Dawar kept saying. "You're absolutely sure of it, Mahmoud?"

"They were knives," said Mahmoud darkly. "I saw them shining as bright as eels!"

"You heard them muttering about robbery? You're quite sure of it, Hamadullah?"

"I wasn't sure of the words exactly, but I was sure of the tone," said the slave-boy.

So they rode into the west, threading their way through the gravelly wastes, now and again catching a glimpse of the merchants' caravan far ahead of them. They rode on until the salt marshes of Persia shone below them and the light crawled over the land like a torrent of lava.

VII

"And what," said the Emperor, "do you really think of us in your honorable country, Monsieur Caille?"

"We think of India as a land of pearls, of tigers and elephants," said the Frenchman. He added hastily, with a sly expression: "And of brilliant Emperors and lovely Empresses!"

"Ah," said Khurram. "I wish it were true."

"Isn't it true?" purred the little Frenchman.

Monsieur Caille had just arrived from the flourishing port of Pondicherry. He was in Agra to negotiate a trade agreement with the Emperor's agents. He was a crisp and animated man with a silky red goatee, a voice as sharp as a needle and eyes as bright as a sparrow's. He whisked a kerchief in front of his nostrils, gave a twist to his beard and said discreetly:

"Times are changing, they are changing with an ominous rapidity, Your Majesty, but human wisdom is slower to grow than human enterprise and human cleverness. Our ships cross seventy seas with silks from China and spices from the Indies, but the subtlety of China and the suavity of the Indies can't be wrapped and sent in a parcel. The Parisians burn incense from Canton, they wear veils from Rangoon, they sniff herbs from Tibet and drink tea from the Himalayas. But unfortunately we can't inhale the wisdom of Confucius, or the piety of the Lamas. We just quietly go on with our own provincial mentalities!"

"Very delicately put," said the Emperor. "But aren't you being a bit of a flatterer? I'm sure that you really think of Paris as much more comfortable than Agra."

"More comfortable in certain ways, perhaps," said Monsieur

Caille, "but much less amusing. Our flora are rather limited and our fauna are distinctly humdrum. I can assure you, Your Exalted Majesty, there are plenty of ladies in Brest or Périgord who would jump at a chance to live in Jodhpur, or even Benares."

"I can't quite think," murmured Khurram, "that it's our spirituality they are longing to imitate."

"Who knows?" said Monsieur Caille. "There are many forms of spirituality."

"Come," said Khurram, tapping the Frenchman on the elbow with his fan. "There is something I want to show you. It's my latest self-indulgence."

Monsieur Caille followed the Emperor down the corridor toward the hall of the artisans, a cellarlike enclosure with heavy grills barring the windows. Here a group of Imperial jewelers, headed by the illustrious Bebadal Khan, were at work on a stupendous new throne for the Emperor. It was six feet long and four feet wide and was surmounted by an enameled canopy. The twelve tapering pillars of the canopy were plated with gold; the jewelers were in the process of studding them with pearls. A peacock with outspread feathers stood on top of each pillar and the golden feathers were inlaid with enormous sapphires and rubies. And in addition to the peacocks there were twelve bouquets of golden flowers, likewise studded with pearls and emeralds, as well as rubies and lapis lazuli.

"Quite incredible," said Monsieur Caille, gazing at the throne with pursed lips.

"The most spectacular throne in the world, beyond a doubt," said Khurram softly. He fondled the pearls on the golden columns and looked thoughtfully at the Frenchman. "Come," he said. "You've seen the throne. Now let me show you the elephants."

They crossed the lawn where Nandini the pet gazelle was playing with the link-boys and Magha, the favorite falcon, sat perched on the gardener's shoulder. They walked into an oval courtyard, descended some stairs and stepped into the huge vaulted stables of the Imperial elephants. It was so dark that the grooms were carrying torches as they fed the elephants. The torchlight shone eerily on their half-naked bodies, but the elephants were almost invisible except for the whiteness of their tusks. The visitors walked slowly along the great row of stalls, and Monsieur Caille could detect the glitter in the eyes of the elephants. They seemed to shine with some deep and inaccessible wisdom: a wisdom which was partly amusement and partly contempt, but under the wisdom lurked a vast and fathomless melancholy.

"They are magnificent," said Monsieur Caille. "I have always been enthralled by elephants. Lions are noble and tigers splendid, monkeys are clever and grayhounds decorative, but there's nothing that combines these qualities so remarkably as an elephant. We have an elephant in Paris but he does not seem very happy. Do these beasts have terrible passions lurking under those witty little eyes?"

"Elephants are bigger and more powerful than men. And wiser, I imagine," muttered Khurram.

"Ah," said the Frenchman, "how does it happen that men rule the elephants instead of elephants the men?"

"You just told me the reason. It's ingenuity which wins, not wisdom. It is enterprise and not nobility. It is ruthlessness, not spirituality!"

"There's no justice in this world," said Monsieur Caille, fondling his goatee.

"No," said Khurram, "there'll never be justice. Only compromise or tyranny."

"And which," said the Frenchman with serenity, "do you choose for India, Your Majesty?"

Khurram's eyes darkened for a moment. Perhaps he was startled by the Frenchman's impudence, or perhaps it did not occur to him that it might be impudence. He clasped his hands and stared bitterly at his favorite elephant, Aja. There was a gleam of understanding in Aja's little eyes. She twisted her trunk affectionately over the Emperor's forearm and then she tapped him very daintily on top of his jeweled turban.

"When I look at a tiger," he said, patting Aja's cheek affectionately, "I realize that the world is filled with a terrible cruelty. I look at a monkey and it's filled with depravity. I look at a parrot and it's filled with a noisy silliness. I look at a beggar and it's filled with fleas. I smell incense and excrement and I know that the darkness is uncontrollable and the whole idea of justice seems utterly preposterous. It's only when I look at the elephants and see the gaiety that survives their suffering that a flicker of hope springs up in me, and I see the reasons for being alive."

"You are a person of pessimism, I see," said Monsieur Caille.

"Not pessimism, Monsieur. Merely moroseness," said Khurram, smiling.

VIII

One evening the Emperor went for a stroll in the shade of the deer park. He walked to the river's edge and stood motionless on the pier. It had suddenly grown gusty. A sultry breeze passed over the water and he drew the purple folds of his cloak around his body. There was a fresh smell of ferns and of flowering rhododendron and the flames of the setting sun shone through the trunks of the alders.

Signs and omens: doubts and fears: prowling mysteries and equivocations. Whatever he did, whatever he ordered or achieved, they still were there. The fog of doubt penetrated even the rustling alcoves of the harem. Even the magnificence of the throne brought no conviction, no absolute certainty. Omens of what? Fear of what? Death, maybe? No, not death, surely. He had never been afraid of sickness or physical suffering. Something else. Treachery? But whose? Ghosts? Phantoms? But what kind? Fear gnawed at his brain, but the roots of his fear he could never identify. It was like trying to hear the words that the wind was whispering, or detecting the source of a shadow among the leaves.

Down on the banks by the reeds he caught sight of a peasant girl. She was kneeling beside the water, combing her long silky hair. She wore a blue-flowered skirt tightly tied around the waist. Her breasts and shoulders were naked; they shone like sprinkled copper. She turned and caught his eye. She shrugged her shoulders and smiled contemptuously and kept on combing her silky black waterfall.

The Emperor felt a tightening in his heart like that of a nightmare; a twinge of guilt and a tickling of pain and a rush of unexplainable longing.

He walked back through the woods and as he stepped into the garden he gave an order to Narayan, the seventh in rank of the Imperial gardeners.

Two days later the girl was brought to a tiny bungalow on the edge of the deer park.

She was different from what he remembered—a bit smaller, a little darker. And the scornful, far-off smile had turned into a furtive look of defiance. She wore a gentian-colored shawl with yellow fringes over the shoulders, and her hair was tied in a big black knot on the back of her neck.

"Forgive me," said Khurram.

"There's nothing to forgive," said the peasant girl sullenly. "You're some powerful sort of person. And I'm being paid. What does it matter?"

"What is your name?"

"Damayanti."

"A beautiful name, I think," said the Emperor.

"Nothing unusual," said the girl. "It's a name like any other."

Khurram crouched on the velvet cushion at Damayanti's feet. He lifted a pitcher and poured some rice wine into a goblet.

"What makes you imagine that I'm powerful?"

"I can smell it," said the girl. "It's a smell like dead lilies. Only the powerful have that smell."

Khurram said: "Are you frightened of me?"

"No," said the girl. She glanced through the curtains. "I'm frightened of women occasionally. But never of men."

"I see," said Khurram intently. "Is it because men are always kind to you?"

"No one has ever been especially kind or especially cruel," said Damayanti. "It's just the way I feel. There's never a reason for how we feel."

"Let me explain," said Khurram quietly. "You will never know who I am. And what's more it's of no consequence. There's only one thing of consequence. Would it make you happy if I loved you, my adorable Damayanti?"

"Neither happy nor unhappy," said Damayanti in her low, hoarse voice.

There was something in her oval face and cynical eyes and pouting lips, and even in her fierce indifference, which stirred a memory in Khurram's brain: long ago, among the trees, by the side of the water, the eyes and the laughter. . . .

"And besides," the girl went on, "I'd be an idiot if it made me happy. You'll love me a week or a month. There's no reason to love me longer. And there's no reason on earth why I should ever fall in love with you."

Khurram lowered his head and stared at Damayanti's feet. They were small and brown and calloused: the feet of a poor, lighthearted peasant. There was something about those feet which pierced his heart like a needle. Those feet, like her oval face and cynical eyes and dark indifference, had something about them which was piercingly familiar.

"I love you," said Khurram, "because you remind me of something I've lost. Of a poppy after the rain, with a single drop still clinging to a petal."

He leaned over and kissed her toes, and then her ankles, and then her calves. But she kept on staring through the rose-curtained window.

IX

The two women were sitting alone in the Pavilion of the Lions, a small wooden summerhouse tucked in the shade near the Tower of Jasmines. It had been built for Nurmahal's wedding and now it was used as the children's playhouse. A row of dolls lay tucked in a cradle and some turbaned soldiers lay scattered on the floor. Octagonal columns of painted wood encircled the whole pavilion, with lions carved in the bases and elephants' heads in the capitals: but the eyes of the poor little lions had been hacked out by the children and the elephants' tusks were streaked with the droppings of birds.

Arjumand was sitting in the couch, leafing idly through a book of poems, and Indira sat by the mirror drawing kohl over her eyelashes. Some sprays of Persian lilac stood in a bowl by the window and their smell filled the room with a drifting disquietude.

There was a bond between the women, one of them dark, frail, preoccupied and the other one blonde and impetuous and emphatic. Arjumand's huge solemn gaze rested tenderly on the handsome Indira, whose Tartar eyes and broad-boned cheeks were more like a man's than a woman's.

"I'm growing old," said Indira cheerfully. "There's not much point in trying to be beautiful!"

"One isn't old at twenty-nine, I should hope," said Arjumand gravely.

"One isn't old but one is afraid. The thing creeps closer," said Indira. She drew her fingers over her cheeks, lifting the skin toward her temples.

"You have a beauty that lasts," said Arjumand, turning a page with a far-off air. "Your bones are good. And your eyes are beautiful. Look at me! I'll shrivel into a little black hag, like the ones in the market place."

"Nonsense, darling," said Indira. "We'll both be dead before we decay. I refuse to grow old and hideous. I absolutely refuse! Do you hear me?"

Arjumand smiled and got up and sat on the bench beside Indira. The two women looked calmly at each other in the mirror.

"I keep wondering," said Arjumand. "What will he feel a year from now? Will he love me more? Will he love me less? Will he love me at all, do you think, Indira?"

"He'll still love you, from the looks of it. But with a queer and crotchety love."

"Is he capable of love?" said Arjumand.

"In his way," said Indira, "obviously." She took Arjumand's hand and raised it gently to her cheek. "Forgive him, Arjumand. He's not aware of the suffering he causes."

"Do you believe that?" said Arjumand.

"I insist on believing it," said Indira. "If I didn't believe it I would flee from this horrible palace. One must accept the bad with the good so long as the good really exists. He has glitter as well as gloom and he has warmth as well as arrogance, and as long as we belong to him we must take the gloom with the glitter."

"Tell me, Indira. Do you really think that he was ever in love with Nurmahal?"

"I don't listen to gossip. There's always gossip when there is mystery. He was impressed by Nurmahal, I imagine. But he never loved her. That I'm sure of."

"Alas," said Arjumand, "my dear Indira, we keep on guessing about people. All day long we keep guessing but the truth still eludes us."

"Khurram," said Indira, "is a murderer by nature, but it's fear that does it, not a natural violence. He hates everything that he is afraid of and his only reaction is to kill. And even the things that he really loves he grows afraid of and tries to kill. He loved Khusru and look what happened. He was fond of Parviz, even though he despised him. Who knows, maybe he even loved that naughty Shahriyar. So it goes. His mind is a labyrinth. Some day he will kill you too, my dove!"

She smiled teasingly at Arjumand, flung a sari over her shoulders, got up from the bench, and stood for a moment in the open doorway. "After all," she said softly, "we mean so little in his life, when you stop to think of it. We are mirrors, nothing but mirrors to reflect the Emperor's own image."

"And that image. . . ."

"Grandeur! Ruthlessness! Omnipotence! Piety!" said Indira contemptuously. "Silly illusions, in short. He's just a boy. He has never grown up."

"And still, when I think of Jahangir. . . ."

"There's no point in thinking of Jahangir. Men grow old just like women, only in a different and sadder way. When a woman is old she learns to accept it, she submits to the bleak inevitable, but a man has his stupid pride and his stupid lust and his stupid cowardice."

Indira glanced into the mirror with a look of sudden uneasiness, then waved her hand daintily and went darting across the garden.

x

The mist was already rising from the damp leafy undergrowth. Indira paused and looked back, then followed the path that circled the stables and entered the cool blue shade of the deer park. The smell of the April twilight went drifting through the air—the whiff of the dangling catkins, the bitter sweetness of clematis. Finally she stopped in front of the hut and rapped cautiously at the windowpane.

An old woman in a black kimono, huge and pendulous, opened the door for her.

"He's on his way. Don't worry," she muttered.

"You're sure, Kausiki?"

"Of course I'm sure."

Old Kausiki had for years been the personal witch of the Emperor. When the monarch left Agra for the Deccan or the Punjab she refused to accompany him and he had to consult less eminent mystics. But in Agra he never listened to anyone's advice but Kausiki's. When he had a toothache he went to Kausiki. When he smelled a traitor he went to Kausiki. And whatever happened, it always turned out that Kausiki was right in the end. Even when she seemed to be in error she adroitly maneuvred the evidence and not once could it be proved that old Kausiki had actually blundered.

She led Indira into a low-roofed chamber with a rattan ceiling. The place was littered with hundreds of strange little objects— hanks of fur, claws of birds, dried-up cobras and disemboweled lizards, as well as a row of jars in which some herbs were obscurely simmering—herbs for impotence or sterility, herbs for dyspepsia, herbs for deafness.

"It's ugly," growled Kausiki, squatting on a cushion by the door. "People dying all over the place. Gujarat, Kandesh, the Malabar coast—nothing but hunger and misery and pestilence."

Indira looked thoughtfully at a little jug which was filled with toads' eyes.

"It's these foreigners," Kausiki continued. "All these men from God knows where. Funny lands like Venice and Turkey. They're all riddled with vermin."

"People weakened by hunger. . . ."

"Nonsense," said the witch. "It's these miserable heathens. They never bathe. They never pray. They'll eat the excrement of a camel. They're pigs, that's what they are. They're carrying the pest in their filthy bodies!"

"It's a punishment from Allah."

"Allah! Allah!" squeaked Kausiki. She wiped her beard on the edge of her kimono. "All this chatter about Allah! It's this talk about Allah which makes men foolish. Even supposing for an instant that there's a personage such as Allah, would he bother about these suffering little creatures down at Gujarat? No, my puss, that's where these notions about Allah fall to bits. It takes hundreds of different gods to keep an eye on all this misery!"

There were footsteps on the path and old Kausiki rose to her feet. She groaned irritably, scratched her back, and opened the door with circumspection. Then she turned to Indira. "Well, he's here. Just as I told you."

"And when do you leave?" whispered Indira, pressing her hands to his cheeks.

"We leave Agra at dusk tomorrow. First we go to Bassein. It won't be especially pleasant, traveling through those plague-infested villages."

"Avoid the villages," said Indira. "Keep to the woods. Keep to the pasturelands."

"Maybe your witch," said the stranger playfully, "can grind a powder to protect us!"

He was a powerfully built young fellow, aggressively handsome in the Portuguese manner, with walnut curls and sea-green eyes, which in the darkness had turned to purple. It was his eyes which she loved the best; and after that the scent of his skin; and after that his purring voice, which was unlike the Hindu's or the Mohammedan's, more resonant than the one and more musical than the other, with a mingling of mockery and a soft drowsy sadness.

His name was Don Fernando. He was the consul at Cambay and a nephew of Ruy Lourenço de Tavora, the former Viceroy. He had met Indira three months earlier at a festival in Ajmer, and he was now returning from Patna, where he had visited the Portuguese mission.

"Are there witches in Lisbon too?" said Indira, half-solemnly.

"There are witches wherever you go," said Don Fernando, glancing skyward. "Every woman has a little witch in her. If she's happy the witch lies sleeping. If she's sad the witch wakes up. I'm always frightened of mournful ladies. I see the witch in their darting eyes!"

He spoke in French, as did most of the Western travelers in Agra; and Indira replied in a tentative, tinkling French which was like a child's. They were sitting on a bamboo bench under the weeping willow, whose twigs were so dense that they completely shrouded the lovers. The night was utterly still; even the Jumna had fallen asleep and a few wips of moonlight hung from the leaves like silver moss.

"Tell me about Lisbon," said Indira.

"What shall I tell you?" said Fernando.

"How do you live? What do you eat? What do you drink in your wonderful Lisbon?"

"We live close by the water and all day long we look at the water. We weave nets to catch fish and braid ropes to haul the boats. We make sails for the boats to sail with, and the girls weave little baskets to carry the fish in while the boys pound the olives for the oil to fry the fish with, and in the vineyards the old women jump on the grapes to make our wine which we drink while we eat the freshly fried mackerel, and the old men tell stories about sailing their ships to India, circling the Cape of Good Hope and splitting the seas by Madagascar, just as Vasco da Gama did a hundred years before them."

"And love? What about love? Is there plenty of lovemaking in Lisbon?"

"My sweet Indira, you can't imagine all the love that there is in Lisbon. The palaces smell of love and the churches smell of love, the gardens smell of love and even the river smells of love."

"Do the men remain faithful to their women in Lisbon?"

"Within reason," said Fernando, rubbing his nose judiciously.

"And what is reasonable?" said Indira.

"Oh, a month or so," said Fernando. "After all, my dear child, if a man goes sailing to the Indies with weeks of nothing but water around him, he begins to hanker for a bit of female companionship!"

"Water, water, nothing but water. Do you think of nothing but water?"

"We think of God, now and again," said Don Fernando, kissing her earlobe.

"And this God of yours: you're sure that he's so much better than other Gods?"

"These other Gods—what are they? Dancing demons and thundering prophets. Is there love in these other Gods? Is there compassion? Is there sweetness?"

"Love! Sweetness! Compassion!" Indira laughed and shook her head. "Those are not the things that we want in our Gods. Those are the things that we want in our lovers! In our Gods, my dear Fernando, we want wisdom and power and subtlety and when we look for a bit of love we turn to our lovers, not our deities."

"Very reasonable," said Don Fernando. "But little by little we grow older and the day finally arrives when we lie down and die. And my heart would beat more peacefully if my God were loving and merciful."

"Look," said Indira, "do you see that bird?"

"Is it a bird?" said Don Fernando.

"It might be a bat," said Indira darkly.

"It's only a moth," said Don Fernando.

The enormous insect flew past them, circling about for a way through the foliage. Its wings caught a flake of moonlight, which turned the velvet into a dancing amethyst. It went swooping past Indira, almost brushing her cheeks. Then it dipped through the boughs and disappeared in the outer darkness.

XII

All over India the sun was blazing, grinding the earth to a thin gray powder. The bullocks were roaring with thirst; the elephants trumpeted in the marshes. The dragonflies hung in the air like chips of isinglass and great crevices split the earth, pouring forth all sorts of vipers.

In the wake of the drought came the terrible famine of 1630. Hunger spread over the Deccan, where rats and lizards were sold in butcher shops. Down in Gujarat the women were offering their pearls for a loaf of bread and in Oudh the dusty highways were blocked with the famished hordes. They were abandoning the towns and villages where nothing was left to eat and went roving over the prairies, gnawing at roots and yellow grasses. With their eyes sunk deep in their heads and their bellies hanging like pouches, they looked more like a tribe of monkeys than like hungry human beings.

The flame-clad bonzes went staggering through the groves with their begging bowls. One could hardly tell the old from the young, they looked so shriveled and pitiful. In Tatta the bones of the corpses were pounded with mallets and ground to powder and then mixed with a bit of flour and fried into pancakes. In Kandesh the townsmen took to the hills and huddled in caves, eating whatever they could find—spiders and grasshoppers and earthworms. And the worst was down in Mangalore, where even the insects had vanished and men were reduced to the desperations of cannibalism.

The Empress had soup kitchens set by the roadside and every morning columns of children crept through the fields on their way to the stalls. She made excursions through the countryside, distributing baskets of bread and barley. But none of this was enough, it merely accentuated the misery; and when Arjumand rode through the villages the people regarded her with a stoical suspiciousness. No one smiled, no one thanked her; they plucked at their crusts with a cringing indifference.

She said to Khurram: "What can we do?"

"Pray for the rain," said Khurram sullenly.

"It won't be enough. Millions of dead—a shower or two won't bring them to life again."

"And what do you suggest?"

"God only knows," said Arjumand. "Something to keep it from ever happening again. Mountains of grain in the store-rooms; seas of water in the reservoirs. How does one save these suffering children from Allah's horrible catastrophes?"

"Do you blame it on Allah?"

"I blame it on things we can't control. And since Allah controls everything it is Allah who must be responsible. And there may be a hidden wisdom or a hidden justification behind it but I cannot imagine it. To me it is horrible and nothing but horrible."

One evening she wandered into a lonely part of the forest, a place that was never visited except by the prophetess Kausiki, who managed to find some rare and benevolent grasses in the thicket. In these black, encircled nooks there was a morbidness in the atmosphere. Long beards of matted moss hung from the intertwining branches; parasitical tufts clung to the web of snake-like vines. A cliff rose out of the tangle and in the side of the cliff there was a cave. It was called the Cave of the Inconsolable Monkey. Ugly stories were told about this cave. A girl named Parmi had been strangled there by a demon and her phantom still roamed through the woods in the shape of a monkey.

Arjumand paused in front of the cave and peered into the darkness. A faint ray of light seeped through a crevice overhead.

It shone on an egg-shaped face which hung suspended in the shadows: a face neither dead nor alive, neither spectral nor wholly palpable.

She was frightened for an instant, but then she grasped who it was. She entered the cave and stood in front of the forgotten Buddha. His arms were covered with moss and scabs of lichen disfigured his cheeks, but the poise, the peaceful sublimity, the impersonal wisdom still were there. His hands were resting in his lap in a gesture of meditation: the right hand slightly raised with the fingers joined, signifying Fearlessness, and the left hand extended with its palm thrust outward, signifying Aloofness. The great stony face was still smiling mysteriously, with eyes that signified Insight and lips that signified Charity.

How very different, thought Arjumand, from the impassioned writhings of Siva and Vishnu; so totally different and yet beneath it there was a thing they had in common. The air of remoteness and ambiguity: the subjugation of human suffering not by an act of compassion or heroism but by a mood of passivity. The disciplines of Buddhism had fallen into decay all over India, where it had been decimated by its self-imposed principles of celibacy; it had fled to the shores of Lanka and the snows of Lhasa and the woods of Burma. But Buddha's smile still lingered on in the smiles of Siva and Vishnu, whose bland, dispassionate faces belied their supple and ruthless postures.

Arjumand's heart was gradually recoiling from the austerities of Islam; she saw in Hinduism a charming poetry, a profusion of meanings, a tense vitality. But Hinduism had always frightened her with its junglelike complexities and it was Buddha who seemed to offer the purity of the one with the profundity of the other.

Lost in thoughts, she walked slowly up the path toward the palm plantations. Suddenly a shadow rose beside her, raising its arms from the sea of ferns.

"It's a dangerous spot, Your Majesty," said Kausiki, fumbling in her sack. "You shouldn't walk here alone. There's mischief lurking in the bushes."

"So I've heard," said the Empress. She stared dreamily at the foliage.

"Were you looking for someone?" said the witch, cocking her head and squinting slightly. Her drooping body, with its greenish warts and bulging eyes, resembled a toad's.

"Perhaps I was," said the Empress cautiously, glancing at the leering face beside her.

"Of course you were," said Kausiki. "We're always looking, perpetually looking. We look into caves and we look into temples, perpetually looking for the face of the beloved. Oh, the folly of kings and emperors! Neither power nor gold brings back our love to us!"

"And where," said the Empress, "shall we find it?"

"In the plants. In the birds and insects. In the claws of the vulture! In the ears of crocodiles! My dear little lady, if only you'd abandon all this fretting and speculation and yield to the Voice of the Forest, what infinite wisdom you would acquire!"

The Empress looked at the witch intently. "Wisdom, Kausiki? Do you call it wisdom?"

"The only wisdom is love," said Kausiki with an air of finality. "If you listen to the Voice of the Forest, there's just one thing that it keeps on saying. If you listen to the lapping of the waves or the twittering of the starlings, it's all the same. I hope you've forgiven me, Your Majesty, for that little episode involving Indira. It was all in the cause of love, and where there's love all is forgivable. Ah, my child, if only you had come to me long ago with your frettings! It's none of my business but I can't help it if I know about secrets which are hidden from the others, and if only you had asked Kausiki, how much happier you'd be!"

PART SEVEN

An Abduction and a Flight

At the beginning of April the Emperor and Empress went for a holiday. They accepted an invitation from an elderly nobleman, Suleiman Khan, who lived in a castle in the Aravalli Mountains. The Imperial procession included twenty Rajput horsemen, a column of foot soldiers and donkeys, and six silk-curtained palanquins. They traveled for three days and it was dusk on the third day when they finally caught sight of the castle looming in the distance.

The rock-strewn valley was empty and desolate. The grass rose stiff and dry. A small village, drab and dilapidated, crouched at the bottom of the hill. The gloomy castle rose from the summit overlooking the village and a narrow gray path twisted up through the rocks. Here and there wisps of shrubbery hung to the hillside like spiders. A haggard goatherd sat in the shade, watching a very old nanny-goat.

Suleiman's castle, like the village below it, had fallen into decay. One whole wing had crumbled to ruin and only a section was still inhabited. The walls looked ominous in their streaky decrepitude. Piles of rubble lay scattered about and rats were nuzzling among the garbage. An ugly stench rose from the gully: over an abyss at the side of the castle hung the wooden latrines, a row of cages overlooking the chasm. Spirals of flies rose from the accumulation of ancient sewage and the ladies drew the curtains of their palanquins as they passed.

But when they entered the castle garden it was an unsuspected paradise. Little statues peeped slyly through the hanging ivy and some slaves in gilded tunics welcomed the guests into the courtyard. Over the doors and windows hung screens of *khas-khas* grass, freshly sprinkled to cool the air and fill the rooms with a smell of clover. Tubs of mint-scented water were brought up for the travelers and down in the patio a boy was playing a harp to soothe their nerves.

It was still dusk when they sat down to dinner in the loggia. Suleiman Khan was a thick, hectic man with the face of an eagle, with ferocious black eyes glittering under bushy gray brows. His wife, Indrami, was an emaciated lady in a silver dress; she had the crêpelike skin and dream-blurred eyes of an opium addict. Khurram wore a plain white tunic with a pearl-embroidered sword-belt and a single huge diamond on the clasp of his turban. Arjumand wore a dress of rosy silk and a short-sleeved jacket of indigo, with elephant-shaped earrings and a triple necklace of pearls.

Aside from the Emperor's assembly two other guests were staying at the castle: an elderly scholar named Duryodhama and a dark young student named Haidar.

"I've been told," said Arjumand casually, as the sherbets were set on the table, "that your castle is haunted. Is it true, dear Indrami?"

"Perfectly true," said Indrami distantly. "We have a number of flitting ghosts—bats and insects, you know, just incidental little phantoms. But we also have two bigger ghosts of which we're rather proud. A crocodile man and a three-winged bird-lady."

"How delightful," said Arjumand. "Do they prowl through the castle?"

"Well, not prowl precisely," said the hostess. "They never creep into the bedrooms. The crocodile clings to the wine cellar, where he shimmers among the jugs, and the bird-ghost hovers in the attic, clawing at the trunks and discarded mattresses."

"Is she looking for something?" said Arjumand.

"So it seems," said Indrami.

"What, for instance?"

"Some old lover. Someone lurking among the bric-à-brac."

"Ah," said the scholarly Duryadhama. "I think I can throw some light on the matter. These elongated bird-ghosts are quite common in the *Brihat-katha,* which refers to them as the Three-Pronged Regrets, or the Feathery Wistfulness. They are women who have rejected their true loves for the sake of advancement. Women in society, you understand, who embark on advantageous marriages."

Duryodhama was a man of a snowy octogenarian beauty. His eyes shone like a pair of icy blue jewels set in a maze of black wrinkles and long silvery hairs. He pressed his fingers into a pyramid and added soothingly: "These little Wistfulnesses, or Regrets, are never malignant in their hauntings. They sing occasionally in a whining way, keeping us awake when we're trying to sleep, but that is usually the full extent of their malice."

"And what," said Haidar, a handsome fellow with auburn curls and the neck of an ox, "what about that crocodile-phantom, my good Duryodhama?"

The oil lamps shone brightly in Duryodhama's magnificent eyes; a flicker of air crossed the loggia, ruffling his hair.

"A crocodile-ghost, I am sad to say, is less innocuous than a Triple Wistfulness. You will find some caustic references to him in the *Suka-saptati,* the Tales of the Parrot. He indulges in spirituous beverages and starts lashing about with his tail, knocking the bottles from their shelves and creating a general confusion."

"Is he wicked, Duryodhama?"

"Alas," said the scholar, "he is his own worst enemy. Wicked? Yes, by ordinary standards. He brings grief and destruction. And why? Because of ambition. He has always wished to be a tiger. And in his failure to become a tiger he seeks refuge from the world of reality. He flails about with his tail, gnashes his teeth and weeps tears."

"So it goes," said Suleiman Khan, gazing tenderly at Indrami. "We must learn to be tolerant. Even the ghosts have their heartaches."

"Do you really believe these things, Duryodhama?" said Haidar.

Duryodhama smiled sweetly. "My dear boy, I am a scholar and not a philosopher. I gather fragments of wisdom but I refuse to fit them into a pattern. My host disapproves of me, and I'm sure His Majesty does likewise. I believe in no God, no Permeating Spirit, no Everlastingness. I believe only in Maya, which is the world that I see in front of me, the perpetual and uncontrollable glitter of change. Call it illusion if you wish. Or call it negation if you prefer. It's the world of the beautiful Siva, the god who dances and then vanishes. He hides among the leaves: and only the leaves keep on dancing."

11

But even here, up in the hills, the heat was like a delirium. No breeze stirred; no leaf moved. The spiders shriveled as they hung from their threads. The dogs lay limp in the shade of the gate and the cheetah panted as she crouched in the portico.

The Empress was sitting alone in the windless silence of her room. She sat by the window; her hand was resting on the side of a water jar. She kept glancing through the window toward the open breach at the end of the valley, a gap in the chain of undulating hills that hemmed them in: and beyond this triangle of open sky, pale as mother-of-pearl, she could imagine another life, both her own and not her own.

The day before their departure from Agra one of the women had brought her a shawl. She said: "I found this in the bungalow at the edge of the deer park." It was a powder-blue shawl with lemon-hued fringes, a cheap cotton shawl such as a peasant girl might wear.

"Whose is it?" said Arjumand.

"I cannot imagine," said the chamberwoman. She glanced shrewdly at the Empress with her wicked black eyes and added blandly: "One of the grooms said it belongs to a girl named Damayanti, who was reading some poems to His Majesty the other day."

Arjumand nodded and said nothing. She laid the shawl in the bottom of a drawer, murmuring some words from an ancient play called the _Nagananda,_ the Joy of the Serpents: "A man is not like a woman and the love of a man is not like a woman's. Nor does love mean to a man what it means to a woman; and infidelity in a man is not like infidelity in a woman."

There were moments when she suspected that she had stopped loving Khurram, and even that she had never really been in love with him, and that her image of love for him had been a self-induced illusion. There were times when she felt a chill of fear, almost of hatred. But then she realized that fear and hatred are quite compatible with love and perhaps even a part of the fabric of love. She was both aware and unaware of the full extent of Khurram's villainy, but knowing him purely by instinct, she was more aware of his inner uncertainty, the true source of his insatiable ambition, his childlike fear, his strange dark helplessness, which in moments of intimacy almost seemed like a kind of innocence. She was aware yet unaware of the complex nature of his love for her, which was a mingling of lust and vanity, of curiosity and scorn and a childish dependence. She had never felt the slightest jealousy toward any of Khurram's earlier wives, who now were relegated to the harem in the role of confidantes; nor was it jealousy that she felt toward the imagined Damayanti. All she felt at this point was a deep, listless loneliness which refused to meditate either on his cruelty or his infidelity.

"Does it matter?" she thought. "Things either happen or they do not happen and under this vast boiling sky it hardly matters if they really happened. All that happens is that one gradually must learn how not to suffer. One must learn to be calm. To be indifferent. To fall asleep."

III

It was late afternoon when the Empress decided to take a stroll toward the fringe of pine wood which crested the hills behind the castle.

"Don't go alone, my child," said Indrami.

"Are there snakes, perhaps?" said Arjumand.

"Do as you wish, then," said Indrami. "It's not serpents that I'm afraid of. . . ."

So the Empress set out, carrying a small blue umbrella. She followed a path through the copse of rhododendron, which gradually darkened into a kind of tunnel, through which the sun dropped glowing embers. The path led over a bridge of bamboo and then curved into a stretch of purplish evergreens. At a curve in the path stood a small *gopura,* no bigger than a wellhouse. It was blackened with age and half-hidden by ferns; it was even smaller and humbler than the little temple near the Agra hunting grounds.

She lowered her head and peeped cautiously into the damp interior. There was nothing at all except a moss-covered rock, which looked like the base of a broken pillar; and on the rock stood a slim black statue, scarcely visible.

She groped her way toward the statue. Her eyes grew used to the cavelike darkness. She recognized the delicate limbs and smiling face of the dusky dancer. This was Siva Nataraja, the Lord of Motion and Perpetual Fluidity. He stood poised with one foot on the belly of a dwarf and his hands were gracefully uplifted, one of them holding a flower and another a rattle, the third pointing upward and the forth pointing down. In this posture he portrayed the universal equilibrium of creation and destruction, as well as the entire flux and ambiguity of human life. A branch swayed over the doorway and with the stirring of the leaves a flicker of sunlight passed over the statue. The look on his face changed for an instant in the passing brightness: it changed from a voluptuous serenity to a look of inconsolable suffering. But then the light died away again and the face sank into shadow. All she could see was the sensual body, the cobwebbed flower and the broken rattle.

She walked through the ferns and started back toward the castle. At that moment a slender figure stepped silently through the trees. The leaves dappled his face with little gray shadows: he looked like some apparition out of the Upanishads of the Forest. But then she recognized Haidar, the young student who was staying at the castle.

He said gently: "You were looking at Siva?"

Arjumand nodded. "I was."

"Yes. I know. You disapprove of him. You despise him," said Haidar. "The world of Islam has no use for sensual fantasies like Siva."

"You are a Muslim, too," said Arjumand.

"Yes, I am a Muslim, too," said Haidar. "I look on Siva not as a God but as a poem, an elaborate metaphor. Siva is even more wicked and intricate than he seems, Your Majesty. He burned his throat long ago when he swallowed the poison which was destroying the world, and after that they called him Srikantha, the Heavenly-Throated. And little by little he acquired certain other more deplorable habits. He haunted cemeteries; he became a vampire; he wore a necklace made of skulls. And he learned how to burn a poor mortal straight to the bone with a single look out of his terrible Third Eye!"

"It all means so little to me," said Arjumand, with an air of impatience.

"If you take it as an actuality, it means nothing, of course," said Haidar.

"And as a metaphor, as you so cleverly put it? What does it mean as a metaphor?"

"A thousand different things, like every metaphor," said Haidar, and a look of speculation crept into his enormous brown eyes. "Time keeps moving and the world streams on through time, perpetually changing. Nothing ever remains the same. What happens is gone irrevocably. Strange, isn't it, Your Majesty? But even stranger is the fact that the past, though it has vanished irrevocably, still keeps lingering and will always linger."

The Empress lowered her head. Then she raised it and looked carefully at Haidar. She said quietly: "Who are you?"

Haidar smiled, but now his smile was of a pained formality rather than a casual intimacy. There was an animal sweetness in his beautiful young face but it was tinged at this moment with a look of bitterness, even of fury.

"I'd prefer not to tell you and I hoped that you wouldn't ask me. But now that you've asked I might as well tell you. I'm Sirkandar's brother."

Arjumand nodded. "Yes, I thought so. There is something in the eyes." She looked dreamily at Haidar and then intently up at the leaves. "How old are you, Haidar?"

"Twenty-three," said Haidar bashfully.

"Ten years younger than Sirkandar. Time passes," said the Empress.

Haidar said cautiously: "Do I look like Sirkandar?"

"Yes and no. You do and you don't." She cocked her head to one side. "You are gentler than Sirkandar. Less impetuous."

"I hardly remember him," said Haidar. "I was only eight

when he died." He stood motionless under the tree, the sunlight touching his shining curls. There was the shade of a mustache on his thick upper lip and his cheeks shone with the sweat of some intense inner excitement, which glowed dimly through the composure and the warm, oxlike gentleness.

"I was very much in love with Sirkandar," said the Empress calmly.

"But you killed him," whispered Haidar.

"Did I?" said the Empress. "Perhaps I did. There are so many, so frighteningly many different reasons for the things that happen. Yes, perhaps I did kill him, since love is only a phase of death and death after all is only a facet of love. You like metaphors, my boy, so I'll let you ponder on that pretty metaphor!"

She continued along her way through the thicket of rhododendron. The path turned suddenly into a grassy glade in front of the bridge. She was blinded for a moment by the flood of boiling light. Then she noticed a silhouette, dark, attentive, at the edge of the path, with the clasp on the turban flashing in the brilliance of the evening.

"I was looking for you," said Khurram.

"Were you worried?" said Arjumand.

"These woods have an ugly name. Nobody walks here," said Khurram. His eyes sharpened slightly as he watched her come closer. "Except the nymphs and the prowling demons. That's what Suleiman tells me!"

Arjumand smiled and took his arm and they sauntered back to the castle garden. The two girls, Roshinara and Jahanara, were playing on the lawn. Roshinara was rolling a nut through a silver bracelet and Jahanara was looking for a thimble which was hidden in the moss. They were engrossed in their queer little games which had no name; they kept whispering and giggling with a secret excitement.

IV

Damayanti struck a flame and lit the candle beside the window. The moths gathered instantly, fluttering in a panic out of the darkness.

She looked through the door and called: "Baji!" Her voice echoed but no one answered. She knelt on the floor and started shelling the big white beans for the evening soup.

It was a dark little hut with thick mud walls and a thatched roof. There was only one room and the only furniture in the room was two beds and a wooden table and some earthenware pots for the water and the cooking. On one of the walls hung several blankets and knitted shawls and laundered loincloths. On another hung a row of spoons, a bottle, a broom, and a sack of rice. Everything was clean and trim and tidy. A smell of charcoal hung in the air along with the smell of dry grass and the curry-like scent of the eucalyptus.

This was where Damayanti lived with her older brother, whose name was Baji. They were orphans: Damayanti earned some pennies sewing dresses which were sold in the market place, and more recently she had been given some coins by the mysterious lover in the Imperial bungalow. Baji worked in the fields. He was a strong, thickset fellow, and he and Damayanti spent most of their time together since the rest of the peasants would have nothing to do with them.

She set the bowls on the table and started to sing a little song which the village girls sang when they walked through the jungle:

"Don't bite, little bee.
I'll bring you flowers as ripe as my breasts.

"Don't bite, little lizard.
I'll bring you flies as sweet as my kisses.

"Don't bite, little snake.
I'll bring you frogs as fresh as my lips.

"Don't bite, my black-eyed lover.
I'll bring you tenderness warmer than sunlight."

There was a sound of someone approaching along the road that led through the woods. She could hear the sound of the hoofs striking the small hard pebbles. She glanced through the window uneasily. Once again she called: "Baji!" Then she rose and closed the door and dropped the thick iron bolt.

She sat motionless, listening. Someone coughed in the darkness. The clattering of hoofs drew slowly nearer and came to a halt. Damayanti crept to the window and peered into the darkness. Very dimly among the trees she detected the silhouettes of the horses. The men had dismounted. There were three of them, it seemed, and they stood under the trees muttering in furtive tones.

She drew the curtains across the window and sat down on the floor again, put the bowl in her lap and stared tensely at the door.

Several minutes passed by. She was about to get up again when there was a violent pounding on the little green door.

Damayanti sat silent, pressing her hands to her throat.

"Open the door!" someone roared in a deep, drunken tone.

Damayanti sat motionless. Her chin started to tremble. There was a beating against the door and then a quick powerful thrust. The bolt creaked ominously; then it burst in a puff of dust. The door flew open and Damayanti saw a man in a plum-blue cloak and a dusty gray turban stand in the middle of the doorway.

"Who are you?" she whispered.

"Never mind," said the stranger. "Put on your coat and come along. There's no time to be wasted."

Damayanti rose to her feet. She was just beginning to scream when the man lunged forward, flung his cloak over her head and carried her out into the night.

v

They followed a bamboo-lined path which ran through the jungle. Now and then as they crossed a hillock she could see the lights of Agra twinkling through the stalks. Then they climbed up a hillside and entered a forest: the Forest of the Humming-Birds, as the peasants called it, which spread over the hills in the direction of the Ganges.

Damayanti rode on the saddle in front of the oldest of the men, a harelipped little ruffian with a foul-smelling breath. She sat silent and sullen; the earlier terror had subsided into a listless, half-contemptuous indifference.

The moon rose, streaking the treetrunks with a pale molten lead. The stirring of the leaves sent silver patches fluttering through the shadows, which mingled and grew confused with the long-tailed moths which floated past her.

"Look! Demons!" said the man with the harelip. "They're on their way from the mountains."

"What are they looking for?" said the man behind him, a dark young Pathan.

"They're all looking for a dying body to glide into, that's what they're looking for!"

The man who spoke was the man with the turban who had broken into the hut. He was riding in front on a large gray stallion.

They kept riding. They came to a clearing on top of the hill. From here they could see the vast and featureless jungle spread below them and far away, so remote that it looked like a cloud clinging to the horizon, the thin moonlit ribbon of the river Jumna.

"Tell me," said Damayanti softly to the little ruffian behind her: "who ordered you to fetch me? There's no harm in telling me, is there?"

The man grunted. "No harm and no good. It's just an order, that's all."

"Was it someone in Agra? Someone powerful up in the palace?"

"It's a secret," whispered the man. "It's a name that can't be spoken."

After a while Damayanti said: "Tell me this, then. Where are you taking me?"

The old man tittered and leaned forward a little, so that his beard tickled her neck. "Oh, a lovely place, my pear-blossom! A cozy place in the city, full of cushions and perfumes!"

The path went downhill again and the tree-shadows deepened. Now and again a lightning bug shone in the gloom, like a spark from a fire, or a drop of resin glowed on a bough like the eye of a cat. The earth grew soft and springy. The horses were panting. She could smell their grassy musk blending with the smell of the evergreens and the lizardlike stench of the man behind her.

After a while she said softly: "I'm just a dull, common peasant girl. Tell me, why are they sending me to that place in the city?"

The man sighed. "Oh, you aren't just a common peasant girl,

my dear. You're special, you've had experiences, you've had privileges, you've had delights!"

"There's no reason," said Damayanti stubbornly, "to carry me off like this to the city. I'm perfectly harmless. I was living quietly with my brother on the edge of the woods."

"True enough," said the old man thoughtfully. "But we're helpless, one and all of us. We enjoy our privileges and delights and the day will come when we pay the penalty. . . ."

They came to a shadowy place on the edge of a brook where the trees formed a circle like the pillars in a mosque. Here the men came to a halt and climbed wearily from their horses. They stood in a row and made water toward the light of the moon and the man in the turban growled casually at Damayanti: "Go ahead. Don't be shy. We're settling for the night. Don't pay any attention to us. . . ."

The young Pathan took a wine jug which was hanging from one of the saddles and he passed it to the man in the turban, who took a great, thirsty swallow. Each of the men drank from the wine jug and then they drank again a second time, and then they passed the jug to the girl, half-reluctant and half-jovial. But Damayanti shook her head and strolled off into the trees, and when she presently came back again the men were lying on their woollen blankets, the old one humming a lullaby, the one in the turban snoring, and the deer-eyed young Pathan with his chin on his elbow, gazing at the darkness.

VI

She tried to sleep but she felt the gaze of the young Pathan fixed upon her, so intent that it ceased being merely the look of a pair of eyes: it turned into a burrowing warmth, it turned into the touch of a finger, it turned into an urgent voice which kept murmuring across the darkness.

But finally she fell asleep and in her dreams she saw an enormous castle, all built out of glass and perched high on a barren rock. She entered the hall, which was quite deserted, and the rooms were all of glass, so that she could see straight through the castle from one end to the other. There was nothing there at all, the place was utterly still and empty, and when she called out "Baji!" her voice went echoing as in a cistern. And then she noticed that all round her there were creatures clawing at the walls of the castle—pitiful beggars in rotting clothes, shriveled women, lepers and cripples, even some ravenous little children scratching at the glass with bony claws.

She woke up with a cry of terror. At first she hardly knew what was happening. She felt a powerful grip on her shoulder and then a hand pressed over her mouth. She struggled frantically and then stopped struggling; she closed her eyes and turned her head away while the breathless young Pathan tore feverishly at her dress.

She whispered wearily to herself: "What does it matter? It is all an absurdity." And she lay inert as the Pathan thrust his knees between her legs and burrowed his frantic way into the folds of her belly.

Finally his body stopped trembling, he uttered a thin little groan, then rolled over on his back and sank into a motionless stupor.

But she still felt the powerful heaving of his big wet body on her belly; she could smell the sweat of his armpits, the stink of his loins, the whiff of semen. She bent over him cautiously and slid the knife from his knifebelt. With a lightning-quick jab she buried it deep in his eye.

He twitched like a fish in a net and let out a great sigh. Then his body grew limp and the blood came spouting over the blanket.

She regarded him thoughtfully and ran her palm over her brow. Then she looked about calmly and went tiptoeing into the forest.

VII

The light was growing rosy over the edge of the horizon when she saw the two horsemen galloping swiftly down the path.

"There! Be careful!" shouted the one in the turban. "It's no use running! Just come along with us. . . ."

"Don't be scared! We won't hurt you!" cried the little one with the harelip.

They halted their horses directly in front of her and jumped from their saddles. The one with the turban took her arm, almost imploringly it seemed, and lifted her gently onto the saddle.

They rode silently toward the east, toward the banks of the river Ganges, whose waters grew bright as the great red sun rose over the rushes.

VIII

It was dusk when they finally rode through the gates of Allahabad. Men were gathering outside the walls, watching some clowns with a pair of monkeys, and by the archway a group of youngsters were beginning to play on their zithers. Some lamps were already shining in a row of tiny stalls where they were selling bits of marzipan, fried pancakes and balls of opium. The scent of the vast anonymous multitude rose out of the city; there was the hum of a thousand voices and the padding of naked feet.

Damayanti sensed something bleak and terribly depressing in Allahabad. There was a heaviness in the air. No one smiled; no one looked happy. The fumes of a bottomless antiquity seemed to weigh on the people. And the dogs: hundreds of dogs, dogs infesting every alley, horrible dogs with bleeding snouts, hairless dogs covered with abscesses, forsaken dogs with trailing dugs and three-footed dogs matted with excrement. It was almost as though the dogs were performing an allegory of human cruelty, with their desperate cringing eyes and beseeching little whimpers.

They followed the darkening alleys until they came to a little *soukh*. Some wooden houses with scalloped balconies stood at one end of the square and at the other stood a long low building of whitewashed stucco. The horsemen halted under a balcony, tied the reins to one of the posts, and then strode through an open courtyard with Damayanti between them.

"Where are we going?" whispered the girl, wrapping her cloak tightly around her.

"Hush, child. It's nothing to fret about," said the harelipped little fellow.

"Is it a prison? Is that what it is?"

"Sh. Be patient. It's nothing to be scared of." The man pressed her elbow and looked at her face with a hint of compassion. "It's often happened before. It will often happen again. It's the way that the world is made and there's nothing we can do about it."

He rapped on a wooden door and a woman's voice squeaked: "Yes? Who is it?"

"It's Ayub!" said the turbaned one.

"Well, come in then," bleated the woman. There was the click of an iron bolt and the door opened slowly and a tremulous old woman peered anxiously out of the darkness. Her hair was entirely white but the whites of her eyes were a dusky yellow and her face was almost black, pursed and jutting, like a monkey's.

She took Damayanti's hand, closed the door and bolted it again. Then she whispered to Damayanti, "They're fools, that's all. Just good-for-nothings!"

She led the way down a narrow corridor which presently branched into another passageway, where soft amber lights shone behind a carved wooden screen. Tittering voices and muffled cries emerged from the room behind the screen and Damayanti caught a faint, agreeable whiff of burning sandalwood. The hag hurried on, wiping her hands on her purple dress, and then paused in front of a narrow black door and drew the latch.

It was a small rectangular room, half the size of Baji's hut, with a bed in the corner and a low round table with a copper basin. The woman lit a candle and at the leap of the flame a horde of tiny cockroaches went scurrying into the corners. There was something vaguely familiar about the smell of the room—it reminded Damayanti of the smell of the dying Pathan. A dark secret smell compounded of dirt and human wickedness, with a faint whiff of blood; maybe the blood of an ancient sacrifice.

"There, there," muttered the woman. "You're all tired out. Lie down and rest." She stared connivingly at Damayanti, baring her broken black teeth.

"Those miserable fools! That's all they are!" She peeped furtively behind her. "Scoundrels and idiots! That's all they are! They bring us trouble, nothing but trouble. . . ."

She closed the door behind her, sliding the bolt into the latch. The sound of her shuffling feet echoed faintly in the vaulted corridor.

Damayanti turned around, stepped carefully on the edge of the bedstead and peered through the oblong window, which was shielded by a bulging grill, so that she could thrust her head through the window and see clearly in both directions. But there was nothing to be seen—just a drab empty alley and two rat-faced little dogs snarling viciously over a bone.

Damayanti clutched at the coils of the black iron grill and cried wildly: "Baji! Baji!" But no one seemed to hear her. The dogs looked nervously about, tucked their tails between their legs and scampered away through a low dark archway.

Damayanti stepped down again and stared at the door. Her eyes were like the eyes of someone who had suddenly gone blind. She stood motionless as a statue in the middle of the room, and then slowly raised her arms toward the ceiling, as though praying. And then finally, after she had stood like this for five or six minutes, she screamed desperately: "Oh, Baji! Tell me! Why is everything so terrible? Why is life so terrible? Why are men so terrible? Why does everything in the end become so foul and disgusting?"

Then she sank on the bed and buried her face in her arms and the flame of the candle shone on her shaking body.

IX

That same evening the Emperor was sitting alone on the balcony when he noticed a procession climbing the road to Suleiman's castle. Little fountains of dust went spiraling through the air as the column of donkeys went stumbling over the boulders.

He called to Tardi: "Who are these people? Are we having visitors, do you happen to know?"

"It's the Empress Dowager, Your Majesty," said the eunuch, somewhat sheepishly.

Khurram sat without moving, staring at the drought-ridden

valley. Finally he rose and climbed thoughtfully into the garden. He heard the tinkling of bells which heralded the illustrious arrival; he saw the slaves with their hampers scrambling up to the gateway. It was nearly dusk and he was sauntering back to the terrace when he caught sight of Nurmahal herself wandering across the lawn.

It was a year since he'd seen her. She had been staying in the Punjab. He had heard of her illness but recoiled from the thought of visiting her. As she crossed the dusky lawn and came to a halt in front of him he was appalled by the incredible change which had come over her. Her cheeks were pitted with pock marks; she had lost her brows and eye-lashes. Neither the kohl nor the layers of powder could conceal her terrible ugliness. Deep furrows crossed her cheeks and her hair had a curious stiffness. The skin on her hands had shriveled to parchment. But there still was a certain dignity in her gaunt, arid mannishness, with suffering stamped in every feature—a deliberate suffering, a pervasion of suffering, a bleak and obstinate refusal not to suffer. Her lips were dry and wrinkled, her chin was as hard as flint, her eyes were those of a condor and her voice was low and grating.

She smiled quietly at Khurram: a frightening little smile. "How delightful. I was hoping to find you alone for a moment."

"Its been long, Mihru-n nisa. Over a year since I saw you, isn't it?"

"Over a year. Yes. A pity." She looked at him intently. "I've changed, haven't I, Khurram?"

"We've both changed," said Khurram evasively. "Everyone has changed. The world's grown older."

Nurmahal nodded. "So it has. Once I was beautiful. Now I am hideous." Her voice softened. "Once you loved me. Now you loathe me. So it goes with us."

"Are you begging for sympathy?"

She placed a finger against her cheek. "Not sympathy, my darling. Merely common politeness."

"They failed to inform me of your visit. It is unexpected, to say the least."

"It is only for a night," said Nurmahal gently. "I'm on my way to Ahmadabad."

"Did you know I was here?"

"I wasn't sure. I rather suspected it."

"Then why did you come?"

"Am I forgiven nothing? Am I allowed nothing?" Her eyes sharpened but in her voice there was a low, tender irony. "Listen, my Khurram. The past is not so easily brushed aside as you think. You pretend to be in love with Arjumand. We both know that it isn't true. Your love for her is a self-delusion. It's a desperate effort to hide something else. Do you know what that something is? Listen. I'll tell you. You still love me. In all my squalor and disintegration you still love me and you'll always love me. You're incapable of any love except this one incongruous love: you love me because I despise you, I see through you, I feel contempt for you, I see the miserable and abysmal weakness which lies at the core of your character. You'll forgive me for being frank. After all, my dear boy, I am still the Empress Dowager and I insist on certain priviliges!"

"You are wrong," said Khurram softly.

"I exaggerate, perhaps," said Nurmahal.

"And as for Arjumand. . . ."

"Arjumand is a delicate and wholly admirable little lady. I haven't the slightest denigration to propose about our Arjumand. Not particularly clever, not especially amusing. But decent, thoroughly decent. Does she bore you a little? Or am I being unfair to her?"

Khurram stared into the darkness, where the fireflies were beginning to gather. They drew bright threadlike patterns, now emerging, now vanishing, as though in a tantalizing game with the bats who came swooping from the eaves in velvety parabolas.

"It is strange," said the Emperor, looking dreamily at Nurmahal, whose face was nearly hidden in the obscurity of nightfall, "but she still eludes me. She is wholly guileless. She is utterly transparent. And yet when it comes to grasping her essence, she darts away like a drop of quicksilver."

"She doesn't love you," said Nurmahal, "and that's the reason. It's very simple."

"She doesn't love me," said Khurram. "Is that all? Is that the mystery of it?"

"Well," said Nurmahal, "if you wish to read an edifying philosophy into it, I can suggest a little thought that I came across in the *Satapatha*. We all live in a dream. We are not individual creatures. We're only fragments of a great endless dream dreamed by the Creator. And that's the reason that everything around us seems so deeply mysterious, without a beginning and without an end, with no visible cause or visible purpose. We're dreams, we're nothing but fantasies. Arjumand is a ghost. We're all just ghosts."

They walked back toward the terrace, where the servants were placing the cushions and laying the bowls for the evening sherbet. The heat had turned sultry; there was a clamminess in the air. Even the leaves seemed to be sweating. Nurmahal turned to Khurram casually:

"What is this odor? I've noticed a curious sort of odor about this castle."

"Something rotting, it seems."

"Rats in the masonry, perhaps."

"And the dampness. There's a dampness oozing from the pine woods," said Khurram.

They climbed up the steps. Suleiman Khan raised the curtains to welcome them and one of the eunuchs beat twice on an iron gong.

X

The Empress was sitting by a table, staring silently into a mirror.
A candle was burning on a bamboo stand beside the mirror.
She was staring at a pale and heavily shadowed little face, in
which the treacheries of age were already visible. The quivering
of the flame accentuated the fine web of lines: tiny furrows
across her brow and purplish threads spreading from the eyelids,
and more than anything a certain tension and aridity about the
mouth. Her pride had begun to sour, as pride must do sooner
or later, drying the sources of her beauty, puckering her lips
and hardening her eyeballs.

She turned around and glanced into the garden. The light
from the gallery was shining through the columns. It dropped a
row of sparkling crescents over the grass and dew-wet shrubbery. Someone was standing under the lime tree with his
eyes fixed on her window. His face was half in shadow but
she recognized him instantly. In that deep, half-shadowed gaze
she caught the gust of his feeling: the intensity of bitterness and
longing which echoed her own deep uneasiness.

She shut the rattan blinds and walked to the bed where Khurram was lying. His eyes were closed; his lips were the only
part of his body moving—the tremor on his lips and the pulse
of a vein in his dusky neck. She sat down on the pillow and
watched him with a deepening curiosity. She looked at the chest
with its firm black nipples; at the dappled belly and the shadowy
sex, which lay mutely expectant, like a ritual offering. She kept
watching and the sense of wonder gradually obliterated the fa-
miliarity. Here was a body she had never penetrated, enclosing a

spirit she had never fathomed. A frail dark creature as mild as a doe, as vulnerable as a caterpillar, as inscrutable as a mantis.

XI

Khurram opened his eyes and looked sleepily at Arjumand.

"You were watching me, weren't you?"

"It was rather odd, watching you sleep."

"Odd? Why?"

Her eyes narrowed. She seemed to be looking at something beyond him, at a fold in the pillow or the shadow on the curtain.

"You looked as though you had turned into somebody else," she said softly.

"Maybe I had. But who?" said Khurram.

"Somebody strange whom I've never met."

Khurram took her arm gently and pressed his mouth to her open palm. "Tell me, my beauty. What's wrong? You're never happy. Why aren't you happy?"

"Am I unhappy?" She laughed wryly and then her face grew tense and solemn. "I feel restless. And why do I feel restless? It's the restlessness in yourself. What is it that you're looking for? I keep wondering. I never know. Is it luxury and still more luxury? Is it power and still more power? Is it the immensity of the Empire? Or a victory in the Deccan? Is it the spreading of Islam and the destruction of alien gods? Is it flattery? Is it glory? Which is it? I do not know."

Khurram stared at her drowsily. "Do you want to know the truth, Arjumand? You don't know and neither do I and questions like these can never be answered. We all keep looking for something or other, we keep groping for a jewel in the darkness, and when we're lucky enough to grasp it we throw it away and look for another."

"I am sick," said Arjumand thinly, "of this air of perpetual intrigue."

"You'll never escape it. It lurks in the palaces. It lurks in the huts, the temples, the jungle."

"Not the things that I'm thinking of."

"What things?" said Khurram quietly.

"No one," said Arjumand, placing her fingers on Khurram's brows, "quite understands you. People have theories. Sir Thomas had a theory. Parviz had a theory. Indira has theories. I've given up theories, I simply admit to a deep bewilderment. I see an image of physical courage, animal decision, single-mindedness. Yes. Ambition. A brute ambition. But there my understanding ends. Under the flame of ambition there lie a hundred shifting shadows. Ambiguities and contradictions. And the image dissolves in smoke."

"And you?" said Khurram listlessly. "Are you any simpler? Are you any more fathomable? My own emotions are clear as crystal when I compare them with your own. I try to place you. What are your tastes? What do you long for? What do you desire? Luxury? I doubt it. Power? Of course not. The grandeur of India? The triumph of Islam? None of these things. Poetry? Music? The charms of philosophy? I rather doubt it. My sad-eyed Arjumand, there are things that you've never chosen to tell me. I keep wondering and guessing but you've never told me. What is your secret?"

"There's no secret," said Arjumand.

"You're lying," said Khurram.

"Very well, then," cried Arjumand. "Yes, there's a secret, a bleeding secret, and the truth is that I'm sickeningly afraid of you! I've always been afraid! I'll always be afraid!"

"Yes. I see," said Khurram after a moment, staring at her grimly. "And what shall we do?"

"Go back to Agra," said the Empress wearily, pressing her hands to her temples.

Khurram reached out his arms and drew her gently to his naked body. "My love," he whispered, "my poor little puss, my black, baffled kitten. We'll go to Agra tomorrow. We'll go to Arabia if you like. We'll climb on a golden-tusked elephant and ride into heaven, if you like."

He clung to her body in a rush of hunger, like a child to its mother. But all she felt was disgust: fear and fury and disgust.

XII

The way back to Agra followed the slopes of the Aravalli and then wound through the thickets that bordered the swiftly flowing Chambal. At dusk they entered a defile between two blood-red cliffs, with a tiny black rivulet gurgling below them. They pitched their tents on a wooden ledge which overlooked the Chambal—the Emperor's tent in the middle, with large rugs spread all around it, and the horses picketed in the distance behind the tents of the grooms and porters. The servants started to unpack the big wicker trunks, laying out the silver basins, the jars and mirrors, the velvet cushions. A campfire was lighted and the silhouettes of the firelit branches swayed slowly on the walls of the circular tent.

After their dinner they sat out under the trees beside the fire. The eunuch Tardi set a large bowl of berries in front of them and one of the Ethiopian slaves began to play on his flute.

Arjumand sat beside Khurram, watching the dance of the flames. Their leaping and writhing was reflected in Khurram's eyes, which kept staring into the night with a mute, brooding sadness. And all of a sudden, for no reason, she felt her love for him awakening again, as though *Emperor* and *Empress* were words that had lost their reality and only the trees, the fire, the night, and the sound of the flute had any meaning.

And yet, ironically, a moment later she felt her remoteness more keenly than ever: as though in the sudden surge of tenderness the invisible wall rose more cruelly than ever, and on the very brink of closeness the threat of distance was darker than ever.

"What are you thinking?" said Khurram softly. "I feel you thinking. What are your thoughts?"

"My thoughts? My darling Khurram, if only I had words for all these thoughts! There's so much that I could say if only I could find the words to say it. So few and such hollow words to say such complicated things. We are Emperor and Empress but that doesn't make it any easier. All around us are hundreds of watchers, hundreds of rituals, hundreds of ornaments, and beneath all these ornaments how can we know what we're really like? To keep our feelings fresh and pure is even harder than for the rest of the world. When I took the name of Mumtaz Mahal I put on a smiling mask and when you took the name of Shahjahan you too put on a mask, and when we were crowned the Emperor and Empress we put on masks of gold and now we're hiding behind these masks and we'll keep on hiding until we die!"

This was the longest speech that Arjumand had ever brought herself to make, and at the end of it she felt weary and breathless and dejected. Once again she had failed to say what she meant. The sound of the flute hung over the fire, so thin and sinuous that it seemed like a flame. The light of the flames and the sound of the flute blended together, and her words seemed emptier than ever, her thoughts seemed hollower than ever, and the gust of rebellious feelings seemed the only thing worth possessing, the only thing that still remained when all the masks had fallen away.

At this moment one of the guardsmen, an elderly Rajput in a

smoke-gray turban, walked up to the Emperor and bowed with outstretched hands.

"It may not be a matter of particular urgency, Your Majesty, but I thought I'd be wise to report it to you. A group of Portuguese have pitched their tents on the opposite shore. One of our men saw the glow of their campfire and I sent him across the river to investigate."

"Merchants, I take it," said Khurram sullenly.

"Some merchants from Goa. As well as a priest."

"What did they say?" inquired Khurram.

"They said nothing, Your Majesty. When they saw Mohammed Ali they took out their knives and made a rush at him."

"But he got away?"

"He ran through the bushes and made for the river."

"An unpardonable impudence," said Khurram. "You have my instructions, please, Mukarrab. Gather your horsemen and see that these travelers are brought to Agra for the appropriate discipline."

The Rajput bowed and retreated, shuffling backward past the fire until his bobbing gray turban finally vanished behind the tents.

XIII

Way ahead of them, at a curve of the river, the light was beginning to shine. It came filtering through the twigs, spreading a haze over the mudbars and sprinkling the current with bright yellow ripples. They rode silently along the shore, Don Fernando on a chestnut gelding, the three merchants on their mares and Father Pinheiro on a small gray donkey.

"Tell me, Father," said Don Fernando. "Do you ever feel homesick for Lisbon?"

"Oh, Lisbon! What a beautiful city," said Father Pinheiro with feeling. He looked down at the muddy river. "I think of the Tagus in the morning ad the sun over Capranica and all those sails flapping lazily." He wiped his nose on his sleeve. "What a beautiful river it is, the Tagus!"

"I personally," said one of the merchants, "have always preferred Coimbra. Lisbon is rich and luxurious. Coimbra is scholarly and fastidious."

"You're a hypocrite, Ferreira," said another merchant in a long black cloak. "Scholarly! Fastidious! Since when do your tastes run in such directions?"

"He wasn't notably fastidious in that place in Benares," said the third merchant, a furtive little man with a bristling blue beard.

"Quite frankly," said the second merchant, "I much prefer Oporto. A clean hard-working city. None of this nonsense about culture."

"Have you ever visited Agarve, Manuel?" asked Don Fernando.

"Never Agarve," said the merchant. "I know Braga and Guimaraës but I've never been in the south. I've no use for all those southerners."

"Thieves and blackamoors," said the second merchant.

"Whores and cutthroats," said the third.

"Almost as bad as the Andalusians," said the first one, smacking his lips.

"When it comes to whores and cutthroats," said the fat little merchant," what about Benares? You'll have to go far to find a dirtier city than Benares."

"Dirty and weird," said Ferreira. "Tell me, Father, what do you think? D'you think there's any hope of ever converting these naked heathens?"

"There's always hope," said Father Pinheiro, grinning slyly at

Don Fernando. "Patience. Caution. And dedication. We must never despair."

"You'll convert a Hindu or two or maybe a Parsee," said Don Fernando. "But never a Muslim. There's an insuperable obstinacy in the Muslims, I've noticed."

"Under Jahangir," said Father Pinheiro, "there was a tolerance and a certain eclecticism. Jahangir's mind was debauched but inquisitive. He always listened to new opinions."

"And Shahjahan?"

"Shahjahan is neither inquisitive nor debauched," said the priest. "He is hard and intolerant. He is villainous and vengeful."

"Strange, isn't it?" said Don Fernando, lowering the brim of his hat. "In Islam, as I understand it, there's no caste or distinction of hierarchy. In Islam, just as with the Christians, all men are equal in the sight of God. Whereas with the Hindus there are a million little merciless distinctions. And yet it's the Hindus who turn out to be kind and merciful and it's the Muslims who are prejudiced and bitter and bloodthirsty."

"So it seems," said Father Pinheiro, looking carefully across the river. "But you musn't judge the Muslims by the Emperor's personal example."

"Maybe not," said Don Fernando. "But the fact still remains. Shahjahan dwells loyally in Islam. Why does he do these terrible things?"

"Because an Emperor's life," said the Father, "is profoundly corrupting and the limitless power of an Emperor defiles the spirit. No man with great power can long remain a true believer. He'll say his prayers and go through the rituals. But the love of power has poisoned the truth of it."

"But Jahangir. . . ."

"Ah, Jahangir," said Father Pinheiro, smiling wistfully. "Poor old Jahangir was a lazy and opium-ridden degenerate. He'd grown sick of his own power. And with that sick imperial lassitude a certain purity flowed back into his soul. But Shahjahan is

still obsessed. He still is blind with the lust for power. And so
India continues to suffer. And our humble task grows increasingly hazardous."

They crossed a sandy estuary and climbed over a hill. On their
left a flock of sheep was grazing peacefully among the willows.
On their right rose a dark and rather ominous stretch of jungle.
The sun now shone brightly on the banks of the Chambal: here
and there a lazy crocodile was dozing among the reeds.

One of the merchants said quietly: "Look. Some horsemen seem
to be following."

"So they do," said Father Pinheiro. He turned wearily in his
saddle.

"I don't quite like the look of it," said the merchant, groping
for his purse.

"Patience. Caution. Dedication," said the Father somewhat
wryly.

They rode casually toward the willows and waited in silence
for the horsemen. The dust from the approaching hooves welled
up over the mudbanks and the sun flashed brightly on the ivory-
hilted swords.

XIV

It all happened with great rapidity. Mukarrab's men rode up to
the travelers, raised the Emperor's emblem and curtly ordered
them to dismount. A panic seized the merchants. They whisked
out their knives and the man from Oporto shouted: "Brigands!
Nothing but brigands!" Mukarrab muttered some words in a
Rajput dialect and the horsemen shot forward, swinging their
swords through the air. Don Fernando sprang from his gelding

and went racing into the thicket. The last thing he saw was the flashing of naked scimitars and the priest's pudgy body shriveling queerly as it fell from the saddle.

XV

He crouched motionless in the shade, waiting for the screaming to die down. The leaves formed a hood over his head like a shield, so low that he didn't move for fear of setting the twigs atremble. There was a sharp falsetto cry. He recognized the voice of the second merchant. Then the noise stopped abruptly. He crouched without stirring, covering his face with his hat to keep off the gnats. He heard a far-off rumbling, maybe the sound of vanishing hoofbeats. One of the Rajputs shouted an order; another one called back. Then there was silence, a silence so intense and microscopic that he could almost hear the creeping of the ants in the foliage.

Then the itching began. It started in his ankles: little pinpoints of flame shot up toward his knees. Then they struck at his wrists, then his shoulders and armpits. He squirmed sideways: he saw that he'd been squatting on top of an anthill. His whole body was covered with ants; blood-red beasts as long as his fingernails. Their sting burned his flesh like some poisonous acid. He plunged frantically through the underbrush toward a small grassy clearing and flailed at his doublet to shake off the furies. The pain grew so intolerable that he bit his fist to keep from screaming. It was more than a horrible itching: it was like wearing a venomous fur whose needles sent jets of hysteria through his system. He climbed on a rock and ripped off his garments, hurling the ants from the folds and scraping them crazily from his skin. Then he

stood for several minutes, frozen still as a statue, trying to cool the
hideous pain by a kind of self-induced coma. Little by little it
grew less. Small red lumps covered his flesh and after a while the
itching dwindled into a dull, throbbing fever. He leaned over and
started to pull on his clothes one by one. The poison had affected
his muscles so that every gesture revived the pain. He knelt down
on the rock in a fit of exhaustion.

He looked around blankly, as though awakening from a trance.
The leaves flickered unsteadily. It was like a scene under water.
And then gradually, as the pain died down, the feeling of relief
grew almost blissful, it turned into a kind of cool floating ecstasy.
The caress of the jungle grew gentle and intimate. His mind sank
into a purring meditation. He noticed the infinitesimal movements that passed through the leaves, the churning of light and
shadow which blended into a magical iridescence, which in turn
seemed to dissolve into a glittering proliferation, as though millions of little lives were being spawned before his eyes. He felt he
was witnessing the whole process of creation: the fusion of the
inanimate into the living and then of life dissolving into death
again, profuse and incessant almost to the point of hallucination.

It must have been noon. He grew aware of a pang in his forearm: it was merely a ray of light which stabbed at his wrist, as
bright as a diamond. He drew back, glanced around, spread his
cloak over the grass, then lay down and fell into a nightmarish
stupor.

When he woke up he saw a brightly colored bird sitting above
him. A parrot; emerald-green with a head of a regal crimson. It
was studying him with an air of disapproving perplexity. He
raised his arms, and lowered them again, as though testing his
muscles. The bird cocked his head and said: *"Kkri-kkri! Kak-
kada!"* Don Fernando looked at the bird with an imploring expression, as though begging it for a bit of comfort and guidance.
But the parrot glared back with an unforgiving look, then shot
off through the leaves and vanished in the maze of jungle.

XVI

He went staggering through the thicket, trying to reach some sort of promontory where he could look over the jungle and get a view of the river. But the land was wholly flat, the jungle was bleakly featureless and all sense of direction had utterly deserted him. Once or twice he caught a whiff of something murky, like the slime of a river. But a moment later it was gone again and there was nothing but thorns and creepers.

He glanced down and caught sight of his shoes, which were coated with mud. He grew fascinated with the shape of his shoes, which made him think of the hoofs of an animal. All of a sudden he felt an excruciating pain in the back of his neck. A great blow from behind had struck at his head like a hatchet. He fell headlong on the ground; his brow struck a rock; the blood went cascading over his eyeballs and nostrils.

He lay stunned for several minutes. A glittering torrent was churning in front of him: then the torrent gradually changed into a great fiery geyser. He tasted blood on his tongue and vaguely realized what had happened. A bough overhead had come crashing on his skull.

He moaned softly, "Mother of God! Jesus and Mary! Beloved Joseph!"

He crawled forward on his belly, clutching at roots and little saplings. The blood was gradually congealing into a mask across his cheeks. A trail of saliva dripped slowly over his neckcloth, cooling his throat with a fleck of moisture. He kept struggling ahead, twisting his way across the pebbles, and after a while he grew aware of the nearness of water. His thirst was so fierce that his mouth seemed to be shriveling. He licked at the air like a fish snapping for gnats.

Suddenly he found himself slumped by the edge of a stream. It was parched by the drought; there was only a trickle of coal-black water which oozed through the layers of mud and detritus. He buried his face in the mud and lapped ravenously at the slime. His whole body was so riddled with misery that he hardly noticed the separate pains—the lumps on his flesh and the gash in his forehead, the fierce little blisters on his knees and elbows.

He caught sight of a deeper shadow under a catacomb of shrubbery—a small muddy hollow where a pool of water still lingered. He crawled on, lunging and writhing across the mud like an epileptic until he felt himself sinking into the lap of the quagmire. It was marvelously soft and cool: it was like floating in a soothing jelly. He lay motionless, feeling the moisture calm his flesh like an unguent. After a while he crawled out again and lay on the edge of the hollow, staring up through the leaves at the shining blueness.

And then he realized to his amazement that the day had come to an end. The light faded slowly. Tiny stars were beginning to twinkle. He felt the mud that covered his body gradually drying into a crust, so stiff that it cracked like a shell when he moved his shoulders. He plucked absently at the little black scales that clung to his skin. Then he reached into the stream and let his hand trail in the water. He felt his being caught up in an uncanny lightness, a lightness of body and of the senses, a delirious lightness of spirit. He grew aware of a curious throbbing in the side of his body. He reached down: something sticky and unpleasantly warm clung to his ribs. He placed his hand against his nostrils. It was only blood; nothing alien. Only the blood that was oozing from a wound in his chest.

The lightness grew eerie. He was rising like a kite. He was floating above the ground: he could almost touch the treetops. He rose higher and higher until he was soaring over the jungle, and then he hovered among the clouds in the coolness of infinitude. He could look across the land as far as the Jumna and even the Ganges, he could see the glittering stars over the Bay of Bengal, and suddenly he saw his whole life illumined by a cold sourceless radiance, without depth, without shadow, without passion or significance. The whole past that lay behind him shone with a pure and shadowless whiteness, as though flashed on a screen by some powerful incandescence. He thought vaguely: "Was I ever alive? Did I ever feel anything? Did I ever do anything? Was I ever really a person?" And then he wondered: "What is my name? Am I really Don Fernando? Is it Fernando who's lying here? In a lonely jungle in the middle of Hindustan?"

And as he lay there, watching the night creep closer and closer, he felt an inexplicable and wonderful thing. He felt a thrill of joy that pierced the blackness like lightning, a joy so intense that it seemed to reach as high as the stars. It soared skyward, shedding a dazzle over the whole hideous jungle, and then gradually it died away like the sound of far-off thunder.

Suddenly he realized that his body was seething with little worms; they were crawling out of the mud and went wriggling across his chest, heading blindly for the cool nourishing dampness of the quagmire. He grew puzzled as he watched the flight of the tiny white creatures, and then quite calmly but unmistakably he grasped the fact that he was dying.

But he grasped it as something casual, episodic, remote: a thing that had nothing to do with the essential Don Fernando. And he felt himself transfigured for a second time by this marvelous joyfulness, which reached out of the sky like a stupendous silver arm.

Visions flickered before his eyes—the bright red sails on the shores of Nazaré, the bulls wandering homeward through the dusk of Alcobaça. And then the great silver arm swept him up like a fallen leaf and his soul entered the darkness that flowed over India.

PART EIGHT

The Snake

On the evening after his return from Suleiman's castle the Emperor was informed that Asaf Khan had arrived in Agra. He rode through the park and welcomed his father-in-law in the hunting lodge. It was hotter than usual and the men sat on the veranda, where the rattan screens had been sprinkled with limewater.

The Emperor wore azure breeches which reached to his heels and a tunic of scarlet interwoven with gold. Across his forehead he wore a row of large emeralds and on his head a white turban with a golden falcon pinned to the middle. Shahjahan was thirty-eight. His body was supple and wiry, but in his face a certain heaviness was already appearing. There were cracks in his brow and shimmering folds in his chin. He still was handsome but there was a faintly oily, dyspeptic look in his face.

Asaf Khan had grown old. His deep disgust with the world had dug lines around his mouth, a kind of perpetual sneer. The look in his eyes was indifferent and desolate. But the Emperor's nervous energy struck a flame in his smoldering embers. He smiled and placed his forefinger on Khurram's red sleeve.

"I haven't been well, you know," he murmured, leaning closer confidentially. "My liver, for example. . . ."

"It is hardly surprising," said Khurram. "All that venison, those curried ducklings."

"It is not a question of food, unfortunately," said Asaf querulously. "Our organs respond to our moods. My mood is a mood of disenchantment."

"Our lives never develop quite as gloriously as we'd like," said the Emperor.

"A surprising statement from you, my dear fellow," said Asaf.

"Do you suggest," retorted Khurram, "that the satisfaction of

an outer ambition inevitably brings with it an inner fulfillment?
We both know that it isn't so. In point of fact, *entre nous,* it's my
very success that leaves me a little sour. While Jahangir was still
alive I had a glittering goal in front of me: the aggrandizement of
an empire, the magnificence of a throne. I've been on the throne
for two years now and already I feel the discomfort of it. And as
for the empire. . . ."

"The world of India," said the old man grimly, "is chaos.
There's no such thing as an Indian Empire. And there'll never be
one, I assure you. What do you have? An enormous seething of
Sikhs and Mahrattis, of Hindus and Mongols, of Pathans and
Afghans and Baluchis and the Lord knows what else. A great
hodgepodge of squabbling provinces and internecine hatreds, all
the way from the rocks of Kandahar to the beaches of Orissa. A
whirlpool of religions so vast and complex that even our eminent
scholars can hardly make head or tail of them. And finally—"

"Yes?" said Khurram, listening attentively. "What else?"

Asaf frowned with the effort of thought. "I keep trying to put
my finger on it. But it eludes me. I feel baffled by this turbulent
land. There's no character, no order, no coherence or cohesion. In
other countries there's a growth toward unity, a gradual blending
into harmony. In India everything multiplies, everything splits
into a deeper diversity. Things keep running to extremes. There's
no measure or moderation. Lust and renunciation, cruelty and
mercy, uncontrollable rage and infinite patience: there they are,
face to face, each of them feeding on the spectacle of its opposite.
Or so it seems. I don't pretend for an instant to comprehend it.
All I know is that when I meditate on the features of India I see
the zest for life's fullness and the passion for death's emptiness
confronting each other like a cobra and a mongoose."

"My fine Asaf," said Khurram, raising his sherbet glass
thoughtfully, "I've given up trying to approach these things in a
mood of philosophy. Things are what they are: their meanings
shift like the shifting waters. My concern is not with meanings

but with outer manifestations. The meanings I leave to the Brahmins, the bickering poets and the pot-bellied pundits."

"Manifestations," said Asaf. "A splendid word. What does it mean?" He plucked a caterpillar from his lap and tossed it airily into the saucer. "What are these outer and visible signs which you seem to regard so highly?"

Khurram rearranged the folds of his tunic with an air of perplexity. "There are clouds on the horizon. Morning and night, month after month. I begin to see signs of order, of organization, even of prosperity, and then suddenly more clouds: a drought, a pestilence, a revolt in the Deccan. Disruptive elements, disruptive elements! Fanatics, spies, crackpots, malcontents. There are moments when I feel positively tempted to abandon it all and just throw the whole agonizing country to the vultures!"

Asaf Khan leaned back in his cushion. There was a gleam in his little eyes. A gleam of scorn or compassion? Of tenderness, maybe? Or merely hatred? He said softly; "You must have a program for the Empire. What is your program?"

"A program for India! As though India were a little playhouse with a brocade curtain!"

"What do you want," said Asaf, "for India? Is it order? Is it stability? Be honest. What you want is simply splendor and power. Your grandfather Akbar, a politician of genius, worked for unity and coherence, and Jahangir, who was a hedonist, believed in the charms of *laissez-faire,* but you, my adorable son-in-law, are neither a genius nor a hedonist and the result is that you live in perpetual torment. For example: you're concerned with religion. You wish to establish Islam solidly. You'd like to raze the Hindu temples and the Christian churches, even the Buddhist monasteries. It's quite useless. You'll never win over the heart of India to Islam. India lies wallowing in chaos and her gods aren't the enemies of chaos but gods who embody and transcend the chaos. They are beautiful dancing gods, six-armed and smiling, with gilded genitals. . . ."

There was stillness for a while. A pigeon fluttered among the eaves. In the distance some boys were leading the elephants down to the water. Khurram looked furtively at the cruel and corroded face of Asaf Khan and what he felt, to his amazement, was no longer hate or resentment but something, in all its reluctance, very close to love. But why? What did it mean? Was love inseparable from hatred? Was every passion inseparable from its opposite, like the two sides of a coin? Did darkness and light draw their sustenance from one another? Did peace draw its sweetness from the thick of disorder?

"By the way," said Asaf casually. "How is Arjumand? Is she well?"

"So it appears," said Khurram, smiling. "She is growing reconciled to the chores of an Empress."

"Is she happy?" said Asaf quietly.

"Well, I hope so," said Khurram. "It is rather difficult to say to Arjumand, 'Be happy, my lamb.' She would look for a trap."

"She is restless," said Asaf. "She's aquiver with nerves. She's like a squirrel." He folded his hands over his belly and closed his eyes for a moment. "There's no truth, I suppose, in this thing I've been hearing?"

"What have you heard?" said Khurram, alert.

"Oh, something silly about a peasant girl. What's her name? Damayanti? It's not a matter of any consequence."

"There's been gossip, has there?" said the Emperor.

"Innuendoes, you might say."

"Sheer impertinence," said the Emperor angrily.

"Well, as I say, it's of no consequence. I merely mention the matter apropos of our little Arjumand. I shouldn't like," said Asaf cautiously, "to see our Arjumand get ideas in her head. She's restless enough as it is. Let her be a squirrel. Let her play with her nuts." He leaned forward and picked up his glass and then said dreamily: "Do you know what Buddha said? He said, among other things, Conquer your anger by love; conquer lies by the truth; conquer greed by generosity; conquer sin by deeds of goodness. Very proper, no doubt. But more than a little nebulous. Still, as I find myself shriveling into a bitter old man, I begin to see truth in such mild nebulosities!"

11

The resurgence of the pestilence was particularly violent in the province of Gujarat. The streets of Ahmadabad were still and deserted. Here and there in a lonely garden a withering fig-tree dropped its fruits; a dove went fluttering past; a curtain swayed in the heat of the evening. But no one dared to go out into the pest-ridden alleys, where the sewage lay steaming under a cloud of coppery gnats. The chickens and goats and even the donkeys had all been slaughtered and the people crouched in their houses, nibbling at corn and pickled mangoes.

Young Haidar had been persuaded to accompany Nurmahal on her voyage and it was on the third day after their arrival that the city closed its gates. They were staying in a blue-tiled mansion which belonged to Nakib Khan, an eminent historian who had been an intimate of the Emperor Jahangir. After the plague had isolated the city Nakib Khan retired to his library and made a point of avoiding his guests, who spent their days in the galleries and gardens. Haidar was a poet; he read his verses to Nurmahal in the cool of the evening while a thickset young Baluchi waved a fan to keep off the flies.

One of Haidar's new poems was called "The Chakora Bird," and it went as follows:

"*The season of love is upon us and I listen to the roaring of the lions.*

*The moon prowls through the darkness and the lotus opens
   her petals.
I keep wondering: 'Is she coming?' I sit silently in the boughs
But the road lies white and empty under the loneliness of
   moonlight."*

Nurmahal listened attentively and then murmured: "It's too
conventional, I'm afraid. I've heard too many poems about the
moon and the lotus. Can we believe in a love that resorts to such
weary clichés? No, my pet, you'll have to invent more startling
phrases if you wish to convince me."

Haidar looked sulky; he lowered his eyes and Nurmahal added
consolingly: "The melody is charming, I agree. But why do you
call it 'The Chakora Bird'?"

Haidar said shyly: "It's the chakora bird which drinks the
juice of the moon rays, and the bird symbolizes the lover, for
whom the nectar is the sight of the beloved. And the lotus, needless to say, is the woman who is in love, and she opens her petals
at the sight of her lover."

Nurmahal pursed her lips a little. "Well, it's all quite pleasant
in a *passé* manner, but I refuse to believe in a love which is merely
a conglomeration of metaphors."

"The love," said Haidar, "exists."

Nurmahal looked at him intently. "Yes," she said. "I rather suspected it. You have fallen in love with Arjumand."

Haidar's chin started to tremble. He looked pleadingly at Nurmahal. "It's utterly ridiculous, isn't it? So blind and hopeless, so
idiotic. I keep trying to persuade myself that it's all just an illusion. But what can one do when one's heart keeps pounding and
one's body is on fire like a brazier?"

Nurmahal smiled somewhat mockingly. "Well, your phrases
are still conventional, but they carry more conviction than those
lotuses and chakora birds. My good Haidar, you're only a child
and your infatuation is that of a child, and I assure you that six

months from now you'll have forgotten all about it. I might add that you scarcely know her, you have built up a creature of fantasy, and I can state that poor old Arjumand is a perfectly humdrum little person who'd be scared out of her wits by all this nonsense about chakora birds. And I might mention, though I doubt if it's news to you, that the Emperor is an irascible character. He'll chop off your head if he ever gets wind of all this frippery!"

III

Two days later, as she lay on her couch, a violent pain gripped Nurmahal suddenly. It seemed to spring from the pit of her stomach and then it exploded into a flame, scorching her lungs and licking at her ribs and tearing savagely at her belly. Her knees shot up to her chin and her hands clutched wildly at the coverlet. She closed her eyes and bit at her knuckles, waiting for the horror to subside a little, and then she screamed: "Menaka! Menaka! God help me, Menaka! I'm dying!"

The old woman came running across the courtyard and stared fixedly at Nurmahal. Her lips twitched slightly and she started to say something. Then she dashed out of the room and came back with a jug of barley water and a bundle of compresses. She said nothing but kept laying the dripping compresses on Nurmahal's belly; and finally the pain died down and Nurmahal sank into a torpor.

When she woke again a feverish, unreal stillness filled the room. Dusk had fallen. A tiny oil lamp was burning beside the bed. She peered at the curtains, which gradually blended into a deep wintery landscape. Towering mountains rose from the plain in a lilac-colored mist: snowy cones like great tents which caught the brilliance of sunset and shifted slowly from gold to a burning amber. She remembered having seen this same landscape long ago. She groped feebly among her memories and was on the brink of recognition when a spasm shook her again, ripping at her bowels with claws of fire. She felt the uncontrollable foulness oozing down over her thighs and once again she howled: "Menaka! For the love of God! Menaka!"

But Menaka was already there, squatting in an alcove by the window. She hurriedly washed the filth away and deftly changed the bed linen while Nurmahal lay panting in a new array of compresses. Menaka kept muttering hoarsely: "There, there, my poor little lady," and she slipped a green lime-pill into Nurmahal's mouth. Then she lit the incense brazier to drive out the stench and tiptoed disconsolately into the kitchen courtyard.

A little later the door opened again and Haidar entered the room. He walked up to the couch and knelt silently on a leather cushion. Nurmahal reached out her hand and started to stroke his silky curls, and then she said:

"Look, my dear, won't you put a screen in front of the lamp, please? I'm hideous enough already and now that I'm dying I must look unspeakable. Do forgive me. It won't be long but a woman looks for a bit of comfort. I'm too tired to think clearly, otherwise I'd make a serious effort and give you the benefit of my final pearls of wisdom. No, thinking is much too strenuous, all I can do is lie and look at you. Would you like me to tell you something? I doubt if it will thrill you particularly, but there's nothing that doesn't provide a bit of food for meditation. Do you remember that little poem of yours about the chakora bird? Well, as you read it a very strange thing happened to me suddenly. I fell in love. Yes, it's true. It never happened to me before. I fell meltingly and deeply and transfiguringly in love. Just an old woman's whimsey, that's what you're probably thinking, isn't it? Call it by any name you wish. It gave my life what they call a 'meaning.' Meanings, meanings—my beautiful Haidar, we must never forget these precious meanings, they're all that we'll carry with us when we tumble out of existence. Every creature, however contemptible, has his own special meaning, quite aside from those other meanings, the religious meanings and philosophical meanings. Am I talking nonsense? There it is. A dying hag spouting platitudes. Look. There's water in that jug. I'm horribly thirsty. Would you give me a glass, please? Thank you, darling. Puzzles, puzzles. How dreadful to die in a room full of puzzles. Hold my hand for a moment. Don't be afraid. You can wash it later. After all, I'm the Dowager Empress and I still insist on certain privileges!"

IV

In the early years of his reign Shahjahan followed his father in his encouragement of the arts. Not that he felt any personal attachment to the charms of poetry or the subtleties of philosophy. Even music left him cold. Painting struck him as vain and frivolous. But his notions of grandeur included a flourishing state of culture and he welcomed "creative" visitors from the great foreign capitals.

The first of these arrivals was the illustrious poet Che-Tsang, who had traveled from Peking with his scrolls and kimonos. A leathery little person with a beard as fine as a spiderweb, he established himself in the guest house and conducted his evening "readings." These included not only the illustrious poets of ancient China but also the Arabian philosophers and the lyricists of Ispahan. His great rival was a portly versifier from Benares named Chanakya, who had invented a number of new and intricate forms of prosody. "I have thirty-three different metres at my command," he said primly. "Even the great Bharavi used only twenty." He employed devices such as lines which were identical when read from either direction, and verses which employed only a single vowel and two consonants, and stanzas with exactly the same syllables as the preceding ones, but ingeniously rearranged so that they created new sentences.

"The five glories of poetry," said Chanakya, bowing to the Empress, "are elegance of shape, intricacy of structure, fluidity of sound, surprise of vocabulary, and subtlety of sentiment. Certain poems have only two or three of these desirable qualities. The great *chefs d'œuvre* invariably have all five. May I give you an example? I am writing a poem about Her Majesty the Empress. What shall I say? Shall I compare her grace to that of a flamingo? Not just an ordinary flamingo but a flamingo seen by moonlight, standing motionless under a willow tree, with a mountain in the distance. In his beak he is holding a rose. Very well. That is the theme. But we must decorate this theme in lines of great complexity, and with syllables that suggest the lapping of pearly waters, and our images must be appropriate, like "feathery wrists" and "beaklike elbows," and the passions displayed must not be vulgarly adulatory but gently crepuscular, and saturated with an indolent refinement."

The listeners applauded politely but Che-Tsang looked stern and expressionless. "I respect the opinions of my venerable colleague," he observed, in a voice so faint that it sounded like a bee buzzing on the windowpane, "but I suggest that the glories of poetry are not five but only two: namely, a purity of texture, so that it feels like the fur of a kitten, and a freshness of feeling, so that it smells like a mountain stream. All these intricacies and ornamentations are a thing of the past. We must look for a new simplicity or we'll strangle the muse with our trickery."

Among the painters that visited Agra was a Frenchman named Le Coq and a thickset, fawning Persian from Shiraz who called himself Mansur. Le Coq's specialty was nymphs and shepherds dancing gracefully among the ruins; their only oddity lay in the fact that the shepherds all wore turbans and the ruins were ivied minarets and moss-covered *stupas*. Mansur was a traditionalist in the manner of the Persian book illustrators. He painted the English ambassador stroking a gazelle in a field of poppies, and he painted the Viceroy of Goa sitting by a fountain with a butterfly on his wrist.

Aside from the poets and painters there were the Emperor's jewelers and architects, and these included a young Italian named Geronimo Veroneo. Shahjahan, who was thoroughly bored by theories of prosody and styles of portraiture, grew fascinated by the plans of Veroneo for the Imperial gardens. Veroneo was a handsome fellow of Italian recklessness and charm, and he pleased the Emperor by adopting the native costume of Hindustan. One evening as Shahjahan was sitting beside him in the Tower of Jasmines, he said thoughtfully:

"What is music? It's only a noise that fades in the distance. What is poetry? Only a jumble of affectations that mean nothing. What is painting? Just gaudy flattery that has no bearing on actuality. The only art that is lasting is the art of marble and lapis lazuli. That is the art that I personally wish to be remembered by, my friend."

"Quite, Your Majesty. And what is more appropriate than a beautiful white sepulcher?"

The Emperor frowned. "I'm not a cowardly man by nature, Geronimo, but I don't feel attracted to the thought of lying in a sepulcher."

"You have a long time to live yet, Your Majesty," said Veroneo suavely. "But in any event, death surely seems less dreadful if it's celebrated in marble. Yes, death is a horrible thought if we think of our bodies crumbling to dust in some miserable field or gloomy forest, with no one to be reminded that we too were once beautiful. But death is bound to come and the next best thing is to try to immortalize it, since nothing yet invented will immortalize our bodies. I suggest that you meditate on the matter, Your Majesty. That sunny spot by the river—what better place can you visualize for a sepulcher?"

"Goodness, no," said the Emperor hastily. "Not for me. Please, Geronimo."

Veroneo smiled. "For the Empress, possibly? Or am I being a trifle previous?"

v

Every evening the Empress visited the little suburb across the river, where the peasants were growing to depend on her charity. She crossed the Jumna in a gilded barge and then followed the mule path, with a slave-boy carrying a parasol and another carrying a fan.

The village was merely a cluster of little mud huts, their roofs just barely visible above the growth of wild cane. There was a smell of fresh dung, the mist of dust and the creak of the water wheel, and then the path entered the clearing where the villagers stood waiting.

They never smiled. They just stood there with their brooding eyes and emaciated bodies, bowing stiffly as Arjumand distributed the rice and flour. Some of them took the trouble to wear their best clothes—a Paisley-patterned skirt, maybe, or a pair of brass earrings—but most of them were too weak and apathetic to care. They just mumbled their thanks and went limping into the shadows.

An elderly couple named Nanda and Padmavati lived in a hut that was larger than the rest, along with an uncle, two aunts and three children. They grew friendly with the Empress and helped her when difficulties arose in the rationing. She would sit in the shade of their hut and chat pleasantly with Padmavati while Nanda doled out the grain in his little black bowls.

It was a pious and punctilious family, very exact in its observances. A patch of grass in front of the hut, carefully trimmed in the shape of a crescent, served as a family altar where the master of the house performed his rites. A fire was lit at the edge of the crescent and offerings of goat's milk were set for the gods. The family gathered for the morning *sandhya:* breathing exercises, the cleaning of teeth, and the recitation of the *gayatri,* and after that they paid homage to the five household idols, which were stones representing Vishnu, Siva, Durga, Ganesa, and Surya. And after this the whole family sat down to its meal of cooked rice.

Nanda explained in lowered tones the nature of his gods to the Empress. There still was Brahma, a rather pale and nacreous figure after all these centuries, having grown a little spectal under the onrush of Hinduism. The most conspicuous deities of Hinduism were four in number: the mighty Siva and the venerable Vishnu, and the legendary heroes Krishna and Rama. The mild and forgiving aspects of Godhead were represented by Vishnu but it was Siva whom the people found vivid and fascinating: Siva the Creator as well as the Destroyer, the Chaste as well as the Unchaste, the phallus become ascetic and thus symbolizing the terror of Godhead. Since he was limitlessly cruel, they called him the Benevolent in an effort to flatter him. In the guise of a dancer he created magic by the rhythm of his limbs, and in this many-armed miracle of balance he represented the purity of a transcendent spirit, which was accentuated by the air of irony and lasciviousness which hovered about him. The followers of Siva and Vishnu formed the two great sects of Hinduism, as Nanda explained it, and these sects had eventually splintered into innumerable subsects, some of them blending the two together, some of them masking them as animals, some of them multiplying them into triplets or even quadruplets. But through it all one thing was constant: a desperate need of god's mercy imperceptibly melting into a desperate fear of God's cruelty.

"And what about Krishna and Rama?" said the Empress, gazing at Nanda, whose sharp little face reminded her of a weasel.

"Krishna? Rama? Well," said Nanda, "sometimes Krishna is really Rama and occasionally Rama pretends that he's Krishna, but personally I have more confidence in Krishna than in Rama, insofar as the two can be readily distinguished, Your Majesty! Krishna is gentle. Krishna is a lover. Krishna's longing is for everybody's happiness. Happiness is finer than sagacity, or even bravery, says Krishna. Krishna would like the elephants to be happy. Krishna would like the tigers to be happy. The happiness of a tiny pink moth is of deep concern to the lovable Krishna. Indeed, such is Krishna, he wishes even the trees to be happy, not to mention the fruits, the eggs, the houses, the spoons, and of course the moon."

"So many things, and all of them happy! Your Krishna sounds charming."

"But sad," murmured Nanda. "He sees happiness float away again. Now it is here. Now it is gone. We keep praying. But when will it come again? And such being the lamentable state of affairs, the lovable Krishna is continually saddened by the elusive nature of human happiness."

VI

There came moments, more and more frequently of late, it appeared, when Arjumand felt that her love for Khurram had died; when Khurram's face and even his nearness filled her with guilt and alarm. And she detected in his lovemaking a hint of absent-mindedness, as though his mind were dwelling on some recollection of other caresses. But there also were moments when she felt that this was only another phase of love, a kind of secret ramification, so that her love seemed actually to deepen in the wake of these estrangements, flowering darkly under the resonance of earlier loves and furtive memories. There were moments of clearsightedness when she saw him as a hard and bigoted despot, with nothing remarkable about him except puerile ambitions and scheming vengefulness. But this too was only a transitory and superficial attitude, and she realized that under his power and intensity and decisiveness lurked fluidity and doubt and an animal hysteria; while under her own outer shyness and dreaminess and indecision lay a secret resourcefulness, a female tenacity. So that in spite of it all it was really she who was the strong one; it was he who was the malleable, the quixotic, the downright feminine.

One evening she went down to the Pavilion of the Lions to sit for her portrait. The pudgy, mild-eyed Mansur was waiting for her among the columns. He placed her in a chair with her back to the sunlight, so that the jewels in her hair created a kind of halo. She wore a dress embroidered with daisies and over the dress a braided jacket. Her hair trailed over her shoulders, interwoven with diamonds. She held a lily in one of her hands and in the other a silken fan. The effeminate Mansur kept fluttering about her, straightening a fold, adjusting a lock, until finally he seemed satisfied. He picked up his brushes.

Indira was sitting on a divan on the edge of the terrace, playing with a small Burmese monkey with blue-dyed fur and an opal necklace.

"I must look rather silly," said Arjumand wryly. "Holding a fan and a flower while all I'm thinking of is that poor little monkey. Does he like being blue? Does he like wearing a necklace? Or does he wish he were back in the jungle, swinging from a casuarina tree?"

"Aesthetic bliss," replied Mansur, "is a strictly human capacity, Your Majesty. I doubt if the monkey realizes how beautiful he looks, all blue and jeweled."

"And does that mean that human beings have lost some other attribute?" said Arjumand. "Does it mean that they've lost the bliss of a jungle freedom and a jungle ignorance?"

"Who knows?" parried Mansur. "Maybe the jungle isn't as free as we think it is. Maybe the ignorance of the animals isn't as blissful as we imagine!"

He cocked his head thoughtfully and applied a highlight to one of the pearls. Then he rose and slightly shifted one of the creases in her sleeve.

"You keep looking at me," said Arjumand, "as though I were a bird, or a fish."

"Neither a bird nor a fish, Your Majesty. A creature of infinite complexity!"

Arjumand tiptoed toward the easel and looked quizzically at the half-done portrait.

"Do I really look like that? So smug and placid? With that sickly smile?"

"It is not intended to be a slavishly realistic portrait," muttered Mansur.

"What is it intended to be, then?"

"Ah," said Mansur: "a distillation! Those bottomless eyes, those smiling lips—they aren't meant to be your own. They're the aura, the ineffable essence which hovers about you, beyond the Reality."

"Well," said Arjumand dryly, "I don't pretend to grasp such high-flown phrases, and after all the important thing is that the picture should please my husband."

Mansur gazed at her soulfully with his little brown rabbit-eyes. She was quite aware of his feelings toward her, which were a mingling of lust and snobbism. And for an instant the glimpse of an affair with Mansur crossed her mind. It was anything but pleasant; but it carried an eerie sort of conviction, just as the thought of Haidar's love had carried the glint of the inconceivable. The very absurdity of Mansur in the role of a lover struck her fancy. And there was something else as well. The vision involved a degradation. It involved an act so distasteful that it washed away her suspicions of Khurram. It was as though, by committing some ludicrous adultery in her fancy, she compensated for the lingering grievance that she felt against Khurram and also calmed the quickening of her pulse when she thought about Haidar.

"Come, Indira. The sun is setting." She walked over to the ottoman, stroked the cringing little monkey, and gently lifted Indira's hand.

VII

The Imperial palace was so large that Arjumand had never explored it properly. It rambled off into innumerable corridors and cloisters and loggias, closed-in gardens and adjoining stables and a labyrinth of servants' quarters. One whole wing adjoining the harem was given to the children and their supervisors, who included a Miss Beecham, recently arrived from Surat.

The boys were Mohammed, his father's favorite: a dark and dismal fellow, deeply interested in astronomy and given to brooding and praying. Then there was Shuja, a muscular boy with the shade of a mustache: and just as Mohammed suggested Khusru in his piety and solemnity, so Shuja suggested Shahriyar in his flightiness and frivolity. He wore bracelets on his wrist and a chain of agates around his neck and spent his mornings with Le Coq, dabbling with pastels and water colors. The third was

Aurengzeb, whom the rest of the boys called the Little Serpent, a tense and sinuous child with a gift for intrigue. And finally there was Murad, a lovable, moon-faced nincompoop who spent most of his time down in the stables with the grooms.

The girls were Jehanara, who was the pretty one, with sea-blue eyes and the cheeks of a Mongol; and Roshinara, the inquisitive one, with jet-black hair and a face like a cat's.

Miss Beecham taught the girls how to play on the gilded harp which had recently arrived from Paris; and she taught the boys how to read Latin, including the *Eclogues* of Vergil and some scattered bits of history and oratory.

"Do they seem to be behaving, Miss Beecham?" inquired the Empress.

"As well as could be expected, or even better," said Miss Beecham equivocally. "Jehanara is a trifle vain, she keeps peeping into the mirrors, and Roshinara is rather nervous, continually rushing along the corridors, but they're both fond of music and their French is rapidly improving."

"And the boys?"

Miss Beecham looked through the trellises with a mouselike expression. "Poor little Murad is a little slow, yes, slow is the appropriate word for him, but his nature is cheerful and he's far from disobedient. Mohammed is clever but I never know what to make of him. He keeps staring into space with those big solemn eyes. Shuja is a darling, full of fun, though I really think it's time that he gave up dolls. As for Aurengzeb, he's a bit of a problem: so darting and mischievous. I found him plucking the wings from some poor little butterfly."

Miss Beecham was a toothy, rectangular woman, with a bellicose gaze which shone through her silver-rimmed pince-nez. When she first arrived in Agra she wore flannels and worsteds but these were soon abandoned in favor of lacy white frills, which she felt were more in keeping with the general atmosphere. These latter had the effect of accentuating her air of transvesti-

tism, what with her deep booming voice and her brusque no-
nonsense gestures. To Arjumand Miss Beecham was always
something of an enigma. But she trusted Miss Beecham; she respected Miss Beecham. And in the end she even grew fond of
the equine Miss Beecham.

"Don't you find us rather odd here in India?" said the Empress
whimsically.

"Well, you're not," said Miss Beecham, "what we'd call conventional in Liverpool. But *chacun à son gout,* as I keep on insisting."

"Are you happy here?" said the Empress.

Miss Beecham lifted her chin a little. "Happiness, Your Majesty,
is not an attitude that I have troubled to cultivate. I am contented,
if you wish, for I feel that I am performing a mission. I insisted on
coming to India, which is a considerable distance from the English coast, and I may state that to my knowledge I am the first of
my countrywomen to arrive in India. I shan't be the last, I trust
sincerely. There is much that we can teach you, if you'll pardon
my saying so. Not only our cooking, which is more wholesome
that these interminable curries, but also—how shall I put it—a
certain emotional self-discipline. Don't misunderstand me, please,
Your Majesty. It's not that the English are frigid, though that is
the reputation we enjoy among the Latins. It is merely that we've
learned after bitter experience that it's better to abandon certain
ultra-romantic notions and be spared, in compensation, the pangs
and flurries, the fleshly fevers. Do I make myself clear? I'd rather
sit with my tea and muffins than indulge in amorous orgies, however colorful these might be. The reason being, if I may phrase it
so, that a cup of tea makes our loneliness palatable, whereas the
orgies (if they really exist, and I am reliably informed that they
do exist) would in the end merely render it bleak and degrading."

After this long and heartfelt speech Miss Beecham got up from
the couch and said, "You'll pardon me, Your Majesty? It's time
for Shuja's Cicero." She bowed stiffly to the Empress, who de-

tected in her eyes, gleaming icily behind their pince-nez, a strange
and secret plangency.

VIII

The intensity of the heat had left an afterglow in the air. A ruddy
brightness clung to the cove, like the flush after a fire, and the cattails rose stiff and black in the shallows. As she walked through
the trees she felt the grass crackling beneath her: the earth was
brittle and parched, on the brink of explosion. She paused on the
edge of the pier. A coppery glaze lay over the water, and as she
stood there the air started to throb with the screaming of insects,
a multitudinous clamor so shrill that it was almost inaudible.

And it seemed, in that stillness which was fringed with an invisible hysteria, that some shadowy coalescence of time was oc-
curring, that the years were melting together, and that the day
was losing its identity, that the future and past were indistin-
guishably blended. There was a shifting of shadows as the light
died over the Jumna; the remnants of another reality were materializing in the half-light. The overhanging boughs were ruffled
by an invisible passenger and a deeper transparency hung over
the tense, burnished inlet.

She grew aware of a voice that was speaking close beside her:
quite distinct, but so frail that it was hardly more than the whispering of an insect. Someone was saying: "Look, Hakim! Do I
see a star? Look carefully, Hakim!" And another voice replied:
"It's the Star of the Golden Crocodile. But wait! Two more minutes! There'll be another one if you're patient!"

She reached out her hand, groping in the stillness like a som-
nambulist. A coolness swept past her, rippling her sari. She felt

poised on the brink of some violent illumination. The reeds shone in the sunset like a row of sabers.

But the moment subsided like a ripple dying in the water. All was silent again as the dusk crawled over the inlet.

As she turned toward the path again, she saw a man standing in the shade of a willow tree. She cried out: "Sirkandar!" But then she saw that it wasn't Sirkandar. It was a youth in a yellow turban who was standing beside the water, eyes fixed on her tensely, lips parted expectantly.

She walked up to him casually and said: "Haidar. What are you doing here?"

He lowered his eyes and blushed. "I hope you'll forgive me. I came on an impulse."

"An impulse! My boy, don't you realize that this is ridiculous? Creeping through the bushes like a brigand—they'll throw you in the dungeon if they find you here."

"It's only for a moment," said Haidar breathlessly, with a yearning look at Arjumand. "Oh, I know that it's ridiculous. Everything about it is ridiculous. Love is ridiculous and hope is ridiculous but there it is. I wanted to see you."

Arjumand clasped her hands together, struggling to keep down her panic. "Haidar, please. Leave at once. Agra is not a healthy place for you. You don't know what it's like here. There are listeners in every cranny. It's a harsh world we live in and there is nothing to be done about it."

"Yes, I know," stammered Haidar, and his hands shook violently. "I'll be going. It's only for a moment. I wanted to look at you, that's all. Tomorrow I'm leaving for Benares and from Benares I'm going on a pilgrimage."

Arjumand looked at him thoughtfully. He looked so pitifully young and helpless, with his great oxlike eyes and his quivering, pleading lips. She looked quickly away and said: "Yes? What sort of pilgrimage?"

"I'm traveling into the mountains."

"Yes? Where?"

"To Kapilavastu. That's the village where the great Siddartha was born. And under the tree I'll shave my head and I'll take up the begging bowl. It's there that I'll find my peace. I'll go wandering through the wilderness."

He spoke with a passionate urgency and stared tensely into her eyes. Then he bowed and said quietly, "Goodbye, Your Imperial Majesty."

"My poor child," whispered the Empress.

Haidar looked at her gravely; a tear rolled down his cheek and he turned away and entered the forest.

IX

The violence of the heat still hung over Agra. The Jumna had turned into a dismal black trickle. The Imperial gardens were a maze of dusty, rattling skeletons and out in the deer park the trees were as brittle as copper. One evening Khurram and Arjumand were sitting in the harem, playing dice. It was a small inner room called the Chamber of Crystal, painted silver and blue, with crystal bells dangling from the ceiling.

Khurram said: "I have just decided. I am leaving for Bijapur."

"Is there anything," said Arjumand sullenly, "of particular interest in Bijapur?"

"Not to you, I should imagine. But to me most definitely. The revolt in the Deccan is spreading. I rather doubt if you'd understand."

"You're perfectly right," retorted Arjumand. "And I'll never understand. Killing, killing, nothing but killing. Will there never be an end to all this killing?"

"Since when," said Khurram frostily, "are you so concerned with political matters?"

"It has nothing to do with politics. I merely loathe this endless bloodshed."

"People live and people die. Death comes in many ways. Being killed on a battlefield is less unpleasant than many other ways."

"You are not especially concerned with human life, I have noticed."

"Look at India!" cried Khurram. "To the west rocky deserts, to the east festering jungles and to the south a boiling sea. And all around us nothing but people, millions of clamoring superfluous people, gaunt with hunger, rotting with sores, worshiping filthy little gods, being born for no good reason and begetting others and finally dying. And why? What's the point of it? I insist on seeing a point in it! The only point I can see is a bringing of order to this insanity, the imposition of power, the creation of a purposeful Empire."

"Don't you ever," said Arjumand, "feel something rumbling deep beneath you? Something churning, like a gathering earthquake? Changes brewing? Terrible changes?"

"There will always be inevitable changes. But they must move in a single direction."

"Oh, this blind fanaticism of yours! This single-mindedness," said Arjumand bitterly. "Yes, there'll always be changes but you won't be able to control the changes. Raging hordes will come sweeping down from the mountains and deserts, men with torches and knives ripping your empire into pieces!"

The Emperor fixed an abysmal black stare on the Empress. "What has happened? Why have you changed so? What have I done? What have *you* done?"

Arjumand looked away quickly, feeling the rage rising up in her. "Precisely nothing. And that is the trouble. Nothing had happened between us. Neither anger nor love and neither tenderness nor understanding, and there might just as well be a wall of ice between us."

"Very well," said Khurram softly. A small blue vein was twitching in his temple. "You are one kind of creature and I am another and there it is. There's no meeting of minds. And there'll never be as long as we live."

"God help us," said Arjumand. "You've always despised me and I've always been frightened of you. I used to hope that something would change, that the ice would finally melt. But now I feel nothing. Not even fear. Merely emptiness."

She stared desolately at the dice, which stared back with their merciless eyes. The light danced about her, setting the crystal bells aquiver. She rose from the table and walked slowly toward the door, groping her way like a sleepwalker through the black hollow blindness.

x

After the Emperor had left for Bijapur a curious stillness fell on the palace. The heat was more sickening than ever, tinged with a clammy gray sultriness. The children went shuffling through the corridors, sweaty and plaintive, and even Miss Beecham looked vaguely cowed and distrait. The whole world seemed to be hankering for the rains to begin and Arjumand clung to the shade of her bedroom like an agoraphobiac.

It might have been merely the weather. Everything she looked at seemed to be burning. Her eyes grew watery with pain when she glanced at the sky. The mere appearance of something bright —a copper basin, a fluttering pigeon—set her eyelids aquiver and reduced her to nausea.

The feeling of dread and frustration grew continually more powerful. She felt an agonizing frustration because she had never found the strength to do what she longed to do until it was much too late and the path she had taken was irrevocable. She felt dread because the man to whose fate she had tied her own was a man who filled her with terror, both spiritual and physical; and if the terror remained to the end a matter of inklings and suspicions, that merely served to make it all the more haunting and inescapable. And she felt guilt not only because she felt responsible for Sirkandar's death, as well as for an inner and subtler death in her own character, but also because she felt somehow associated with Khurram's atrocities, and in her closeness to him she had absorbed the aura of evil which surrounded him. Indeed, it almost seemed that her role in his life was more wicked than his own, since hers was a conscious complicity and his was an uncontrollable drive.

And still, when she stopped to think of it, it seemed that there had never been an alternative. Was this what life was intended to be? That nothing could ever be what one hoped for? That life's glories could remain untarnished for the simple reason that they never materialized, and that the deepest emotions could stay poignant only in frustration? If she had fled with Sirkandar, her life with Sirkandar might have crumbled to boredom; and if she had accepted the love of Haidar, her life might have rotted to self-disgust. It might, it might. She would never know. Who ever can tell us what *might* have happened? All she knew was what really had happened—a life of guilt and frustration and dread, tinged with stray little moments of inexplicable joy and secret beauty. And whether some other kind of existence might have brought her a deeper fulfillment, that was something she couldn't know and would go to her grave without knowing.

More and more she turned to opium for relief from this sickening oppression. And after five or six minutes she could feel the heaviness fall away from her. The throbbing in her temples subsided and she felt herself floating in mid-air, gently fanned by invisible wings. She would lie half-undressed and face down on the bed, one arm trailing on the floor, lazily inhaling the eerie sweetness. Her hair slid over her shoulders, sleek and cool as a viper, and the unfolding of the atmosphere was like an opening of petals.

In her dream she saw herself spread over the sky like a bird, a three-winged vulture with the head of a woman. Her serpentlike hair floated in the starlight as she flew. She flew and kept flying, crossing deserts and jungles, listening to the wail of the jackals and the whimpering of hyenas. She crossed volcanoes that vomited their flames over the prairies. She crossed lakes where the cranes dipped their beaks in the crystal waters.

When she rose from her trance it was a descent from the clouds. There was a buzzing in her ears; blue-hot arrows flashed in the air. She focused her mind on the gradual reconstruction of the outer world, like the pieces of a puzzle gradually materializing out of the vapor. She glanced at the mirror: a ravaged countenance looked anxiously back at her with big, glassy eyes that bulged over their pouches.

She looked through the window into the L-shaped courtyard. Her favorite horse, the snowy Fatima, was being brushed and rubbed down by a big black groom in a yellow loincloth.

There were footsteps behind the curtains. Indira entered the room. She had just stepped out of her bath; her face was rosy with health and energy. She wore a dress of green muslin with a camellia tucked in her breast. She leaned over and kissed Arjumand playfully on the cheek, and Arjumand caught the fresh, teasing scent of acacias.

"You look happy. A secret messenger?"

"No, nothing so grand as a messenger. Just that green-toothed Kausiki, whom I met down by the water."

"And what did she say?"

Indira laughed. Her beautiful face was illumined with mischief.

"Do you know what she said? 'You'll be seeing him soon. Just be patient a day or two. He's coming.' That's what she said!"

"My darling," said Arjumand, "doesn't it occur to you that you're playing with fire? It's all just childish recklessness. It's terribly dangerous, what you're doing."

"Of course it's dangerous. Why shouldn't it be dangerous? Everything precious is alive with danger, and if the danger isn't an outer one it's an even more insidious inner one. And of the two I prefer the outer. At least I'm able to take precautions!"

"Just as you wish, my chick," said the Empress. "Please don't think that I'm being envious. I wish you every sort of happiness. But I can't pretend to be optimistic."

Indira shrugged her shoulders. "We're alive only once. When they told me that Fernando had gotten away from Mukarrab's horsemen I knew that it wasn't luck, it was a special deed of destiny. And who am I to fight destiny? Love is love. And love is rare. Long ago I loved Khurram. So long ago that I can hardly remember it."

Old Draupadi came limping across the tiles with a tray. She set it on the table between the two women and poured the foamy milk into tall silver beakers. She leered cheerfully at Arjumand, muttered "Health to you, Your Majesty!" and shuffled back through the thick mauve curtains.

Arjumand lowered her head and placed her thumb on the edge of the beaker. "When love loses its freshness everything else grows stale too. Life grows tiresome and squalid and nothing has much point to it."

Indira glanced at her thoughtfully and said: "We mustn't expect men to behave like women, when it comes to this queer little business of lovemaking."

"I never expected fidelity. All I hoped for was tenderness. Even betrayals," said Arjumand, "are unimportant if the love is there."

The two women sat silently, each lost in her thoughts. Finally Indira got up, pressed her palms to her cheeks, and said brightly:

"Dreams, Arjumand! You must stop all this vaporizing. To abandon oneself to drugs is stupid and deadening."

"I'm perfectly willing," said Arjumand, "to live in a world of hallucinations."

"So long as they're sunny and cheerful."

"Even if they're dark and disturbing. The world is ugly. We need illusions. We need opium. There's no way out of it."

Indira looked at her solemnly. "The world is ugly if we submit to it. You're submitting: that's the trouble. You're surrendering. When you needn't surrender."

"Do you call it surrender? This perpetual fever, this agitation? You think you can escape, do you? Riding into the wilderness with your lover's arms around you, heading for some unimaginable freedom and some paradisical happiness. How I wish it were true. Yes, I suppose such things do happen. But I've learned to be pessimistic. I see danger, nothing but danger."

"Well," said Indira, "whatever the priests or the Brahmins may say about it, we're alive only once and I refuse to surrender. If I live after death I'll be a turtle or a mosquito but now I'm Indira and I insist on being Indira!"

She walked softly across the room, cast a quick sharp look through the lattices and hurried along the corridor, singing a song as she went.

XI

Down by the Pavilion of the Lions the boys were playing on the lawn. It was a Siamese game which had recently become fashionable. A net of green raffia had been stretched between two stakes, and Shuja was hitting a ball over the net with a giant spoon while

Murad on the other side was trying to catch it. Indira watched them for a while and then sauntered down the path, past the crumbling stone wall which was covered with clematis.

At the bottom of the path stood the big old willow with its trailing branches. She slid through the leaves and sat down on the wooden bench, and as she sat there she tried to remember what it was that Fernando had said to her: all those words about ships and water, about sails and ropes and fishes. But her joy was so exultant she couldn't concentrate on the words, she merely remembered the sound of his voice and the fluttering of a moth among the leaves.

As she sat there, wrapped in her visions, she felt a stirring close beside her: an undulation along the edge of the log-woven bench, deliberate and abrasive, like a long stealthy finger. She looked down. One of the arms of the bench had come to life: it was gliding slowly toward her with a suave, uncanny grace. She sat motionless. The snake floated lazily across her lap, raised its hooded head inquisitively, as though suddenly startled, and then passed on its way, drifting quietly over her elbow toward the opposite end of the bench.

An uncontrollable scream rose from the bottom of her throat. She flung out her arms and leapt wildly into the darkness.

XII

After Indira had left the room Arjumand sat motionless in front of the looking glass. The haze of opium still lingered in her senses; everything around her looked blurred, disconsolate. As she stared at her reflection she felt that she was utterly plain and colorless, without character or individuality or any sort of vividness.

Her features melted as she stared at them: she watched her face turning into a mask and then from a mask into a ghostlike vacuity. And then she felt that life itself was melting into a spectral fluidity and she was aimlessly floating over an empty gray sea, and the people all around rose and fell like the wandering waves, and she herself was nothing but froth tossed about by the waves. Who was she, after all? Just a bewildered and restless woman, starting to gray a bit at the temples, with mournful pouches under her eyes. Much less clever than Nurmahal, much less charming than Indira, much less beautiful certainly than the invisible Damayanti. She kept staring; and suddenly it occurred to her that she was no longer alive, that the actual Arjumand had died at some point not quite identified, and that her death was merely this watery succession of images, this vista of intimations which haunted her night and day. She kept staring; and then a wasp came darting across the light; it buzzed angrily against the mirror and fell tumbling on her wrist. And the wasp suddenly reminded her that she was still alive after all. Still alive! And life so short! So unrecapturable! So fearfully precious! She glanced at a string of pearls that lay in front of her on the marble demi-lune. What were pearls, what were the ornaments of every palace in Rajputana? Hurry! Hurry! No time to be wasted! So much to do! So far to go still!

The curtains parted behind her and she saw, reflected in the mirror, two young gardeners in sweat-stained loincloths carrying a bundle between them: a limp, long-haired body in apple-green muslin.

XIII

The shutters were drawn. A ladder of light fell on the coverlet, weaving its bright golden slats through the embroidered lotuses. Nagasena, the palace doctor, was sitting beside the couch while a boy waved a fan of palm-leaves behind him.

The blood had been let; the flesh had been seared; the herb-pastes were bubbling and the prayers had been uttered. But Arjumand knew that Indira was dying and that it all had happened too late, there was nothing more that could be done about it.

The smell of opium was still in the air. But this time it was Indira who had taken it, and the pain it was meant to soften was a real and not an imagined one. The Empress leaned over and looked at Indira: at the broad Tartar face with its blue, wide-set eyes, and the full-blown lips that had always been so quick to laughter, and the hair that was so shiny that it looked like a hood of satin.

She said softly: "Do you hear what I'm saying, Indira?"

But Indira lay motionless. Only her eyelids flickered faintly.

Nagasena sat with his head sunk low over his chest. After a while he looked up and said quietly to Arjumand:

"So it goes, so it goes. We all look for someone to blame. The snake is not to blame. He was merely the tool of the ice-eyed Mrityu. Nor is Mrityu to blame. He was guided by Kali, the Mother of Destiny. And what about Kali? Even Kali isn't really to blame. After all, everything that Kali decides springs from our earlier lives, our *karman*. So it goes. Evil exists because we were the ones who created it. It's only we ourselves who can cure the evil in our future existences." He glanced mildly at Indira through his heavily lensed spectacles, behind which his dark, solemn eyes bulged like a frog's. And he kept on muttering softly: "Impermanence! Evanescence! It's the misery, Your Majesty, of human evanescence!"

It grew darker. A bell started to ring in the Tower of Jasmines. Down in the courtyard by the stables a donkey was braying. Arjumand closed her eyes and leaned back in the chair. She fell asleep, or half-asleep; time and place shed their identity. She felt that someone had come and sat down beside her: another woman, intensely familiar and at the same time frighteningly strange, slenderer than she, still young and pretty, with a pearl on her forehead. She sensed all these things even though her eyes were still closed, and she whispered to the newcomer: "Tell me, what have I done wrong? Where did I make my fatal blunder? Is there anything I can do still? Or is it all over?"

She opened her eyes. No one at all was sitting beside her. The room was nearly dark and Nagasena was kneeling by the couch, his hands clasped together, his face pressed into the coverlet.

And she thought: "Very well. I've been stupid. Murderously stupid. We live only once in this world and I've been stupid."

PART NINE

The Search

It was midnight when the Empress went tiptoeing down the stairs, dressed in a brown linen cloak, with a long black shawl over her head. She had darkened her cheeks and drawn lines over her brow. The watchman in the courtyard glanced at her casually and turned away again.

Down by the lodge old Draupadi and the groom were waiting in the shrubbery. They walked silently down the path, Draupadi swinging her lantern, and they came to the wicket gate in the southern wall of the park. Jali took out his key and turned it softly; the gate creaked open. A thin, filtered starlight hung over the road that pointed to Delhi.

Three horses were grazing among the trees by the road: not the beautiful Fatima, of course, who was too delicate for this kind of voyage, but three little mares, two black and a chestnut, from the officers' stables. Jali tied on the hampers and held out the stirrup. Arjumand mounted the chestnut mare and they started down the road.

They rode quietly under the stars, feeling the warmth ooze up from the valley. Dead leaves and dry twigs kept crackling under the hoofs. Now and again a heap of pebbles went tumbling as they crossed a hillock. Once they saw the flames of an encampment on the slopes beyond the river.

After a while, to relieve the loneliness, Draupadi started to chat. "Listen," she whispered. "There are hundreds of noises if you only listen carefully! Things rustling and rattling. Worms creeping. Grasshoppers clicking."

And then she said: "Just look at the stars! Thousands and thousands! What are stars? Are they torches hung in the dark there by the All-inquisitive Siva? Or are they diamonds which the sky-nymphs have scattered across the heavens?"

And finally she said: "Yes, it's difficult, this business of being a woman. Daughters are the slaves of their families. Wives are the slaves of their husbands. Spinsters are the slaves of their virginity and harlots are the slaves of everybody. I've decided to become a nun, Your Majesty. Only the nuns belong to nobody. I'll go riding into the mountains, and after you've left me I'll keep riding till I find a nunnery."

They rode for six days. They passed through Oudh and entered the hills. They crossed range after range, split by deep and waterless torrents. They looked down on thirsty valleys and dusty ravines. Now and then they came to a spring trickling feebly out of a rock and Draupadi filled the goatskin while Jali watered the horses. The villages along the way looked grim and half-deserted: there was only a scattering of bow-legged patriarchs and insectlike children, too listless and enfeebled even to glance at the passing voyagers. Once they passed a long caravan on its way from the Himalayas, carrying furs and Chinese silks and bags of asafoetida, which would be bartered in the west for Persian rugs and Arabian pearls. On the slopes they saw the skeletons of camels and donkeys and occasionally a jackal lurking in the underbrush. One evening they passed some pilgrims on their way from Nepal. They cried out to Jali: "Turn back, boy! There's plague in the villages!" But still they kept riding, heading for the great Siddartha's birthplace, and the thought of Haidar with his begging-bowl kept hovering in front of Arjumand. And then finally they came to a village, a jumble of huts among some junipers, and they caught the sweet raisinlike smell of the floating pestilence. Old women couched by the road, scooping the earth over the corpses, and a *saddhu* stared skyward as he burned a sacrifice to Kali. The three travelers folded their cloaks in front of their faces and rode with lowered heads into the rhododendron forests.

Northward they rode, continually northward. Away from all the stink and squalor, away from all the savagery and sadness of humanity. Toward the freshness of the ferns and the hush of the woods and the chill of the mountains. Gradually Arjumand began to feel that she was riding into a deeper darkness, not only her own earliest beginnings but the very beginnings of the world, with its fog-swept forests and vast inhuman silences. As she lay in the dark on some miserable mattress in a lonely rest house, all the memories of the past grew trivial and irrelevant. All the festivals and ceremonies and all the squabbles and reconciliations were only scenes in an empty dream and the true reality was a dreamless darkness.

11

But the curious thing was, as they finally entered the mountains, that the image of Haidar grew increasingly nebulous and it was the image of Khurram which was beginning to obsess her. First she visualized him as a pursuer, surrounded by his shaggy Rajput horsemen, but this picture of him faded and another rose instead: a grim and brooding figure sitting alone in his bedchamber, with the candlelight shining on his wet throbbing temples. And this image was followed by another—a gray, pathetic Khurram, strangely troubled and terrified, lying alone in the grip of midnight. It was the third of these images which became the most convincing and Arjumand leaned over her saddle and said to Draupadi: "It's strange, isn't it, Draupadi?"

"What, Your Majesty, is strange?"

"There's a darkness that creeps over us when we grow too powerful."

"So it seems," muttered Draupadi. "The good and the bad intermingle."

"Odd, isn't it?" said Arjumand. "I came to fear and detest him. And I could see in his eyes that he scorned and distrusted me. And the world kept on thinking we were blissfully happy."

Draupadi nodded. "So it goes. None of us ever understands another. He's a wicked villainous man, he's a man with a stone for a heart, and I hope you'll excuse my impudence in saying so, Your Majesty. He has a nickname in Agra. Do you know what it is? They call him the Cobra. He kills when he strikes. There's no point in looking for pity in him, they all keep saying. But men are queer creatures. Deep in his blood there's something hidden. Deep in his bones there's something innocent, judging from others that I've known. Maybe it will stay there forever, maybe it will never see the daylight, but there it is, deep inside him, like the gold buried in a mountain."

Arjumand looked over the valley where the heat was bubbling like lava. "I wonder what's been happening to me all of a sudden? What is it, Draupadi?"

"Well, I'll tell you," said Draupadi. "You are looking for a new, fresh soul for yourself."

"I am sick of the old one," said Arjumand bleakly.

"So it seems," said Draupadi. "But remember, my child, one doesn't achieve a self-renewal merely by suddenly deciding to do so. One doesn't shed one's emotional habits as one does a cloak, by shaking one's shoulders."

"How does one do it then?" said Arjumand.

"Time and patience," said Draupadi. "Patience and humility. Humility and solitude. Solitude and suffering. Suffering and tenacity."

"All those things!" said Arjumand mournfully.

"Call it love," said Draupadi. "That's the word that covers everything. With love there is hope and without it there's nothing."

A breeze passed through the spruce trees. The sun was slowly sinking and in the north, vast and fiery, rose the fangs of eternal snow. They passed a humble shrine, a barrel-shaped hut made of pine logs, and farther on, at a curve in the road, rose a rambling little rest house.

III

As Khurram's forces crossed the prairies on their way to Bijapur, they passed through a land of famine and desolation. The fields lay parched, the woods were shrunken, the streams were waterless and the cattle were dying, and a cold black loathing shone in the eyes of the peasants. But the Emperor rode on, ploughing through the dust and the brambles, and one evening he finally arrived on the outskirts of Bijapur, where his army pitched camp and embarked on its siege of the rebels.

It was a long, savage siege. The Emperor's men laid waste the countryside, plundering the crops, burning the villages and desecrating the temples, turning the girls into harlots and the boys into simpering ephebes. And the Bijapuris themselves completed the destruction in self-defense, burning the stocks that were left in the storerooms and killing the oxen in their stables, setting fire to the farm lands, dropping hemlock into the cisterns. So that the plains beyond the city looked like a landscape in hell: black and charred, littered with bones, stinking with rot, steaming with insects, with nothing but lepers still scrounging in the refuse. Even the Emperor's own camp grew dirty and drab as the days wore on. The soldiers, limp and demoralized, lay naked under the tamarisks and at night by their campfires they found relief in the arms of their catamites.

The Emperor had brought along young Veroneo, his architect,

and one still evening they sat in his tent, gazing at the scrolls on the bamboo table.

"It's a bit in the Persian manner, I should say," said Khurram thoughtfully.

"But not in the Persian spirit. The effect will be of impeccable purity."

"Purity. I see," said the Emperor, frowning a little. "A dome of blue-veined marble. Four towers similarly of marble. A pool lined with cypresses. A little austere, I can't help feeling."

"Please consider," said Veroneo, "the quality of the ornaments, Your Majesty. Inlaid flowers of crystal and jasper, sapphire and amethyst, coral and turquoise. Hardly austere, to my way of thinking. And try to visualize the ultimate effect. The actual tombs, I should think, would be placed in the downstairs vault, in which silver would be the dominant theme of decoration. And I hope to design the cupola with considerable ingenuity, so that the murmuring of prayers will rise and echo in the arching hollows. Splendor of detail; subtlety of acoustics; and there's a third effect to consider—that of the light continually changing in the course of the day. This exquisite white dome will be tinted with rose in the morning, it will shine like snow at noon, and in the deep glow of sunset it will turn to a filmy gold, so that the marble will melt into the light of the clouds. And at night, if the moon is out, it will look like a silver bell, so melodious that people will hear the echoes lingering in the distance. And if there happens to be no moon the effect will be even stranger—a vaporous silhouette, more like a ghost than a mausoleum."

"How long," said Khurram carefully, "would it take to finish the building?"

Veroneo scowled slightly. "Twenty years, if all goes properly. Two thousand workmen, including the jewelers. Quite an investment, needless to add. But the achievement will be unparalleled. Nothing in the world will rival its loveliness."

Some half-formed misgiving seemed to be lurking in Khurram's mind. He placed his chin on his palm and ran his thumb over the scroll. "You've almost converted me when it comes to the minarets and the marble, my dear fellow. But another idea occurs to me. I have a passion for symmetry, as you've noticed. Not an exact and slavish symmetry, but a suave, implicit symmetry, and while marble and whiteness seem exactly the thing for Her Majesty, now that I visualize her character in the coolness of distance, I can't help thinking that something dark, maybe porphyry, would be more appropriate for me. Two such sepulchres, identical in structure, one of them white and the other black. The idea has a very definite appeal to me, Geronimo."

"Well," said the Italian, smiling coquettishly, "it's a thought worth considering. But first let's tend to the white one; there'll be plenty of time for the other. One white and one black. You have a fanciful touch, Your Majesty."

IV

"Tell me, Geronimo. You've come from a very different part of the world. Some call it more civilized and some call it less so. Such things are a matter of personal opinion. I don't deny that the life in our villages leaves considerable to be desired, but on the other hand I wonder if it isn't much the same everywhere—there are always the rich and the poor, the latter inevitably more numerous, and the delicacies of life will always be in the hands of a minority. So it was, so it is and so it will continue to be until the volcanoes pour forth emeralds instead of lava. And such being the case, in a land as vast as India, anything that remotely resembles justice is out of the question, and anything like human prosperity is also out of the question. And as for religion, I've given up hoping that the purity of Islam will ever appeal to these groveling hordes. Two things remain, and it seems reasonable to hope that they'll eventually be achieved. The first is to weld these scattered provinces and rebellious sultanates into a coordinated empire, for without that India will never achieve her true destiny, she will never even exist as India. A bit of luck, a bit of patience, a bit of ruthlessness and it will be done. The second thing is this: when I look across this land and see nothing but endless squalor and a devastating anonymity, it strikes me that something is needed to exalt our sense of individual dignity. Cringing in front of naked idols, rubbing cow dung in the hair—these aren't things which will ever inspire us with a sense of exaltation. Some day when I'm sick of Agra (and, frankly, I am already wearying of Agra) I plan to build a fortress of red sandstone in Delhi, infinitely grander than my grandfather's fortress in Agra, and Delhi will become the capital of my great and final Empire. I can't help feeling that old Akbar made a terrible blunder of Fatehpur-Sikhri—all these sprawling pagodas just for silly entertainment, and all of it done in a vulgarly synthetic Buddhist style. Do you see what I'm driving at? What India needs is magnificence. Less of this flesh-defiling spirituality and more awareness of human power. I refuse to accept this fatalistic Hindu passivity. I'll build a sepulcher which will symbolize the triumph of the human spirit not only over misery and monotony but even over death itself. That's the point of it, Geronimo. To celebrate not human death but the human triumph over the darkness of death."

Khurram delivered this speech in a deep, urgent voice, with his fists clenched over the table and his eyes fixed on space. Suddenly his body slumped a little, as though gliding out of a trance, and his eyes grew soft and intimate as he looked at Veroneo.

"What do you think of it, Geronimo? Do you see what I'm trying to say?"

Geronimo's ironical smile grew gentle, almost pitying. "Oh, most definitely, Your Majesty, you are trying to say something which is deeply important to you, and which, if you'll pardon my saying so, explains your whole character. Human magnificence, human grandeur—all these things which seem to obsess you, what are they after all but a frenzied protest against death? You cry out against death with fortresses and sieges, with thrones and sepulchers. Maybe you've even cried out against it by bringing death to others. Men have cried against death with exquisite music, deathless poetry, sublimity of thought, selfless suffering, and ironically enough with cruelty and bloodshed. So it is. All that's marvelous and immortal in man's achievement can be traced, if we just look deep enough, to his passionate awareness of death's terror."

Khurram looked at Geronimo with his black fanatical eyes. He reached across the table and took his hand in his own. He held it tenderly, almost amorously, with his eyes still fixed on Geronimo. He breathed a deep sigh, as though remembering a long-lost secret, and a shy furtive smile passed over his face, half-reluctantly.

"My boy, you've got a way of coming to the heart of the matter, haven't you? There's truth in everything you say, though I rather doubt if it's the whole truth. What we feel is never simple. It can't be put in a single word. Our reasons for what we do are always a hundred different reasons. Yes, I feel I'm growing old already when I look at you, Geronimo. I was once as handsome as you, and just as clever, and just as brave. But time passes, everything passes, the brow grows wrinkled, the hair turns gray, and what's left for us in the end is only a bundle of weird little memories."

v

Soon after dawn, as they stood on the porch of the rest house, the ladies were joined by an elderly monk. His name was Bilhana, he said, and he was also traveling to Kapilavastu. He was a weather-beaten man who had come all the way from Kandy. There was a mole on the end of his nose, which he stroked with a thoughtful air, and merry pink creases spread from his eyes like the rays of a sunburst. He rode next to Arjumand on his cinnamon-hued donkey, and as they rode he told her about the life and meditations of Gautama.

Queen Maya-devi, so he explained, had conceived a supernatural being, a tiny elephant which entered her body through a fold in the robe; and six months later, amid portents and prodigies, a wailing of birds and a falling of stars, she gave birth to the incomparable Buddha in the garden of Lumbini. Maya-devi died of a fever some days after his birth and her sister Mahaprajapati reared Siddartha (which was his personal name) in considerable wealth and comfort, in a setting of fountains and oleander blossoms. He grew into a good-looking youth and married his cousin, Yasodhara, who bore him a son whom they called Rahula. One day as he left the palace he met an old white-haired man who was limping along, hunchbacked and haggard, clutching at his cane. And a little further, under the trees, he saw a cripple covered with sores. Some minutes later a funeral procession walked past him on the highway, and when he came to a bridge he saw a blind ascetic sitting in the sunlight. These four successive visions carried the impact of a revelation: he saw in a blaze of light the spiritual enslavement that comes from suffering. And that night, alone and secretly, he rode from his home, even though his heart was torn with grief at the sight of his wife sleeping in the darkness. He rode southward, bartering his clothes and jewels to keep alive, and he sought the great Yogis, the dove-voiced Kalama and the hawk-eyed Ramaputra. But their teachings left him still troubled and unsatisfied, and he wandered through Magadha in the direction of Patna. By now he was lean and ragged, wearing the garb of an ascetic and practicing the keenest, most formidable austerities. And finally one night as he was meditating under a fig-tree in Urubvila, seven years after he'd started on his wanderings, came the great Illumination, the *samyak-sambhadi*. And henceforth he was Buddha, free from the temptations of Mara the Wicked One, the god of love and decay, who had offered him the delights of the world. He had passed beyond the capacity for pain or for pleasure; he had finally discovered the secret of all being. He stood above good and evil, and beyond the demons and divinities. He saw the One True Way which leads to deliverance. He set out for Benares on the following morning and there he preached his sermon on the Wheel of the Law. Disciples gathered about him and his fame spread through India, over the water to Bangkok and northward to the Brahmaputra. He kept wandering and preaching for forty-three years, excluding the rainy seasons, until he was a wrinkled man in his seventies. One night near Kusinagara he came to the hut of the blacksmith Chunda, who gave him a plate of freshly cooked boar's meat. That night he felt sick and the spasms crept over him. He called his favorite disciple to his side and muttered hoarsely: "Nothing lasts, my sweet Ananda. Everything passes. Everything vanishes." And thus he finally attained the state of Nirvana.

The light of the sun fell through the dry, spicy pine needles. Jali the groom and old Draupadi were riding behind Arjumand. They passed a great waterfall which tossed rainbows over the valley as though they were veils of many-colored silk. And now

Bilhana, having finished his narration of Buddha's life, started to tell about the faith and wisdom of Buddha. He pointed out that the essence of Buddhism resided in the Three Great Jewels: the figure of Buddha himself, which he had just been describing; the *samgha*, or community of believers, of which he himself was a wandering representative; and the actual law, the *dharma*, which he was about to explain to Arjumand. He mentioned casually that he himself, being a member of the clergy, was forced to abstain from any form of sexual intercourse; he owned nothing but the heap of yellow rags he was wearing, as well as a spoon and a rice bowl, a razor, a needle and a sieve, this latter being essential to protect the tiny water-beasts from being swallowed while he was drinking.

"And what are the teachings of Gautama?" said Arjumand.

"His teachings," said Bilhana airily, "are the teachings of the Middle Way, which is based on the recognition of the Noble Truth, the *aryasatyani*. The truth of pain: all that exists in the world is subject to suffering. The truth of the origin of pain: suffering springs from desire. The truth of the alleviation of pain: which lies in the suppression of desire. And the truth of the elimination of pain, which lies in the Noble Eightfold Path—the rightness of intuition, of will, of speech, of behavior, of habits, of aspiration, of thought and of concentration."

"I'm afraid," said Arjumand, "that it would take me many years to achieve these rightnesses."

"To achieve them fully, perhaps," said Bilhana, smiling cheerfully at Arjumand. He snapped a dead leaf from an overhanging bough. "But is it really so intricate? What are the enigmas in our life, the terrors? They are suffering, age and death. And why do we die? Because we are born. And why are we born? Because we thirst for existence. And why do we thirst? Because we hanker for pleasure. And why do we hanker? Because we imagine that we really exist as people, we think that the contacts between our flesh and the world are real contacts, whereas the truth of the matter is that these contacts are quite illusory, since we never exist as entities and live in a state of perpetual change. We *become* rather than *are;* there's nothing in us which is firm or lasting. And please remember, my dear lady, that the human mind, such as it is, doesn't reflect the truth like a mirror, it must shine with the truth like a lantern. It isn't knowledge which must be achieved, it is vision and understanding. Not a multiplicity of facts but a harmony of insight."

They paused for their noonday rest in a little village in the middle of the woods. Some raffia awnings had been set on poles in a circular market place, and the people from the adjoining valleys had come for their weekly marketing. Fruits and spices, dappled with sunlight, lay heaped in yellow baskets. One old man was selling rice-spirits; another was selling sherbets. The voyagers ate and drank and then lay down in the shade of the temple. A boy up in a tree started to play on a flute. And one by one they spread their arms and closed their eyes and fell asleep.

VI

The Empress woke to the sound of drumbeats deep in the valley. The sunlight over the trees had changed into a grape-tinted darkness. And as she sat there, rubbing her eyes, the raffia awnings started to tremble and the villagers snatched their baskets and went scurrying toward the temple.

"Wake up, Draupadi," cried the Empress. "Jali, wake up! Wake up, Bilhana!"

And they picked up their spoons and hurried down to the horses, which were flicking their tails in the clearing below the village.

"Shall we stay, do you think?" said Jali. "Or head for the rest house before it rains?"

"It's not far," said Bilhana. "A bit of a soaking—what does it matter?"

So they started through the woods, feeling the air grow cool and agitated, smelling the menace in the trees, listening to the rumbling in the gullies. A black cloud moved out of the east, from the vale of the Gogra. It changed shape as it went: from a toad to a camel, from a camel to an elephant, and from an elephant to a whale. The rumbling became a roar. The branches swayed frantically. The horses took fright and went galloping through the forest. A great streak of lightning set the landscape on fire. The cliffs turned to platinum and the pines dropped white-hot needles. The foliage started to rattle under the great leaden drops. Suddenly the sky burst wide open and the air turned into a torrent.

After the first violent outburst the storm steadied down. The travelers were drenched; they leaned low over their saddles. Great streams of pink mud started to spurt out of the hillside and the road was transformed into a web of rivulets. Everything looked flattened and disheveled in the valley below: crashed trees, battered thickets, twisted ferns flung hither and thither, and a foamy cascade gushing from the lip of the gully.

They rode on, scarcely able to find their way through the downpour. The light grew so dim that dusk seemed to have fallen. The chestnut mare and the little donkey were just as black as the other two. Their manes hung down streaming; their necks looked scrawny and elongated. Arjumand felt an icy trickle run down her breast, as sleek as a lizard. Her saddle was swollen and slippery with water. She clutched at the reins, fixing her eyes on Jali in front of her, and then the rain started to lessen and the roof of the rest house shone through the evergreens.

VII

The following morning the sun came out. The whole landscape lay transfigured. The dusty grayness of the valley had burst into a wild surge of greenery. Foamy waterfalls came spouting out of a hundred crannies and the air was filled with a multitudinous water-music. Everything sparkled; tiny beasts were crawling out of their shelter; baby snakes and frogs and turtles all came wriggling out of the slime.

The Empress was sitting on the rest house veranda, basking in the sunlight. Suddenly she called to Draupadi:

"Draupadi! Come here, please!"

The old woman looked at her thoughtfully. "It's much too strenuous, this mountain traveling." She moved closer, looking intensely into Arjumand's eyes; she nodded judiciously and ran her palm over her forehead. Then she whispered: "Why didn't you tell me, my poor little swallow? You're with child and here you go galloping over the hills in search of a lover."

"Draupadi, bring me some tea, please."

"You're all of atremble, my child. Rest—that's what you need. Sleep and comfort. And a dose of realism."

"I've made up my mind, Draupadi."

"Yes? What about, Your Highness?"

"We're leaving for Bijapur."

"God help us!" cried Draupadi. "It's a long way to Bijapur, and the roads all covered with water. Wouldn't it be wiser to stay here in the hills a while, Your Majesty?"

"I don't need your advice, thank you kindly, Draupadi. Pack the hamper and explain to Jali. It sounds impetuous but there it is." She reached out and took the old woman's hand in her own. "Forgive me, Draupadi. I feel dull and depleted. I've done what I needed to do. A woman must learn to abandon her dreams."

They said goodbye to the smiling monk; it was nearly noon when they mounted their horses. They rode back to the village with its sun-spangled market place and then started on the long twisting road into the valley. The slopes were littered with débris; uprooted saplings, broken cartwheels, dead birds and dead rabbits, and once they saw the corpse of a child. But the smell of disorder was mixed with the scent of budding and blossoming. Flowers sprouted along the roadside; the meadows were all aglitter.

Arjumand's thoughts, as she rode along, kept drifting insistently back to Khurram. A violent trembling took hold of her, for no good reason that she could think of. Suddenly the image of Khurram set her heart pounding violently, and her eyes filled with tears when she thought of Khurram close beside her again.

"Tell me, Draupadi. Why is the world created with so much superfluous misery? Is it the reason that Bilhana told us? Simply our yearning to feel alive?"

"That's what he said," said Draupadi, scratching her earlobe reflectively, "and I couldn't help feeling that there was a definite grain of truth in it. And yet, now that I think of it, there's something unexplained. There's something about it that he didn't consider sufficiently."

Arjumand looked at her anxiously. "And that something? What is it?"

Draupadi shook her head. "I'm an ignorant woman, Your Majesty. It's rather ridiculous, this notion of my turning into a nun. Nothing in the world could be more silly than Draupadi becoming a nun. There are things in our stupid hearts that are more powerful than Buddha's wisdom, and if we suffer for it, Your Majesty, very well, then let us suffer for it."

VIII

That same morning young Prince Aurengzeb went riding into
the forest. A brownish haze crept over the sun and puffs of powder burst from the hoofs. His horse, Hamadullah, was a sorrel
gelding with a thick white mane. He stepped daintily over the
dust as though it were a carpet of velvet, trying to avoid the fallen
twigs and keeping an eye out for the snakes. He was fond of his
master Aurengzeb; he sniffed gratefully at the woody spices; but
he whisked his tail nervously, there was restlessness in his eyes.

"What do you think, Hamadullah? Am I cleverer than Mohammed? I'm much cleverer than Murad, certainly. Murad is a
halfwit, but I'm fond of Murad. Old Draupadi said that Shuja is
heading for corruption. She can see it in his eyes, she said. He'll
end up like our uncle Shahriyar. And Miss Beecham says that
Mohammed is turning into a bookworm. A bookworm becoming an Emperor! It's absurd, Hamadullah, isn't it?"

The horse kept flicking his ears as he listened to Aurengzeb.
But he gave no reply except for the whisking of his tail.

The bridle path curved through a stretch of brittle evergreens.
The pine cones kept bursting under the hoofs like hollow shells.

"What about it, Hamadullah? Shall we stay here in India? Or
shall we ride out to the west, toward the Kingdom of Sindh?
There are wonderful beasts in Sindh; I've read about them in a
book. Great silver-tusked camels, snakes with rubies set in their
eyes. Or we can ride to Kabul, which is even stranger than Sindh,
with birds as big as elephants that fly over the mountains."

The air was so tense that the sweat burst from his temples. The
light became greenish. A smell of phosphorus was in the air. In

the distance he could hear a stealthy rustling among the saplings, like some great beast of prey prowling closer through the thicket.

"What's the point of it, Hamadullah? Here we are, you and I. To a bird up in the sky we're no bigger than a couple of ants. Why were we born, do you imagine? Just to fill a bit of space? Just by an odd sort of accident? I keep wondering but I can't explain it. Here we are, just the two of us, and you're the loveliest horse in the stables and I'm the cleverest of the princes, and we're riding through the woods. It can't just be an accident, can it, Hamadullah?"

The heat welled about them like the steam of a geyser. Way in the north there was a rumbling: the far-off galloping of a herd. The light suddenly turned into a turtle-brown shimmer. A zigzag of lightning split the overloaded sky.

And then it came. First a fluttering among the boughs, tense, excited. The leaves turned their pale yellowed undersides toward the dimming light. When Aurengzeb looked up he saw a great mass of darkness, like a range of blue hills, suddenly rising over the jungle. A shudder ran through the park: and then the thunder exploded, a roar so stupendous that Hamadullah reared frantically, twisting his head back and forth and lashing desperately with his tail. A large drop, warm as blood, fell on Aurengzeb's forehead, and this was followed by another and then immediately by fifty others. A scurrying darkness covered the woods, split by shots of greenish light; the dust went spinning about in little white whirlpools. The balloon which hung over Agra burst into a great sheet of fire and the rain started to slash at the land with a million knives.

I X

There was a tumbledown hut where the Emperor's woodmen kept their tools, and here the boy took refuge with his horse Hamadullah. The storm snapped at the shingles and rapped savagely at the door but there was a deep, earthy peacefulness inside the hut, like that in a cave. Some logs were heaped in a corner, exuding a smell of fresh sap. A saw and a hatchet gleamed faintly in the darkness. Flashes of lightning shone fitfully through a crack in the door, turning the rain into a cataract of white-hot needles.

The horse stood motionless in the corner with his ears flattened backward. Now and again a kind of spasm went rippling over his belly. The boy stripped the dark dripping clothes from his body and tossed them over the logs and curled up on a burlap sack. He closed his eyes and waited. And after a while he fell asleep.

He dreamed that he was riding over the mountains of Afghanistan. The hills kept on rising until they were a part of the sky; and all around him swarmed the clouds, waving their trunks like a herd of elephants. Suddenly a voice rang out of the clouds, deep and strong, like a bell. It said: "Aurengzeb! Aurengzeb! Wake up out of your dream! The Gandharvas are waiting for you! They are weaving your fate with their long white fingers!"

And Aurengzeb woke up again. He listened to the drumbeats on the shingles. The rage of the tempest had turned into a powerful steady downpour. He lay motionless for a while, watching Hamadullah's shadow, which shifted uneasily in the cavernous half-light. And then gradually, almost subconsciously, he grew aware of another presence. Some sort of creature, maybe a monkey, sat huddled beside the door. He could hear the faint dripping of the raindrops from its arms; a thin slant of light fell on a shiny brown head.

For an instant he was filled with terror: this wasn't a beast, nor was it a man. Could it be some wicked swamp sprite, or one of the wild Rakashas? Or the Lord of the Estuaries, the hairy-faced Hanumat? He crouched on his sack and cried out, "Who are you?" The creature turned slowly and looked at him with its great black eyes. And then he realized that it wasn't Hanumat, it was only a child, some little waif, some lonely wet creature that had crept out of the storm.

"I'm Mandanika," said the girl in a hoarse, timid voice.

"Where do you come from?" whispered Aurengzeb.

She said faintly, "From down by the river. My father is Pandu the fisherman. I was walking back home when the skies cracked wide open. And then everything grew dark and I started to run through the woods."

"I see," said the young Prince thoughtfully. "I don't wonder that you're frightened. It's a terrible storm, isn't it? Never in my life have I seen such lightning!"

Mandanika pressed her hands against her cheeks and said darkly: "Do you know why it is? The Heavenly Spirits are furious. Someone or other has been doing a thing that he shouldn't be doing. Maybe someone has done a murder, or insulted a Brahmin. It's a punishment, that's sure, sent down on the city by the fierce Gandharvas!"

Aurengzeb moved closer to the girl so that he could see her a bit more clearly. Her hair hung over her shoulders in long dripping strands and her wet, narrow face was white with alarm. She might have been fourteen or fifteen. Her dress was drenched with the rain and it clung to her body like the skin of a catfish.

"Those Heavenly Ones," said Aurengzeb: "are they really so powerful?"

"They watch everything that we do. They're clever and cruel," said Mandanika.

"Do they weave out our destiny?"

"So they say," said Mandanika. She leaned forward a little and placed her hand on Aurengzeb's elbow. "They're the ones," she said, awestruck, "who decide what's to become of us. Not only now, while we're still alive, but even long after we're dead. They can turn us into a cricket, or a bush, or a grain of sand. It pays to be friendly to those watchful Gandharvas!"

She spoke with such solemnity that Aurengzeb believed her. He felt the warmth of her body stirring close beside his own. He suddenly felt that he had known Mandanika years ago—in some other guise, conceivably; maybe as a chipmunk or a swallow. He put his arm around her shivering shoulders and said: "Listen, Mandanika! The sky is spitting with rage at that wicked Agra!"

Mandanika said nothing. She pressed her body against Aurengzeb's and he lifted her chin and kissed her tenderly on the face: first on the brow, then on the cheeks, and then impulsively on the mouth. And then, as though he were following some whispered instructions, he drew her dress from her knees and very deftly over her shoulders, and then he tucked it on top of an empty bucket which stood beside them. The rain kept on pounding as they clung together silently, feeling the warmth creeping back into their storm-soaked bodies.

x

One day two young travelers arrived at an inn in the mountains. The wind was rattling the boughs and the flames danced uneasily. A stout broad-cheeked woman took a kettle from the stove and poured out the tea for the sunburned visitors.

One of the men was a strong, handsome fellow in his early twenties. The curly growth of beard made his face look older than it was, but the blue watchful eyes were the eyes of a child. He had tossed his shaggy cloak over a hook behind the door and was lolling beside the brazier, legs sprawled lazily in front of him.

The other was a dark-skinned youth, smooth and frail and faintly effeminate, with an almond-shaped face and black locks that covered his brow. He wore a thickly padded coat of crimson wool embroidered with black; he was sitting by the table with a small white kitten in his lap.

"Yes," said the girl, flicking a bread-crumb from her apron, "that's what they've been telling us. A traveling monk from Sikkim saw him too, maybe a month ago. He was walking across a bridge and lo and behold, there he was, squatting in the middle of the torrent, as big as a buffalo."

"What was he wearing?" said the man in crimson.

"Nothing at all," said the woman cheerfully. "Thick black hairs all over his body to keep him warm, even in the wintertime."

"Are they sure that it isn't a woman?"

"His voice is too deep for a woman's. Once in a while you hear him roaring down in the valley. He sounds like a tiger."

"You've never seen him?"

"No, not I! I keep away from the woods at night, let me tell you. Suvarnakshi says she's seen him but Suvarnakshi's a bit of a liar. She says she was bathing down in the pool one morning and suddenly she saw him peeping through the bushes, all queer and shaggy."

"Some kind of demon," said the man in red, scratching the cat on its belly. "Down in Gondwana there was a demon of the type you're describing. Black and hairy, as big as a donkey, prowling at night on the edge of the village. He had long yellowish tusks. The little girls were scared to death of him."

The other men, who had listened silently, glanced through the window and said mildly: "Look, Shahji. The sun is sinking. We'd better get going before it's night-time." He turned and looked at the woman. "How long will it take us to reach the monastery?"

"Just an hour, if you take it leisurely. Or an hour and a quarter maybe." She ran her broad fingers over her thick braid of hair. "The path goes straight and easy except for the stretch beyond the waterfall. It twists around the chasm. Then it climbs up to the monastery."

The man got up from the floor, placed a coin on the middle of the table, plucked his cloak from the hook and flung it casually over his shoulders. "Demons," he muttered. "I don't believe in them. They're just men who've gone into the wilderness. Hermits, lepers, halfwits, pariahs. Nothing to be scared of. Just the unlucky ones."

The black-haired boy took the kitten and laid her gently in front of the brazier. He sighed and tightened his collar and leaned down to fasten his boots. He glanced lazily at the blue-eyed fellow; a furtive smile moved over his lips. Then he rose, picked up his sack and murmured drowsily, "I'm ready, Haidar."

XI

They climbed the stony path and entered a frozen stretch of forest. In the hard narrow stretches it was Haidar who led the way, probing the stones with his stick and digging his heels in the frozen gravel. The air had turned cold now that the sunlight was fading; but in the treetops the ice-coated twigs were still glittering and the last flakes of light danced like fire in the shivering pine needles.

"Look: that cloud there," said Haidar. "I don't like the looks of it."

"Dawdling about with that stupid woman. Serves us right," said Shahji sulkily.

The sun sank abruptly and the light grew green and ominous; the sky darkened rapidly and turned a bloated violet. The boughs crackled brittly. Then everything grew still. Not a breath stirred the bushes; not a sound rose out of the wilderness. A single huge flake came floating slowly in front of Haidar, and then he saw a second flake and a moment later a hundred others. They were falling so slowly that they seemed to hover in mid-air. A tuft landed on his sleeve and clung there like a feather. He stuck out his tongue: the melting flakes tasted like metal. He felt a tingling on his eyelids, crisp and sharp, like chips of glass. It was the first time in his life he'd seen the snowflakes falling. First they struck him as merely strange, and then as delightful, and then as frightening. The air was possessed by these seething white multitudes, which looked like a migration of millions of moths. They fell more and more swiftly and grew smaller and icier, and then a wind shot through the forest and sent them spinning in ghostly whirlpools.

From the bottom of the valley rose a deep, spreading roar and a ripple of hysteria came whistling through the air. The far-off summits seemed to melt and evaporate. Night fell and the snow changed from white to a furry blue. The flakes went spinning about in an aimless frenzy, rushing hither and thither in the icy confusion. Gusts came swooping across the path and whisked the snow from the ground and little pale flurries rushed past them like phantoms. Now the peaks were completely hidden, not a thing could be seen, neither the trees nor the bushes, only the blinding veil of snowflakes. The air grew cold as a hatchet. Haidar's eyes were watering with the cold; drops of ice hung from his eyelashes and jets of pain stabbed at his temples.

The wind grew more violent. The boughs creaked and chat-tered. He turned his back to the wind and took hold of Shahji's elbow. "Hold tight!" he screamed hoarsely; he could hardly hear the sound of his voice. They went staggering through the trees, clinging blindly to one another, heads lowered against the wind and elbows raised to shield their faces. The miserable Shahji was trying to say something but Haidar couldn't hear him; all he heard was the feverish clattering and whining in his eardrums.

Now they knew they had lost their way. The path had vanished without a trace. Every five or six steps they had to pause to catch their breath. Their cloaks were stiff with ice, flapping about like sheets of metal. Their beards had turned white and their purple cheeks were burning with tears. Their nostrils were choked with snow so that they had to breathe through their open mouths, and their tongues grew numb with the melting snowflakes. The snow now came racing in a single direction, building drifts around the treetrunks and turning the bushes into igloos. Fallen trunks and tangled roots floated like wreckage on waves of snow and soon even these were submerged in the powdery flood. A thin, steady whimper came oozing out of Shahji and Haidar patted him briskly on the back to encourage him. Now and again poor Shahji stumbled and fell headlong into a drift and Haidar had to kneel and tug desperately to help him up again.

And then casually, as though a curtain had been flung from the Himalayas, the snowflakes stopped falling and a thousand stars shone over the mountains.

XII

And suddenly the landscape grew tranquil and clear under the starlight. The wind died away, echoing faintly in the distant valleys. The woods grew eerily still. The only sound was the squeak of the boots and the coppery click of the ice-hardened cloaks. Tufts of snow, light as foam, lay afloat on the branches; now and again a plume of powder sank through the darkness and vanished.

The snow was up to their knees. It was like wading through quicksand. They plowed ahead grimly but the woods grew still denser—aisle upon aisle of shrouded evergreens and froth-dappled saplings.

"What now?" whispered Shahji.

"It can't be far," said Haidar gently.

"What's the point?" muttered Shahji. "We can't go on. There's no use trying."

"We'll look for a place to rest a while," said Haidar, glancing about him.

"Yes? And then?" said Shahji miserably.

"We'll wait till it's morning. The sun will be out."

"The sun!" whimpered Shahji. "That marvelous sun down in the Deccan! How I hated that horrible sun! Oh, how I wish that the sun were shining!"

"Hush," said Haidar. "Stop chattering. We'll look for a place to rest. In the morning it will be easier. The snow will start melting."

On they went, struggling through the snowdrifts, clutching at the boughs to keep their balance. In spite of the hacking cold Haidar's face was covered with sweat. The thin mountain air set him gasping and panting. His heart pounded feverishly. He tasted blood in the back of his throat.

The woods ceased abruptly and they came to the edge of a precipice. The valley lay spread below them, a gulf of frozen breakers, and beyond rose the Hills of Heaven, range after range of steel-blue summits. Now the moon came rising slowly from an eastern peak, like a silver bubble; the snow began to glitter; a silky sheen spread over the valley. The stillness of all those summits was so huge and intense that it seemed to burst out of its own immo-

bility. Streams of quicksilver poured from the slopes and wands
of phosphorus danced on the pinnacles; the whole valley was
simmering with white-hot lava. Never had Haidar seen a sight so
inhumanly terrible and yet so magical. He forgot the pain in his
flesh as the glow of wonder swept over him. He stood motionless,
staring at the mystery and majesty which confronted him: so vast
that the very thought of human suffering seemed irrelevant and
the suffering itself was soothed and extinguished.

He caught sight of a shadow in the side of the hill, a small
snout-shaped hollow that looked like a cave. He tugged briskly at
Shahji's elbow and dug his way through the drift and five minutes later they were crawling through the mouth of the cavern.

XIII

The entrance of the cave was half-covered with a snowdrift but
further back there was only a sprinkling of snow on the pebbles.
Haidar crawled on all fours toward the back of the cave while
Shahji waited near the opening, whining softly and shivering
violently.

"What's it like, way in back?"

"Nothing but dust and stones," said Haidar.

"No snakes? You're sure?" said Shahji.

"Come," said Haidar. "You need some rest, my boy."

They found a small nook where some moss covered the stones
and lay down with their arms wrapped tightly around each other.
Shahji's teeth were chattering crazily and a feverish trembling
shook his body. He kept nuzzling against Haidar, trying to ab-
sorb a flicker of warmth, but the ice-hardened cloaks were like a
coat of mail between them.

After a while he said softly: "I was a fool, wasn't I, Haidar?"

"Hush," said Haidar. "Stop talking. Try to sleep. You're all worn out."

Shahji pressed his frozen cheek against Haidar's affectionately. Then he closed his aching eyes and after a while he stopped shivering. Haidar spread out his cloak so that it covered both of their bodies; he breathed on Shahji's face, trying to bring a little warmth to it. The wind had died down. The world outside was pale and motionless. All he could see through the mouth of the cave was a slit of sky and an icy pinnacle, so sharp and shiny that it looked like a dagger. The mere sight of that arrowing summit was acutely painful to him: it was as though the point of a knife were probing delicately at his eyeballs.

Time passed; he dozed fitfully. In his dreams he saw a river, and a woman dressed in silver sat weeping by the edge of the river. When she saw him she grew terrified and ran crying into the jungle. He ran after her, begging for forgiveness, but she darted into a temple and when she stepped out of the temple her face was transfigured: it had turned from a shining freshness into a yellowish mass of wrinkles. He fell on his knees and cried: "Darling! My darling!" But she turned away her face and her hair grew gray and furry and suddenly she turned into a great silver moth and flew into the darkness.

He woke up. Someone was calling from the mouth of the cave. He lifted his head and listened intently, waiting for the voice to call again. There was nothing but silence but his heart still kept pounding. He looked at Shahji sleeping: he touched his forehead and then his cheeks. They were stiff and cold as ice. He cried softly: "Shahji! Shahji!" But Shahji lay motionless. He rose to his knees and started to crawl toward the mouth of the cave.

All around him rose the Heavenly Mountains, some of them close and eerily clear, every crevice and defile vivid and sharp, as though seen through a telescope; others veiled in a far-off mist, half-suspended in the air; others blazing like sabers, white with a cold which resembled heat, piercing the starlit blackness with their mineral fury.

The fir trees below seemed to stir very gently. But it wasn't the wind, it was merely the boughs shedding their burdens. Haidar could sense that even in the stillness there was something continually happening; millions of secret little dramas and struggles and annihilations. Miraculous crystals were falling apart, splitting and cracking and disintegrating. Tiny jewels of a dazzling delicacy were congealing into a mass of ice. And when he looked at the stars the infinitesimal blended into the infinite. A single snowflake, if one looked at it carefully, was as intricate as an entire galaxy. Just as the cold dissolved into heat, just as the ice blazed up like fire, so the infinitely small blended into the infinitely vast and a single passing moment blended into the silence of eternity. Haidar felt that he was hovering on the very brink of illumination: one more moment, one more thought, and the whole of life would reveal its meaning to him. He reached out his hand to grasp the meaning like a falling snowflake: but just as he finally caught it, the meaning crumbled and melted away.

He thought of calling to Shahji to come and share in this thrilling vision. But then it occurred to him, as an afterthought, that Shahji was dead and that Shahji was already aware of the whole white dazzle of illumination. A pang of pity shot through him when he thought of Shahji dead and frozen. But then he knew that it hardly mattered. Shahji had entered a new identity and the only thing that mattered was this glowing sense of wonder, this splendor of divination which was slowly sweeping over him.

He thought vaguely: "Am I dying?" But the thought of death had lost its density. The pain had gone from his limbs and all he felt was a simmering peacefulness, a craving for sleep which generated a warmth of its own in his arteries. A warning flashed like a flame: something cried out in him: *"No, no, Haidar!"* But then he realized that the cry of warning was merely the residue of illusion and the only reality was this whiteness which was ma-

terializing in front of him. He cried joyfully, "Shahji! Shahji!"
Shahji reached out his hand and smiled at him. He felt himself
rising and swelling and suddenly bursting: and then he turned
into a little gray bird which fluttered and soared over the Heavenly Mountains.

XIV

The rain started pouring with a lunatic violence, turning the Imperial camp into a mass of stinking puddles and mildewy tents.
Tiny worms started to creep into the rice bags and barley sacks.
The saddles started to rot; the swords were beginning to rust.
Khurram felt tempted to abandon the whole ridiculous siege but
rumors reached him that matters were even worse in Bijapur itself—fetid food and empty water tanks, festering sewage and
creeping dysentery, and the whole population on the brink of
hysteria. So he lay in his tent, grumbling at his guards and curs-
ing his captains, waiting miserably for the day when the gates
would swing open.

As he lay there, half-dozing, listening to the raindrops on the
canvas, he saw himself wandering through a vista of fog-
wrapped memories, like a pilgrim crossing a landscape on his
way to a far-off shrine. He felt that his body had sheltered a
whole series of personalities who had only two things in common:
their flesh and their memories. And even the flesh and the memories seemed to suffer a continual change, dropping a few threads
of hair or a yearning or a hatred, putting on a bulge of fat or a
grievance or an apprehension: his identity seemed to flicker with
doubts and ambiguities and he felt a kind of dizziness which was
almost like a fever. Now and again in the middle of the night he

was seized by a powerful longing, nothing with a name, nothing tangible, nothing to do with Agra or Arjumand, nothing to do with India's glory or a golden throne or a marble sepulcher: a passionate longing for something new, some unimaginable freedom which flickered through his mind like light through a gully.

One evening he sat on his couch with Geronimo beside him. The wine jug was empty; a bowl of almonds stood on the table. The drops kept tapping dismally on the roof of the tent. A small iron brazier was glowing behind the bed.

"Tell me about your city, Geronimo. What's it like, this famous city of yours?"

"Well, it's difficult to describe, Your Majesty. It's built on stakes in the middle of the water, and you'd think that a breeze could blow it down overnight. There are columns of braided marble and carvings so delicate that they look like the foam on top of a wave. There's a piazza with a golden temple and wherever you look there are golden lions and gold-embroidered flags that flutter in the wind from the Adriatic. There are bridges so frail they look whittled out of ivory and balconies so white you'd swear they were made of porcelain. There are bells that keep ringing, bells of iron and bells of bronze, and if you sit and just listen there's sure to be music somewhere or other. Maybe it's only the boatman singing, maybe it's the violins in the palace, maybe it's the boys in the temple, maybe it's the waves on the *fondamenta*. It's a city of gold and marble and sometimes gold inside of marble, and here and there a bit of suffering and sadness, I suppose, but the marvelous thing about it isn't the gold or the marble, it's that blue Venetian sky filled with clouds that are whiter than snow. It's the sky and the clouds that gave them the idea for the gold and marble."

Khurram folded his arms and leaned back and peered at Geronimo: at that beautiful young face with its full-blown lips and teasing eyes, the chestnut curls shining on the temples, the ivory teeth, the equivocal smile.

"What do you think of it, Geronimo? What's the point of a man's existence? Is it to achieve the greatest possible fulfillment within himself, the flowering of his nature, a final richness of thought and character? Or is it to achieve some outer ambition, something shining and unmistakable to prove that he really existed?"

"Some think the one and some the other," said the Italian evasively, "and there are some who think that the one is inevitably linked with the other. It's difficult to say. I've known men in my own city who created glorious masterpieces and yet led lives of filth and debauchery. And I've also known men who created nothing except a marvelous sweetness of character which blossomed for a while like a flower and then vanished."

"Strange," said Khurram, nodding thoughtfully. "And what shall we make of it all?"

"Only that life glides on mysteriously," said Geronimo, lifting his brows a little. "Only a fool lays down a law on what is the wisest way to live it. You've mentioned two philosophies but there's a third one that I've heard of. It says that the end of wisdom is neither the inner nor the outer achievement. We must snatch our little moments of pleasure as they come along and in the end just hope that somehow we've managed to make the best of it. We've been true to our instincts, at least, neither flattering nor degrading them."

"That," said Khurram, "hardly deserves to be called a philosophy, my boy. That's the way most of us live, just muddling along, hoping for the best. It's the way that the animals live. I refuse to remain an animal."

"True," said Geronimo. "It's the way of the animals and it's not exactly inspiring, just eating and snoring and pissing and copulating. But sometimes it occurs to me that there's a marvelous beauty in it, and that there's nothing any lovelier than the humblest expression of nature. And in our crazy human longing perpetually to improve on nature we merely degrade what is pure in our own natures. We lose sight of the magic and we tarnish the very essence. And in shedding our primitive ignorance we slip into a deeper, uglier ignorance."

"Well," said Khurram, "it's all very well to speak of magic and so on, I know quite well what you mean and I also lament the loss of it. But men are thinking creatures; there it is; it can't be altered. It goes against their grain to live a life of primitive ignorance. Whatever the arguments for simplicity, and I don't deny there are powerful arguments, the fact is that we've left our simplicity behind us forever. Our task is to discover a philosophy which lets us think and yet be happy." He glanced wryly at Veroneo and spread his fingers across the cushion. "Tell me, Geronimo. What's wrong with me? Why do I feel lonely? Why am I unhappy? Why does the horizon look so bleak? Why does everything seem so flavorless? I used to feel a wonderful glow which was like a lantern in the middle of a forest. Now the lantern is extinguished. I feel cold and bored and hollow."

"There's no question," said Geronimo, "that there's a puzzle in you, Your Majesty. I'll never know what exactly it is and neither will you, in all probability. I keep looking into your eyes and I see a bottomless darkness. You've been spreading your powers and triumphs over the face of India, you've built fortresses and palaces, you listen to the philosophers and the poets, you give gold to the mollahs and mushtehids, and it's all just a desperate pantomime you're performing. Behind it lurks terror. Of what are you terrified, Your Majesty?"

"Ah," said Khurram, sighing deeply, "you're a brilliant man, Geronimo. You're the only one who's troubled to probe into this miserable soul of mine. Yes, you're right, there are two separate men perpetually at war in me. One is the restless, violent soldier driven on by a hidden demon. The other is the shy, brooding mystic worn by anxieties. And there's a third who lurks in the corner and quietly watches the conflict—a lizard, cold and calculating, who lurks at the very bottom of me. I grow older, the mystic ponders, the soldier roars with impatience, and all the while the lizard sits in the darkness, watching slyly."

"You seem capable," said Geronimo, "of an amazing self-perception, Your Majesty."

"Listen, Geronimo. There's something else under it all which still eludes me. I've always found it difficult to love and yet I know there's a capacity for love in me. I'm afraid to love deeply and yet there's a powerful need to love in me. I keep floundering about like a madman, bringing destruction to the ones I love, just because I can't bear to submit to this love. Idiotic, isn't it, Geronimo? I need love. And still I rebel against it."

"There are so many kinds of love," said Geronimo, blinking his eyelashes, "and there are some we shrink away from out of pride or panic or vanity."

"And the more we shrink away, the more we submit to their fascination. So it is, my lovely boy. Men are fools. Frightened fools."

x v

After Geronimo had left the tent Khurram sat alone by the table, leafing idly through a sheaf of maps which Ahmed Khan had left that morning. The raindrops kept rapping; the wind rippled the curtains. The flame swayed nervously over the swan-shaped oil lamp.

The rug which hung over the entrance parted abruptly. Mukarrab stood in the doorway, dripping and spluttering, with his saber in front of him.

"Forgive me, Your Majesty! There's a stranger who wants to see you!"

"Yes? Who?"

"It's a woman. A kind of hill-witch, I'd say, from the looks of her."

He bowed and stepped aside with a grunt of apology. A shabby, shivering creature slid through the entrance of the tent. She stood motionless and stared at Khurram with big, bloodshot eyes. Her dress was spattered with mud; her shoes were ripped to shreds. A rain-soaked shawl clung to her bony little shoulders.

She limped wearily across the carpet and picked up a glass from the table. "I'm so thirsty, so terribly thirsty. Could they bring us some wine, please, darling?"

XVI

"And after this," continued Arjumand, "I will leave you for ever. This one last child I'll bear you. After that I shall go into the mountains."

Khurram sat by the couch and stared bleakly at the oil lamp. The dance of the flame shone in the sweat on his forehead. She picked up his hand and pressed it gently against her mouth. She said quietly: "I'll leave you behind me. You and the world. And even myself."

After Khurram had gone to his tent she snuffed out the lamp, drew the coverlet over her shoulders and stared emptily at the ceiling. She tried to fall asleep but the darkness was too alive. It was alive with the noise of the raindrops and the creaking of the tentpoles; it was alert with the passionate tension which her meeting with Khurram had left in its wake.

Somewhere a dog began to yelp. Footsteps shuffled behind the tent. Someone cursed in an unknown dialect; there was a ripple of high-pitched laughter.

And then abruptly the pain took hold of her. It struck at her body like a beak, hacking away at her abdomen with a vulturelike fury. Then it turned into a claw, reaching deep into her belly and tightening its grip till she gasped like a stranded fish. She tried to cry out but the sound was trapped in her throat. She rolled sideways, clutching at her knees and biting crazily at the clammy cushion.

Then it left her for a while. She was soaked with sweat and panting violently, but the relief was so intense that it was almost like ecstasy. Her mind grew eerily lucid as she rose out of the pain: both lucid and at the same time darting and intricate, mercurial. She thought calmly: "Is it really so? Do I really have to die? Just to teach him how to love? Just to help him understand?" And a voice in the back of her brain answered, ever so softly: "No, it's not so simple as that, nor so ugly or cruel. We all must finally die in order to understand these things ourselves."

She looked around quickly, thinking that someone had entered the tent—the sense of another presence was so dense and oppressive. "No," she thought. "I'm still alone." But the presence wouldn't leave her. It took on a deepening identity, a kind of feverish exactitude: a middle-aged man with bushy eyebrows was sitting beside her, head sunk, hands folded, staring intently at the carpet. Who was he? Did he exist? Did he have a name? Did he have a purpose? The phantom grew blurred, the brooding face melted away. She caught the echo of lapping water and the smell of tar and mossy lilypads.

And then the sound of the ripples spread into the roar of far-off waves. The pain came swooping down again, but now it had turned into something else: it was more like a great avalanche tumbling out of the darkness. The world split apart; a streak of lightning shot through the wilderness. And she felt herself floating through the rain, light as a feather.

PART TEN

The Sepulcher

There was a looking glass in his cell, speckled by flies and badly blistered, but still clear enough for him to recognize the change in his features: the gradual shrinking of his cheeks, the sprinkled white on his temples. Every year on his birthday they brought him a duckling garnished with gooseberries: and every year he nodded his head and muttered vaguely, "I'm sixty-two," and the following year, "I'm sixty-three," and one year later, "I'm sixty-four."

To pass the time he had formed a habit of drawing patterns across the wall. At first with an ink-brush, while they still allowed him his diary; and then with the edge of a knife or a broken spoon or a splinter of charcoal. Magnificent patterns: cone-shaped summits receding into shadowy distances; huge cobwebs spreading outward like the ripples in a pool: flocks of birds that kept flying toward an invisible destination.

When he grew weary of visible patterns he invented invisible ones. He drew patterns in his mind—lists of words beginning with *K*, lists of phrases in the Koran, lists of plants, lists of jewels, lists of cities, lists of ancestors. And when these mental patterns bored him he got up from his couch and walked slowly across the floor, creating patterns among the tiles—squares, zigzags, arcs and triangles, five-peaked stars and parallelograms. And finally, when he had exhausted all these patterns of his own invention, he sat down by the guttering flame and studied the patterns of his body: the bulging veins in his wrist and the intricate branchings in his palms, the creases on his knuckles, the hairs that hung from his nipples. He began to feel toward his body a mingling of wonder and disgust—disgust with the gradual rot that was spreading through his tissues and wonder at the marvelous intricacy that still survived the rot. There were moments when he felt that age had turned his body into something alien—it was no longer Khurram's body, it was merely a shriveling, sickening encumbrance, a ghostly kind of effigy that had been mysteriously substituted for Khurram. And there were moments when he felt the opposite—that this was his only true embodiment, that the supple creature of forty years ago was a wholly different character, likewise called Khurram by some weird coincidence but unimaginably different, with nothing in common in mind or body, poignantly handsome, radiant with youth, neither cruel nor vicious but merely misguided, and still performing in the theatre of his memory a series of meaningless little pantomimes—now sly, now audacious, spattered with slime or sleek with unguents, cloaked in black or gold brocade, galloping through the rain, lolling in the sunlight. And though he recognized the décor, the soul of the dancer was infinitely alien, more remote from his being than the groveling turnkey who crouched by the doorway.

11

The turnkey opened the door and an elderly visitor entered the room. It was the poet Abdul Rahim, a portly man with a crimson beard, a friend of Khurram's childhood who called on the prisoner twice a week.

"Sit down, Abdul. I feel bored. I'm in the mood for a bit of gossip."

Abdul shrugged his pudgy shoulders. "Gossip, Khurram? I wish I had some. I've grown old just like you. Nobody bothers to tell me the gossip. People are marrying and dying and being naughty, the same as usual. Old Mukarrab died last week. Who's still left of our generation? Ahmed Khan, Suleiman Khan —they're all gone, like the leaves in autumn."

"There was a commotion in the gardens yesterday. A procession of elephants. Some sort of victory?"

"A victory, no doubt," said Abdul. "Down in Orissa if I'm not mistaken. He's a brilliant young general. More of a general than a monarch, frankly."

Khurram's eyes were dark and expressionless. He muttered, "Aurengzeb, Aurengzeb! He's an evil, ungrateful son, Abdul, isn't he? Isn't he?"

"I've heard him speaking of you," said Abdul, lowering his voice judiciously, "and his tone is neither evil nor ungrateful, it is merely impersonal. He is young; that's the point. As an Emperor he's far from popular. But he has energy; he has passion. Listen, Khurram. You must be reasonable. When he usurped your golden throne he justified his usurpation by dwelling on your indiscretions. Indiscretions—is that the word? Let's be frank and call it brutality. He clapped you into prison. Well, it wasn't especially nice of him, but do you happen to remember what you did to Khusru and Parviz and Shahriyar? One grows old and as I say, one must try and be reasonable. I know you better than most of them, I still remember you as the golden Emperor, and I might add that seven years is a long, long time in people's memories. Most of the courtiers have conveniently chosen to forget your existence. The only thing that still reminds them of it is that building down in the gardens. It's a pity you've never seen it now that the dome is finally completed."

"Oh, I've seen it," said Khurram wistfully. "Bihari took me for a walk one day. Only as far as the pavilion, mind you. I could see it through the foliage."

"Yes," said Abdul, "it's a building such as will never be built again till the world stops turning and the sun stops blazing. Every day I watched it grow, glory upon glory, splendor upon splendor, and it seemed that the very perfection of man-made beauty had been finally achieved. People have wandered from all over India just to peer at the snowy dome. People have come from Smyrna and Ispahan, they've come from London and Alexandria, just to look at those marvelous mosaics and jewel-encrusted columns. Oh, my Khurram, nothing more beautiful was ever created in this world. And yet I wonder: has it made us happier? Has it made us wiser? Has it made us more virtuous?"

Down in the gardens of the Taj they were setting off the fireworks. There were brisk little explosions rapidly following one another and then sprays of blue chrysanthemums soaring up through the blackness. The two old men turned their heads and glanced through the iron bars. The sulphur-blue light shone on their faces and was gone again.

"Victories, victories," muttered Abdul. "One day it's Berar and the next Gondwana. And what does it matter, Khurram, I ask you? This whole idea of a Mogul magnificence—it is merely a chimera which hangs over a dark and suffering continent. Have these victories brought peace? Or better food? Or better weather? Have these victories made the thought of our extinction any less horrible?"

"My dear friend," said Khurram, tremulous, "let's not talk about these matters. It all sounds strangely familiar. I'm no longer interested in these victories. I look at my face in the mirror every morning and what do I see? A face like a withered mushroom and hair that's floating as white as thistledown. I look as though some witch had scattered dust all over my body. What does my life amount to nowadays? I wash my face and I drink my soup, I pluck the lice from my miserable body, I think my thoughts and I mutter my prayers, and finally I lie down on that filthy bed and try to sleep. A stupid old man paying the price of his early wickedness. What's happened to us all?

Have we forgotten the meaning of happiness? Tell me, Abdul, was I ever alive? Was I ever the real, full Khurram?"

"There was a time," said Abdul vaguely, "when you were in love. That surely was real enough."

"I was in love? Is that what you said, Abdul? You're sure? You're utterly sure? Was I really in love with Arjumand? I wish I knew. I can hardly remember it."

"There's that building down in the gardens to prove it," said Abdul quietly.

"It proves nothing," said Khurram with vehemence, raising his fists in front of his face. "The only proof, if proof exists, lies buried somewhere in the dark of my heart. Mumtaz Mahal! Do you want the truth, Abdul? I can hardly even remember her. A mousy little woman with big brown eyes—that's all I remember. And as for my own beautiful emotions, God only knows what they really were. Guilt, pity, remorse, curiosity—I can't even remember. Call it love if you want to, Abdul, but it's on your own responsibility."

The light was beginning to fade; the muezzin called from the tower. The sky beyond the grill turned a deep, hollow lilac. The two old men sat silently, waiting for the bells to start ringing. And then they rang, globes of sound that rolled through the dusk like chains of iron.

"It still keeps haunting me in the night, that dreadful memory of it, Abdul. That poor little woman lying in the tent there, all dark and wet and shrunken, and the pattering of the rain and the dismal howling of the pariah dogs—oh yes, I'm quite sure of it, I felt a frenzy of grief and loneliness. But was it really love, Abdul? When I never understood her?"

"The true depth of love," said Abdul thoughtfully, "is deeper than insight. It's deeper than this triviality of understanding another character."

"Words of wisdom, my dear Abdul. They're lovely words.

Let's hope they're true. There I was, crouching by the bed, clutching at the pillow, sobbing crazily. And do you know what happened then? I looked up and glanced at the mirror. Lo and behold, the Emperor of India, brought to his knees with love and sorrow! There I was, still self-absorbed, still self-adoring and self-dramatizing. What is grief? What is love? Just another facet of self-love? It's a frightful thing to say, but I can't help wondering, my good Abdul."

Abdul's eyes shone in the lamplight like tiny black cherries. He lowered his bearded chin and looked intently at Khurram.

"If you're suffering still, my friend, then your heart is still alive. You're speaking with despair, but even the despair is a sign of vitality. You feel guilt about that glimpse of your suffering face in the mirror, but the very guilt is a symptom of your love, if you want my opinion. And I have another opinion about it. Love can grow and keep growing long after the object of our love has left us forever. Whatever you felt that night in the tent, and I'm sure that it was a mixture of different feelings, it's obvious that your memory of it has marvelously deepened. And the irony is that whatever you may have felt when she was lying there, now that she's faded into a phantom the thing you feel is truly love."

III

Night after night there was nothing but a long, black vista of dreams: one hideous dream following another with a mad incoherence and at the same time a fierce and strangely rational inevitability. Three dreams kept recurring. In the first he woke from a dream within a dream. He was lying in a hut in the middle of the jungle. There was no light except for a thin slant of starlight seeping through the blinds. He heard a sound, nearly inaudible, of watchful breathing close beside him. He could sense another creature lurking intently in the darkness. He peered into the gloom: all he could see was a hairy bundle; gradually the bundle took on the contours of an enormous crouching ape. He discerned the gleam of a knife and two little eyes, primeval, cretinous. A feverish panic took hold of him. He darted wildly from corner to corner, trying to escape the gorilla-faced enemy. But the eyes drew steadily closer and the knife shone more murderously until in a wild, gurgling spasm he woke up to reality.

In the second dream he was lying in a hammock in the shade of a deodar. He grew aware of a strange corruption that seeped through his limbs, and then he saw that his body was seething with worms and a large blue rat was gnawing at his belly. One of his arms, half-severed, was dangling from the hammock, and to his horror he saw a leg lying on the ground, still twitching feebly. He picked up the leg and clutched it desperately to his thigh, hoping that somehow it might grow to his body again. But the leg broke away and went limping over the dust, and then it turned and looked back with the pale, sad eyes of his brother Parviz.

In the third of his dreams he was lying in a subterranean tunnel, totally dark except for the faint phosphorescence of the dripping walls. He was trapped in a narrow passage; he could move neither forward nor backward. He kept twisting about frantically, but with every movement he was gripped more tightly. He could feel something fetid approaching in the blackness, but the thing remained faceless, intangible and unimaginable. Nothing happened, nothing at all, there was only the suffocating darkness and the slimy, intestinal clutch of the tunnel, but the terror of this dream was even more potent than that of the others.

The deepest part of his terror was that it seemed to be he who wielded the terror: he himself was the clutching tunnel, the dark gorilla, the gnawing rat. And thus he was in a manner not merely the victim who was tortured and haunted, he was also the secret torturer, the faceless phantom who had come to haunt him.

IV

He still was wearing his beaded slippers and pearl-embroidered tunic; but the years of imprisonment had rotted the satin and worn it threadbare. His beard had turned silver but his little eyes were as bright as always—not with the fire of ambition but with the flicker of self-knowledge. Twice a day he was led by his turnkey to the latrines behind the stables, and there he squatted while the grooms and the link-boys peered at him curiously. During the night he knelt by the bed and pissed into the basin that was brought from the kitchen. Little by little the room took on a nightmarish atmosphere—the walls all covered with scrawls, the floor reeking of urine, the mattress dank and dirty and the jeweled robes disintegrating, and the smell of the sleeping elephants creeping in through the window. And every night, during those black and feverish hours of insomnia, the shadows in his room turned into other and more eloquent shadows—the table into a throne, the jug into a parrot, the mirror into a mountain.

Sometimes the faithful Abdul Rahim read him some lines

from the *Ramayana,* and as he listened the verses took on a strange, contradictory meaning. Words like *gold, cloud* and *palace* turned into *night, guilt* and *loneliness* and the meaning of the poem was suddenly turned upside down. And it seemed that the entire world was standing on his head and the whole of human history had been strangled with illusions.

One evening he said to Abdul: "What's that noise I'm hearing, Abdul?"

"There's nothing," said Abdul; "it's only the wind down in the rushes."

And a moment later: "Listen, Abdul! There's somebody calling! Can't you hear it?"

"It's only a cricket out in the bushes," said Abdul Rahim solemnly.

And then the pain was suddenly on him. A white-hot needle shot through his belly, his lungs contracted violently and the sweat burst out like a fountain. "Quick, Abdul! Give me some water! I'm burning up!" he screamed hoarsely.

Abdul Rahim knelt by the bed and sprinkled water over his temples; then he started rubbing Khurram's chest with an ointment of camomile. The pain gradually lessened but Khurram finally whispered: "It's useless. It's all over. I'm crumbling to bits. I'm dying, Abdul."

v

The sun was already rising when they carried him to the Tower of Jasmines. Two of the eunuchs, Ali and Iqbal, took him gently in their arms and climbed the dark stairway to the Room of the Sixty Crescents.

He lay on the couch by the window with Abdul sitting beside him. Iqbal waved a peacock fan while Ali lit the incense brazier.

"Lift the curtain a little, Abdul. There's one of the towers I can't quite see."

Abdul raised the edge of the curtain; the dappled light fell over the couch and clung to the long, silvery hairs of Khurram's beard. Pain and weariness had shriveled his face beyond recognition: he looked like some crumpled old *saddhu* out in the desert.

He craned his yellow neck and peered blearily into the gardens. The dew still shone on the cypresses; the pool lay still as a mirror. The snowy-white marble was flushed with the rose of early morning.

"Move the pillow, please, Abdul. There, that's better. Look, Abdul! The whole Taj Mahal's turned into gold all of a sudden!"

"Is it as lovely," whispered Abdul, glancing at the dome, "as you'd imagined it?"

"Oh, Abdul, sweet old Abdul, I'm too weary even to think. Yes, it's lovely, it's even lovelier than I dared to imagine. Is that what the poets tell us? That things keep their loveliness as long as we never defile them by looking at them?"

"A symbol," said Abdul wistfully. "That's what it is. A miraculous symbol."

"Of what?" said Khurram, stammering.

"Of human love, of course," said Abdul.

Khurram's eyes turned in their sockets and stared filmily at Abdul. "A symbol of human love? Is that what you call it, Abdul? Do you know what it really is? It's a desperate scream of anguish! It's a symbol of human suffering and corruption and mortal terror, all masked in slabs of marble and delicate gold mosaics!"

Abdul nodded and stroked his beard. "So it is. Just as I said. A symbol of human love. And infinitely lovely, just as I said."

Khurram seized Abdul's hand and held it tightly against his chest. His chin started to tremble. "Yes, Abdul, so it is. All triumphant and shining, if one only has eyes to see it!"